Snowline

By John Witte

ISBN: 978-1-57833-833-7
Library of Congress Control Number: 2023903267

Book Design: Scott Elyard, 𝕿𝖔𝖉𝖉 𝕮𝖔𝖒𝖒𝖚𝖓𝖎𝖈𝖆𝖙𝖎𝖔𝖓𝖘
The typeface for this book was set in Minion Pro.

❄ Apun Publishing
2224 Kissee Court
Anchorage, AK 99517

First printing April 2023

Distributed by:

𝕿𝖔𝖉𝖉 𝕮𝖔𝖒𝖒𝖚𝖓𝖎𝖈𝖆𝖙𝖎𝖔𝖓𝖘

611 E. 12th Ave. • Anchorage, Alaska 99501-4603

(907) 274-TODD (8633) • Fax: (907) 929-5550

with other offices in Juneau and Fairbanks, Alaska

sales@toddcom.com • **WWW.ALASKABOOKSANDCALENDARS.COM**

Printed in China through **Alaska Print Brokers**, Anchorage, Alaska

Prologue

Rusty Connelly pilots the stolen pickup west, through the black night and blacker mountains. He checks the rearview mirror anxiously, certain flashing red and blue lights will appear in the distance. They never do.

"C'mon motherfucker," he mutters to himself, refocusing his gaze on the narrow, potholed single-lane highway ahead. "You're almost there."

He squeezes the steering wheel until his knuckles turn white and his fingernails dig into his palms. The pain is intense. He fixates on the sensation, hoping it keeps sleep at bay. It's not the cops that should worry him now—it's exhaustion. To his right, walls of rock loom in the darkness. To his left, a yawning river canyon snakes parallel to the road. If he nods off, this drive may be his last.

In his sleep-deprived delirium, the abyss is almost tempting. The drive has been the hardest of his life, a true test of endurance. It would be so easy to gun it through a gap in the guard rail, launch into the void, and crash in a fiery wreck in the riverbed. So easy to check out.

Squeezing the steering wheel, Rusty realizes, isn't enough. He slaps himself forcefully across the cheek—he didn't drive this far to die. Sighing, he reaches for an unlabeled pill bottle on the dash, then shakes out a couple of translucent orange capsules. He thought he'd popped his last Dexedrine, at least for a while. He washes the pills down with the dregs of a Red Bull, grimacing as a floating cigarette butt bumps against his upper lip.

Thankfully, the cocktail of caffeine and amphetamines kicks in before he succumbs to sleep. A familiar synthetic energy pulses through his body. Rusty loosens his iron grip on the steering wheel and starts drumming on it instead with his thumbs.

He's humming a Red Hot Chili Peppers tune, in the apex of an impassioned drum solo, when a feeble glow materializes on the horizon. Rusty blinks repeatedly, rubs his eyes, and slaps himself once more, just in case he's staring down the headlights of an oncoming semi-truck, or it's some hallucination, the exhaustion and drugs playing tricks on him again. But the road is as empty and desolate as the wilderness it cleaves through, and the glow slowly brightens as the miles roll on, which can only mean one thing: Anchorage. The sight brings him to the brink of tears.

Rusty glances sideways at his brother, James, who's fast asleep in the passenger seat. James had faithfully accompanied Rusty's humming and drumming with his usual snoring—and the occasional fast food-induced fart—and remains out for the count. Rusty considers waking him to watch the city lights come into focus, but quickly thinks better of it.

It was James who insisted on a disciplined exodus, James who insisted on Alaska. Aside from a couple of nights spent recuperating in a grungy Indianapolis motel, the brothers stopped only to refuel, shit, or hot-wire a fresh ride. They ate at drive-throughs, slept in shifts, pissed in empties. Fueled by fear and desperation as much as energy drinks and uppers, they drove and drove.

Anchorage isn't just another waypoint, thinks Rusty—it's a shimmering finish line. It's sleep. Stretching out his aching limbs in a real bed. Buying a toothbrush. Taking a shower. Scrubbing himself clean.

Yet as soon as they pull into town and check into a motel, Rusty ducks out for a drink. His heart's still hammering away from the dex, and he's craving real food—a burger, maybe a steak, definitely a beer. He wouldn't mind momentarily forgetting his troubles between the thighs of a sexy stranger, either. Mostly, though, he just needs a breather from his brother's increasingly sour moods.

Following directions from the front desk attendant, Rusty

walks swiftly through the foreign streets, keeping an eye out for cops and cursing the chill that cuts through his thin leather jacket.

"Not my fault I didn't pack a parka," he mutters to himself. "I wanted to go to fuckin' Panama."

He almost overshoots his destination, a shabby pub sandwiched between an abandoned Victorian-style hotel and a furrier—Anchorage immediately strikes him as bizarre. He yanks open the door, eager to get out of the cold. The air inside is stale with smoke and heavy with liquor, like the hot breath of a wino. He claims a wonky barstool and rubs his hands together for warmth, scanning the saloon's disheveled clientele for a suitable distraction. Unfortunately, there are no women to be found, save for the morbidly obese bartender trundling toward him. Tonight, a burger will have to do. And tomorrow, Rusty vows, he's not driving anywhere except the strip club.

"Can I please get a cheeseburger and fries?" he asks the bartender.

"Kitchen's closed," she grunts.

Rusty sighs. There's a Taco Bell across the street from their motel, although he'd been hoping for something more substantial.

"A shot and a beer, then. Jameson, and whatever's cheapest as far as beer goes."

The bartender busies herself with his order, and Rusty takes in his surroundings. The place seems unabashedly Alaskan. Dollar bills, defaced with autographs, expletives, dates, and doodles, paper the ceiling. The wood-paneled walls are warped, yellow as smoker's teeth, and decorated with faded photographs of dogsledders and fishermen. If the walls could talk, they'd have emphysema, cirrhosis, and a few decades' worth of sloshed stories to tell.

The bartender slides him a shot and a beer across the bar with the accuracy of an Olympic curler.

"You want to start a tab?" she asks.

"Sure," he says.

Aside from the lack of females and cheeseburgers, Rusty concludes, the dive isn't half bad. He raises the liquor to his lips, but stops short of tipping it back, cringing as he catches a glimpse of his fatigued reflection in a grubby mirror behind the bar.

The Connelly brothers both have their mother's fair hair and green eyes, but that's where the resemblance ends. Before they dropped out of high school, the boys often got into scrapes with classmates who implied they came from different gene pools. James, like most of the men on their mother's side of the family tree, is stocky, with a broad brow and squashed nose, like a wrestler whose face has been rammed into the mat so often that it's been permanently flattened. Rusty, on the other hand, inherited good looks and a tall, lanky frame from their father. His arching eyebrows are delicate, his cheekbones pronounced—fine features that almost clash with his prominently veined, tattoo-covered forearms and battered knuckles. "Almost" being the operative word. Rusty's always made it work. Back home in Queens, his looks opened legs quicker than he could jimmy a car door with a crowbar. He had a well-deserved reputation as a player, which he referred to as "free marketing." His hypothesis, one he often extolled to drinking buddies over beers in their booth at The Jack of Hearts—"Jackie's" for short—was that chicks from the neighborhood knew what they were getting into when they took a tumble in Rusty's sheets. That was the only way to explain why so many risked the wrath of significant others, fathers, and brothers.

"They know I'm a dog," he used to joke. "And they got pussy-ass cats at home."

But that life is over, and the handsome, devil-may-care playboy is gone, too. The mirror doesn't pull any punches. Rusty's aged seven years in as many days. Patchy scruff darkens his jaw, purplish rings circle his bloodshot eyes. In his rundown state, the likeness to his father is starker than ever. Looking into that mirror is like looking through the thick, smudged bulletproof glass in the Rikers visiting room.

Dad would've loved this dive, muses Rusty, wrenching his gaze from his haggard reflection to take in the scene. Growing up, if Patrick Connelly wasn't in prison, the pub was a safe bet. He wasn't a strict parent, but he had a strict drinking routine; he'd cross himself, tip back the booze with the grace of a sword swallower, promptly take the Lord's name in vain, and order another round. Profanity notwithstanding, Patrick was a devout Catholic. He refused to come clean to the assault and grand theft auto counts that sent him back to Rikers, but he regularly confessed (to anything less than a felony, at least) in church.

"Always pray before you take your first drink of the night," the old alkie would say, his Irish accent thick as Guinness, pressing whiskey into his sons' hands long before they were legally allowed to drink. "Even if God ain't listenin', or, heaven forbid, he's an eight-armed elephant or a bearded bloke named Muhammad, hell, smart thing to have an afterlife insurance policy."

Prayer hadn't done shit for Patrick, may he rest in peace, but it can't hurt now. It's been nearly eight years since Rusty prayed, at his father's funeral, no less, and he doesn't remember the last bit of the Lord's Prayer. Rather than blunder through it anyway and chance the cosmic repercussions, he closes his eyes and thanks God for granting them safe passage to Alaska.

He thanks God for guiding the bullet away from James' femoral artery.

He thanks God for giving him the patience to deal with his brother's prickly moods.

He asks that God continue to keep police from their path.

Then, grinning at the thought, Rusty asks a favor of the Big Man Upstairs - to transform the hefty barmaid into a slender blonde, preferably five years younger, with prodigious tits and a nose ring.

Rusty kicks back the Jameson, savoring the warmth of the whiskey. He cracks an eye open, ever hopeful, and looks at the bartender. She's still as vast as a beanbag chair. Oh, well. It was worth a shot.

7

He puts the pint to his lips, and his grin disappears. It should've been easy. In and out. That was the plan.

Rusty's nursing his beer, playing back the botched job on a loop like an obsessive detective with a CCTV tape, when a gravelly voice derails his train of thought.

"Why the long face, partner?"

An old man climbs onto a stool to Rusty's left. He's skinny, but his frame is padded by a buckskin leather jacket with fringe running down the sleeves. Gray sideburns curl out from under a black cowboy hat. The flat brim casts shadows onto a weathered face dominated by a drinker's nose and deep-set eyes. To Rusty, a New Yorker from Queens, for whom a brush with wildlife is kicking a rat down a subway tunnel, this man looks like he stepped straight out of an old western.

"None of your business," says Rusty, feigning hostility. Part of being on the run, as James continuously reminds him, is not being too friendly.

"No need for that," says the old man, amused. "If you'd prefer I keep my nose outcher business, that's fine. But I won't tolerate lip from you, son. Not in my bar. See this?"

Grunting at the effort, the old man gets off his barstool and points to his seat with a gnarled finger. "This stool right here has my name on it."

Carved into the wooden stool are the words "Bishop, Bush Pilot, Esquire."

Bishop nods at the bartender. "The usual for me, Britney. And while you're at it, the same for my cantankerous young neighbor." He jabs a thumb toward Rusty. "Maybe it'll teach him some manners."

"Esquire, huh?" asks Rusty, beginning to take a liking to this crackpot.

"Don't forget it," says Bishop.

Britney pulls an unmarked bottle from beneath the bar and splashes clear liquid into a pair of questionably clean glasses.

"Here ya go, Bishop," she says.

Bishop raises his glass and gestures Rusty to do the same. "Here's to you, sugar. If you were any sweeter, I'd leave this place with a cavity."

Britney blushes. Bishop tips back the liquor, and Rusty—briefly pondering the horrendous footage that might be acquired if these two Alaskan animals ever drank enough to copulate—follows suit.

It hits like ethanol.

Rusty gags, then gulps his beer to put out the flames. Bishop lets out a laugh that's more like a fit of wheezing. Britney raises an eyebrow.

"What the fuck is that?" says Rusty, eyes watering.

Bishop chuckles. "Hooch. Best in Alaska. Well, strongest in Alaska. One more, would ya, darlin'?"

Britney pours Bishop another. She raises an eyebrow at Rusty, who shakes his head weakly.

"There are tampons in the women's restroom if you need 'em," she says. To another chorus of Bishop's raspy laughter, she fetches Rusty a fresh beer.

Bishop downs his second shot without so much as a twitch.

"Where you from, son?"

"New York," says Rusty. He's not supposed to tell anyone where they're from, either, but to hell with James' rules.

Bishop whistles. "Long way from home."

"It's not home anymore."

"Why's that?"

Rusty sips his beer and shrugs.

"I see. You got a name?"

"Rusty," he says, breaking rule number one—no names, ever.

"What brings you to Alaska, Rusty?"

Rusty runs a hand through his greasy hair, yet another reminder that he needs to shower, then retrieves a battered pack of Marlboros from his pocket. He lights one up, then holds the pack out to Bishop, who nods graciously and accepts the last bedraggled cigarette and the lighter. The old man's weather-beaten hands tremble as he sparks the cigarette and puffs contentedly.

"Well," says Rusty, thinking of one of James' tall tales. "Me and my brother, we're writers. Screenwriters. We came to escape the city, settle somewhere off the grid and finish the script we're working on."

"A writer, huh?" says Bishop, clearly tickled. "You ain't exactly the most articulate man I've met, but what do I know? I'm just a bush pilot. Couldn't spell my own name if it weren't carved into my stool."

Bishop waves Britney back. She brings an ashtray and splashes more moonshine in his glass. The two men watch the television behind the bar—a basketball game neither cares about—in silence and smoke.

"You know what, son?" says Bishop out of the blue, twirling unruly sideburns with crooked, ringless fingers. "I may be able to help you and your brother out."

He stubs out the cigarette, waiting for Rusty to ask how. Rusty obliges.

"I got myself a trapping cabin. A hundred and fifty miles from the nearest road. Not so much as a lick of electricity, none of this internet crap. Don't use it in the winters, don't have the heart for trapping no more, tell the truth, and I've been hopin' to rent it out."

"Really?" says Rusty, intrigued.

"Now, I ain't no writer, but I do my best thinkin' out there— mountains that make skyscrapers look like sandcastles, river valleys that could swallow a city whole, a night sky that makes you believe in God. You believe in God?"

Rusty nods, but apparently not vigorously enough for Bishop's liking.

"You ever seen the northern lights? The scientists are full of shit. Those lights are cold, hard proof of one thing and one thing only in my book. And that's God. People say heaven is all white, fluffy clouds and whatnot, but I reckon I've seen heaven, and it's green and bright as that there sign."

Bishop points to a neon Heineken sign on the wall and smacks at his moonshine. The old man is a salesman, Rusty has to give him that. He pictures himself swathed in fur, trekking across the tundra, a rifle slung across one shoulder, aurora borealis glowing overhead.

"I never have, but I'd like to see them," says Rusty.

"They're indescribable, really—I shouldn't try, ain't doin' 'em justice," says Bishop. "Anyways, this cabin, it ain't five-star accommodations. Two beds, no running water, outhouse. Rustic. But it's warm enough, so long as you tend to the fire. How's about this? Four hundred dollars a month for rent, and for an extra thousand, I'll fly y'all out and back. Matter of fact, make that two thousand, and I'll help you shop for food and gear and teach you how to use it. Something tells me you city boys don't know jack about survival."

Rusty can't believe his ears. A place to lay low. They'd traveled all the way to Alaska on a lark, but they didn't have a plan beyond getting a motel. And here's Bishop, a barstool blessing. God, Muhammad, the eight-armed elephant—whoever was listening to his prayers might not have transformed Britney into a pretty, young blonde, but Bishop was better. In the cabin, they'd be all but invisible.

Four days later, Rusty and James are scrunched together like bobsledders in the back of Bishop's 1957 Piper bush plane. Bishop might be a shaky son of a bitch on the ground, but in the cockpit of his canvas-wrapped single-engine plane, he's an artist. The pilot expertly guides the plane along a loose northeast heading, out of the city and the suburbs, over forest and foothills, between mountains that make the Adirondacks look like molehills. The Hope River, a colossal gray-blue braid of waterways, writhes beneath them. Rusty is in awe. He hasn't seen the aurora borealis yet, but he catches Bishop's drift—God isn't up for debate when surrounded by such majesty.

James, on the other hand, is numb and nauseous, courtesy of a hangover and his now-customary regimen of painkillers, a six-month supply of which is packed in his duffel. He shares none of his brother's wonder as the mountains flash past, only tries not to

11

think of the plane for what it truly is - a death trap hurtling toward the middle of nowhere. He wants to blame Rusty for the harebrained decision to hide out in the Alaskan bush, but the guilt is his to bear.

The brothers were in Indianapolis, a full day's drive from the Mexican border, holed up in a motel room with a broken air conditioner. Rusty wanted to splurge, stay someplace fancy, but James refused. He was paranoid, coked-out, and sweating. His knee throbbed. The Veterinarian—a preferred medical advisor to the Bonanno crime family and an associate of their father's—stitched James up after hours at his Long Island practice and said the knee would be fine so long as James rested and kept the wound clean. Despite the pain, James still limped to the window every ten minutes to survey the street below.

Less predisposed to paranoia, Rusty channel surfed and chopped up lines of blow with the hotel room keycard. He flicked past the news and cartoons and paused momentarily on a nature show—shots of a grizzly snapping at salmon in the midst of a rushing river, dogsledders mushing through the snow—before continuing on.

"Stop, go back to the bears," said James.

"I'm looking for the Yankees game," said Rusty.

"Go back."

It was an exposé on Alaska. Normally, it would never have caught James' eye, but the snow-capped mountains looked so damn refreshing. It was a record ninety-four degrees in Indiana, an uncharacteristic autumn heat wave, and James had to take a cold shower before bed just to fall asleep. The notion that it might be even hotter in Mexico was appalling.

"Every criminal heads south," said James, rapt, a coke-coated finger tracing his gums. "Dependable as those migrating fucking butterflies—what are they called?"

"Monarchs," Rusty said. "They travel thousands of miles and sleep in the same trees every year and shit."

"Exactly," said James, hobbling to the window to peer through the blinds. "Monarch fucking butterflies! Going to Mexico? We're a walking cliché! And what happens to clichés?"

In answer, Rusty snorted a long line and slapped the coffee table. He'd learned to ignore his brother's rhetorical questions long ago.

"Clichés get fucked! And you know who goes north?" James paused for effect. "No one, that's who. People who don't want to know their neighbors. Hunters. Fishermen. Lone Ranger, Clint Eastwood, motherfucking cowboys. It's the perfect place to hide out."

Rusty was unconvinced, but there was no arguing. The next morning they drove north and didn't stop until they hit Anchorage.

"Comin' in hot," says Bishop over the mic, snapping James to attention. "Good thing, too, wasn't sure we'd have enough fuel!"

He smiles over his shoulder at the alarmed Connelly brothers and hoots. "Hot damn, you should see the looks on your faces."

Bishop nods to the left.

"You'll see my only neighbor's house in a second. Jean Pierre. French dogsledder. It takes him two full days to get back to civilization. He's a long walk southwest from my cabin if you follow the river—twenty-five miles or so, down on a little pond there, right where it meets the Hope—if you need to borrow a cup of sugar."

Rusty peers out the window and sees a long, relatively narrow lake and Jean Pierre's metal roof glinting through the dense spruce tops.

Bishop descends gradually. He aims the plane at a swatch of gravel along the river. The Piper's huge rubber wheels bounce twice and the plane cruises to a stop. Bishop shuts down the motor.

"Welcome home, boys," says Bishop.

The brothers unload and follow Bishop up a narrow, overgrown path. The cabin is rickety and small, but inviting all the same, tucked into a grove of spruce a stone's throw from the river and set against a backdrop of snowcapped peaks. Two square windows are cut into the notched log walls flanking the front and only door, which opens to the dilapidated deck. A black metal chimney juts crookedly out of a triangular galvanized tin roof.

"Built it in just three summers," says Bishop proudly, ushering the brothers inside.

It takes the Connellys a moment to adjust to the dimness—the one-room cabin is overwhelmingly brown, austere, cobwebbed and dusty. In the center of the room, two brightly colored piles contrast the dark wood and curtains—one of outdoor gear, one of food, both of which Bishop had hauled on previous trips. True to his word, Bishop had taken the brothers to the hardware store, camping store, and grocery store, where he got them outfitted with a rifle, several fishing poles, traps, additional hunting and fishing supplies, bear spray, winter clothes, backpacks, sleeping bags, flashlights, lanterns and fire starters, among other essentials, plus nearly two thousand dollars' worth of food, mostly canned and dried goods, not to mention enough whiskey to knock out a frat house. In their motel room, the piles seemed excessive. Here, facing an entire winter in the wilderness, they look woefully inadequate.

"You sure that's enough?" asks James, pointing at the pile of food.

Bishop chuckles. "I'm sure it's not enough. That's why I lugged that pile of huntin' and fishin' crap out here, too."

A kitchen table and two chairs are positioned in front of the wood-burning stove, on top of which is a large pot for melting snow, a battered teakettle, and a cast-iron skillet. A rocking chair—Bishop's one apparent luxury—sits in front of one of the windows. A row of peeling paperbacks lines the sill.

There's a ladder to a small loft, and Rusty climbs up to investigate. Two twin beds sit side by side, a small bedside table between them. Furs and wool blankets are stacked at the foot of each bed.

"How's it look?" asks James skeptically, not eager to climb the ladder more than he has to.

"Cozy," says Rusty as he descends.

More furs are tacked onto the walls, and a stuffed wolf head reigns over the room.

"Is that a wolf?" asks James.

Bishop laughs. "It ain't a coyote." He catches concern flitting across Rusty's face. "Don't worry, they won't bother you none. It ain't the wolves you need to worry about—the grizzlies neither, at least in winter."

"What should we be worried about?" says James disdainfully. "Feral salmon? Bloodthirsty mice?"

"No, son." Bishop chuckles again, then grows somber. "It's the cold. And the darkness. Some days, you won't see the sun."

Over the following days, Bishop does his best to teach the boys the basic skills they need to survive: how to split and stockpile firewood, set traps, skin game, load, aim and shoot the rifle, navigate with map and compass and cure meat and fish. After much pestering from Rusty, Bishop shows the boys how to get the Piper taxiing, although he doesn't let them fly the plane. "How the hell am I supposed to get home if one of you boneheads totals my ride?" he says.

On the fourth morning in the cabin, over a breakfast of coffee and skillet-fried cornbread, Bishop says, "I saved the best for last - today, we're going fly-fishing."

"We've been fishing," says James.

"Fly-fishing?" asks Bishop incredulously. "In New York City?"

"What's fly-fishing?"

"You ain't been fishing, boy." The old pilot breaks into a ten-minute sermon on the virtues of fly-fishing, calling it "God's gift to man" and "the ultimate teacher of patience." He helps them rig up their long, slender fly rods, tying on small insect imitations made of feather, wire, string, and foam. He schools them on the pair of relatively short, fat ice fishing rods he'd helped them pick out, too. "We won't use these today, but they're easier to operate than the fly rods—a Neanderthal could do it blindfolded. Still, ice fishing is a mighty fine way to spend a winter afternoon, particularly if the larder's low," says Bishop. "Not as challenging or fulfilling to the soul as fly-fishing, in my own humble opinion, though it offers more time to test the liver."

On the rocky banks in front of the cabin, they practice casting for an hour—it's tricky work, the perfect cast "a lifelong pursuit," according to Bishop. Rusty struggles, his long arms not seeming to understand the rhythm, and he gets his fly tangled every other cast. But James picks it up fairly quickly, flicking out semi-straight line and occasionally hitting his target, a large, smooth boulder thirty feet away. Bishop whistles and claps in approval. It's the first time Rusty's seen his brother smile in days.

Once they have a grip on the absolute basics, they follow Bishop downriver. From the cabin, the braided river winds lazily along a gentle slope, splitting into forks and bending back together again, fed here and there by streams of snowmelt. Bishop points out productive seams and holes and regales the brothers with fishing tales—trout caught, salmon escaped, steelhead that gleamed as if their scales had been hammered from silver.

The gentle rush of the river steadily amplifies as they get farther and farther from the cabin. After fifteen minutes of walking, the roar grows so powerful that Rusty can feel it vibrating through his entire body. Suddenly, the fork they've been following drops off a cliff and into space.

"We're here," yells Bishop, grinning at the awestruck expressions on the boys' faces. "Careful now, slippin' ain't an option."

Taking his warning to heart, the brothers tiptoe cautiously to the cliff's edge so they might marvel at the source of the sound in its entirety. The thundering cascade, a brilliant, bowed pillar of white, rejoins the main branch of the Hope in a stunning blue pool some one hundred fifty feet below—a sapphire shining in the forest's never-ending carpet of green.

Bishop leads them away from the void so they need not yell.

"The fishing is decent above the waterfall," he says. "I like to walk down here, then fish my way back. Better to fish from downriver so you don't spook the fish with your shadow. But some mornings I'll just come without my rod and sit and watch the sun peek out over yonder peaks."

"I can't believe we get to call this home," says Rusty, shaking his head.

Even James is stunned. "Incredible," he murmurs.

After a successful day of fishing, the trio celebrates Bishop's last night at the cabin with a feast of breaded trout over spiced potatoes, sautéed carrots and fried onions. The brothers kick back at the kitchen table, stuffed and satisfied. Bishop excuses himself, presumably to take a whiz off the deck, then returns moments later with a bottle of moonshine and a deck of cards.

"Cabin-warming gifts," he says slyly, clearly pleased with himself. "I had 'em stashed in the plane."

Rusty groans. "James, this is that firewater that I was telling you about."

"I could use some medicating," says James, clapping his hands.

"Good lad," says Bishop. He hands James the bottle and fetches tin mugs from the kitchen. "Pour us a drink then, will ya?"

The old man eases into his chair, then slowly peels the plastic packaging off the deck of cards. "Rusty, put a pot of coffee on. The good stuff, none of that decaf crap. Tonight, we're staying up for the northern lights. The way you boys been snoring' up in that loft soon as the sun sets, you'll never see 'em unless I turn you into night owls. And grab a bag of dried beans while you're at it, the red ones will do. I'm gonna teach you boys one last thing—how to lose at cards."

Rusty and James have both bet on sports plenty back in New York, never with much success, and played a touch of Texas hold 'em, too, but other than that, they're fresh to poker. Bishop shows them a variety of games—five-card draw, seven-card stud, Omaha Hi-Lo, Iron Cross. The bottle and kettle both slowly empty. Piles of beans grow and shrink in the lantern light. For the first time in many years, Bishop realizes, laughter fills his cabin to its hand-hewn eves.

It's near 3 a.m. when James wakes with a start at the kitchen table. The room is spinning, a dim vortex of timber and animal hides and playing cards. Damn moonshine.

He wants water, his mouth is drier than hell itself, but someone's shouting outside—and they're shouting his name. Grizzlies tearing Rusty in half like a wishbone and snarling wolves run through his mind, and James remembers the rifle leaning against the doorframe. He jumps to his feet, knocking over both his chair and the empty moonshine bottle, the shattering on the floor, then promptly trips and goes sprawling himself.

The yelling outside stops, and Rusty and Bishop appear at the door just as James gets to his feet again, cursing and wobbling like a sailor having just returned to solid ground, using the rifle as a crutch. They catch one look at James, glance at each other, and burst out laughing.

"What's going on?" barks James, sobered by both the fall and his amused audience.

Rusty doubles over, Bishop hacks like an asthmatic smoker who just can't quit. Neither says so much as a word for a few long, aggravating seconds, but Rusty recovers enough to point at the small mirror above the kitchen sink.

"Look at your face."

Wincing at his smarting knee, James limps toward the mirror. "What the fuck?" he says.

To an encore of laughter, he reaches up and plucks several dried beans from his forehead, leaving behind blotchy, bright indents.

"You fell asleep while we were playing cards," chortles Rusty. "Protecting your beans, apparently."

"I heard you yelling my name."

Bishop, having reined in his wheezing, wipes a tear from the corner of his eye.

"C'mon, James Bean, Alaska's got something to show you."

"James Bean," chuckles Rusty as they follow Bishop outside. "Good one."

"That's why we was yellin'," says Bishop, nodding toward the heavens. High above, spectral swathes of iridescent green and purple snake through the clear, black night.

"Aurora borealis," intones the pilot, gravely, as if invoking a magic spell.

"The northern lights," echoes Rusty, brimming with awe.

"God's country," says Bishop. "That'll give you boys something to scribble about."

Rusty, unable to take his eyes off the shimmering skies above, suddenly feels a confusing pang of affection for Bishop and remorse for having lied to him. The old man's done so much for them. Maybe it's the moonshine, or the lightshow in the moonless sky, but he's compelled to tell the truth. "You know we aren't writers, right?"

Bishop smiles wryly into the dark. "I had my suspicions. I never met any writers before, but I was fairly sure you two ain't writing no screenplay. Hell, I ain't even seen so much as a pad of paper in that mess."

"We never even graduated from high school," says Rusty.

"I asked you once, but seems like a good time to ask you again. What brings you to Alaska, then?"

It's James' turn to laugh, but it comes out harsh and forced. "Same reason I'm always limping around—there's a sliver of a bullet in my knee."

Bishop continues examining the arctic sky. Everyone comes to Alaska for their own reasons, Bishop included. Alaska, he's always believed, is a haven for both society's unwanted and those who want nothing to do with society. Who cares why the brothers hid the truth? That's their prerogative.

"I shouldn't have asked," he backpedals. "Ain't no business of mine."

"No, it's not," says James. "Don't worry, though. I'm fine telling you. You're family now—right, Rust?"

Rusty, apprehensive, says nothing, only nods slowly.

"A cop shot me," says James. "When we were escaping from a robbery in New York. That's why we're here."

"Robbery," repeats Bishop, torn between changing the subject and unearthing the truth. "That explains the crispy cash."

"Well, there were a few bills with my blood on 'em, but we didn't think you'd want those," says James drolly.

"That cop who shot you. You shot back?"

James snorts. "Of course I did."

There's another question on Bishop's lips—whether that cop lived or died—but he doesn't ask. "Some regular cowboys in my cabin. This goes without saying, but your secret is safe with me."

James claps him on the shoulder and says reassuringly, "I know that, Bishop. Wouldn't have told you otherwise."

James takes one long, last look up at the night sky, then limps back to the cabin, whistling.

The next morning, Bishop wakes with a searing hangover. Rusty, bleary-eyed, fixes coffee.

"Coffee will be ready in a minute," he says. "Pancakes, too."

"Thank God," says Bishop. "I'm afraid if I tried to fly home without coffee I wouldn't make it."

"Not you," says James, climbing down from the loft. "You're a wizard with that plane of yours. I'm sure you can fly it drunk."

"Course I can fly it drunk. I'm a functioning alcoholic. Now, hungover? That's a different beast. Might as well be a kamikaze mission."

The sun's out, so they eat breakfast on the porch, James sitting on the steps while Bishop and Rusty occupy the deck chairs.

"Quite a view," says James, looking out at the river and the forest, the foothills and mountains beyond.

"I second that. It put on quite a show last night, too," says Rusty. He lifts his coffee mug toward Bishop. "Thanks a ton for, well, everything. All your help and hospitality. We couldn't have done it without you."

"You haven't done it yet, son. Long winter ahead. But you're welcome," says Bishop sincerely, sopping up maple syrup with his last bite of pancake. "I'll fly back in a couple months when the lake freezes and I can swap my tires for skis. I'll bring some fresh vegetables, more moonshine, too, maybe a pizza if you're lucky."

James stands and shakes his coffee dregs onto the dirt.

"I'm afraid that's not necessary," he says, and suddenly swings the tin mug at Bishop's head like a prizefighter throwing a right hook. Bishop doesn't have time to yell before the mug connects with his temple and sends him into blackness.

Rusty jumps to his feet. His plate and silverware clatter onto the deck.

"What the fuck!" he screams.

Breathing heavily, brandishing the blood-spattered mug, James turns to Rusty. "He knows who we are. He knows what we've done. He has to go."

"He knows because you fuckin' told him!" shouts Rusty.

James shrugs. "You brought it up."

He drops the mug and drags Bishop's limp body out of the chair. "You just gonna stand there?"

Rusty, swearing, comes to his brother's aid. Together they carry Bishop out toward the river.

"What are you going to do with him?" asks Rusty, trying to keep his voice from cracking.

"We," grunts James, "are going to send him off right."

They stuff Bishop into the pilot's seat and strap him in. James climbs into the plane as much as he can, half sitting on Bishop's lap and half holding the struts so he doesn't fall out. Eventually, after some trial and error, he coaxes the propeller to life. At the sound, Bishop groans.

"No you don't, motherfucker," says James. He clocks Bishop with an elbow and the pilot's eyes roll back again.

James gets the plane taxiing and steers downriver for three quarters of a mile or so, then, once he's satisfied with the speed and trajectory, jumps out of the open door. He tries to roll like special agents do in the movies but bangs his bum knee into the ground and yelps in pain. Grimacing, he gets slowly to his feet—just in time to watch the plane dive-bomb off the cliff next to the waterfall.

"Bingo," says James as he hears the explosion.

He's walking toward the crash site, the waterfall growing louder with each step, when Rusty tackles him from behind like an NFL linebacker.

Rusty flips his older brother onto his back, pins him to the ground, and punches him in the face over and over again. Then he wraps his hands around James' throat.

"You psychopath! You lunatic! We're gonna be stuck here for the rest of our miserable lives. Why the fuck did you do that?"

James gasps for breath, blinded by his own blood. He tries to punch back, but Rusty has longer arms. Shadows creep into his vision like velvet curtains closing across a movie screen. Terrified, James flails frantically for a weapon. He grabs a smooth river stone the size of a baseball and smashes it into the left side of Rusty's ribs.

His younger brother rolls off him, howling in pain, two ribs cracked.

James drags himself to his feet, spitting blood. He feints as if to smash the rock into his brother's head but stops an inch away. He lets the rock hover there for a moment.

"I did what had to be done," he growls.

He releases the rock and offers Rusty his hand. Rusty curls up on the ground and doesn't take it.

"Like it or not, we're in this together," says James. "Bishop might've been your friend, but I'm your brother. Your blood."

Rusty grits his teeth. Still ignoring James' hand, he pushes himself to his feet. In silence, the brothers limp slowly to the waterfall. Rusty, to say goodbye. James, to make sure the job is done.

Chapter 1

Richard Maynard can afford better coffee. That much is evident from the state-of-the-art kitchen in his riverside home, with its stainless steel appliances, ostentatiously high ceilings, imported marble countertops, and twelve-person, solid walnut dining table. But Richard, a self-made businessman who started with less than nothing, sees no reason to splurge on highfalutin coffee beans. Much to his wife's chagrin, he feels about coffee the same way he does about wine—the cheap stuff gets the job done just fine.

He presses a button on his coffee maker and waits as it burbles to life. The pungent aroma conjures up memories; his father spooning instant coffee into a hammertone green Thermos before heading down to the docks, and, years later, his first job as a newspaper delivery boy in high school. Every morning, he used to speed through the empty streets of Astoria, pretending the papers he chucked into driveways were touchdown passes. Back then, cheap coffee and sports radio were his saving graces. Swap sports radio for sports podcasts and the same holds true over three decades later.

It's dark out, but in the conic glow of the porch light, Richard watches snow fall in light eddies, brushing the backyard in white. Which reminds him—he has chores to do. He extracts a pen from the chaos of the junk drawer, the one comforting bastion of disorder in an otherwise spotless kitchen, and starts a list:

Friday, To Do.

Item one: *Work out.* He writes it down and crosses it off, just for the satisfaction.

Item two: *Change snow tires.*

He should've swapped tires weeks ago. Numerous snowstorms have already come and gone, and the days are steadily getting shorter. In Richard's defense, he's been busy, at his desk from dark till dark for weeks on end. Had he known that selling his company would be such a torturous task, he would never have entertained Aleutian Energy's offer. But the due diligence is almost over. Hopefully, he'll sign the final paperwork before Christmas, and the new year will bring a fresh start. He'll have more time for family, more time for adventures, more time to do chores around the house.

Of course, Richard could just pay someone else to change the tires. He is, after all, a pragmatic businessman. He owns a two-hundred-person trucking business that hauls pipe and raw materials for oil companies, and he understands the arguments for delegating tasks and valuing time better than most. But he's also old-school, and he believes that each time you let someone else change your oil or fix your sink, you chisel away at your masculinity.

Richard aims to pass that sense of self-sufficiency down to his children, despite their upbringing of wealth and privilege. Maybe he'll ask the kids to help him after school. He'll teach them how to jack up the car, swap the tires. They can order a pizza, listen to loud music—just like old times.

As Richard racks his brain for more items to add to his to-do list, he taps the pen on the counter, sips his coffee, and studies the photos on the kitchen walls. Anne's interior decorating tastes change from year to year, and she's currently in a minimalistic phase. Family photos from elsewhere in the house have been replaced by spacy abstract art—or nothing at all—and relegated to this corner of the kitchen by the fridge, so close together their frames are nearly touching. Caleb dubbed the corner the "Scrapnook," which stuck, and it's become one of Richard's favorite spots in the house, aside from the garage—his true haven—and the game room in the basement, replete with a billiard table, vintage arcade games, and pennants and memorabilia from University of Oregon and Seattle sports teams that Anne is forbidden to remove.

There are countless photos of the kids—kicking soccer balls, going fishing, learning to walk, awkward school photos. There's a picture of the whole Maynard clan at a family reunion in Florida— the kids look so young, the twins were barely out of diapers—and another of Richard happily losing his money at a charity golf tournament. The small, grainy picture of Richard with Jim Sullivan at senior prom always makes him smile—they're wearing top hats and tails, big cigars hanging out of their mouths. Jim's been Richard's best friend since football tryouts their sophomore year of high school. They look so young and confident. At that point, Richard only had dreams of playing in the NFL.

Among the photos is a newspaper clipping from the front page of the local section of *The New York Times* that Anne framed many years ago. There, preserved behind the glass, is Richard, fifteen years younger, eyes bright and burning, muscular frame yet to be padded by a fatherly paunch. He still has a decent head of hair, too, before he bit the bullet and shaved his head clean. He's standing in the middle of Sixth Avenue in Manhattan, looking over his shoulder at blurred buildings, the unmistakable blue and red of a cop car's flashing lights in the background. Their honeymoon was an eventful one, to say the least.

"Good morning, honey."

Anne, wrapped in a robe, her wavy, dyed-blond hair ruffled, kisses him on the cheek, gently stirring him from his memories. "Aren't you sweaty."

"Morning," says Richard. He's already lifted weights, hit the rowing machine and loosened up with a quick yoga flow downstairs in the home gym. Richard's always been a weightlifter, but he's new to yoga. A former tight end for the University of Oregon, he's six foot four, with wide shoulders, a thick neck, and legs that Anne described as "concrete pylons" when they first met, although these days they're more flabby than firm. When he was playing college ball, he bulked up to two hundred seventy-five pounds. He was a machine—an All-American his sophomore year with the potential to go pro. He's two-eighty now, but muscle has little to do with it, and he's getting a head start on his New Year's resolution by hitting the home gym hard. Sarah recently told him that, with his shaved head and goatee, he looks like "an elderly member of a biker gang." Talk about motivation to get in shape.

If it were up to Richard, he'd strictly lift heavy and forgo the yoga. But back injuries stopped his football career short and have since been a constant source of pain. Both his personal trainer and Jim encouraged him to give yoga a crack. Reluctantly, he opened his mind and started to open his hips. All the stretching and bending is growing on him, though. It's certainly preferable to wincing every time he attempts to touch his toes.

"Are the kids up?" asks Anne, tightening her robe. "It's chilly down here."

"Sarah's doing her makeup. Sean and Caleb are moving," says Richard. "And it's snowing outside."

"Oh, boy," says Anne, sighing as she peers out the window and fiddles with the thermostat. "How slowly are the boys moving?"

"I believe they're alive—I saw them twitch."

"Very funny. They've got their first ski team meeting and team dinner of the year today after school, so no need to pick them up."

"I know, love. I'm on it. It's on the calendar," says Richard teasingly.

Flustered, Anne peers at the calendar—twelve months of Georgia O'Keeffe paintings. It's stuck to the refrigerator with alphabet magnets that are meant to say "The Maynards" but instead have been rearranged to say "Yam Hen Darts."

"Caleb's work?" asks Richard, referring to the misspelled magnets while eyeing O'Keeffe's tulips with good-natured skepticism—the pitiable American public, duped into finding flowers erotic.

"Can't say he's not creative," says Anne.

O'Keeffe and her contemporaries were, indirectly, at least, the driving force behind that fateful trip to Manhattan. Richard proposed while Anne was finishing a degree in art history from the University of Washington. When he asked her where in the world she wanted to go for their honeymoon, she said New York City.

"I want to visit the museums, to experience paintings in person I've only seen in textbooks." she explained. "They're so two-dimensional on the page."

"All paintings are two-dimensional," parried Richard, purposefully riling up his bride to be. "They're paintings."

The jab backfired, and she dove into a fervent dissertation on brushstroke depth, and the palpable difference between a print versus an original. "That's like saying watching a football game on TV is the same as taking in the stadium in person," she lectured smugly, knowing she'd driven her point home.

"All right, all right, New York it is," Richard surrendered, amused. "But we're going to a Jets game, too. Deal?"

"Deal," she giggled, extending her hand to formalize the pact.

Richard would've preferred to go fishing in Belize, or on safari in Tanzania. Anywhere, really. Cities were boring—for business, not pleasure. But he was hopelessly in love. And when that slender art student talked about MoMA like it was Mecca, and her eyes sparkled at the thought of Picasso and Cézanne, and she chattered on about skyscrapers and subways, he acquiesced. He always did for her. He always would.

And back then Richard was relatively anti-art—he valued practical skills like architecture and glassblowing but saw no utility in painting or sculpture. He considered the latter a waste of time and energy—creativity for creativity's sake. In middle age, he'd come around a bit, having taken to the therapeutic act of woodworking. Still, O'Keeffe's supposedly sensual blossoms never worked their magic on him like they did Anne.

Luckily, there's a strict calendar constitution in place in the Maynard household; every year a new family member gets to pick the fridge calendar. In a month, it will be Sarah's turn. Five years ago, she picked horses, but she seems to have outgrown her love of ponies, and Richard has no idea what it will be next. Boy bands? Pop singers? Male models? The thought makes him appreciate O'Keeffe's flowers.

And what of the boys? Sean assuredly will pick skiers, or maybe snowmachiners—either way, that's a win. Caleb is tougher to pinpoint. Last time, when he was nine, he picked landscape photographs: eerie barns swathed in fog for fall, snow-cloaked pine trees for winter, rivers swollen with snowmelt for spring, high-alpine meadows abloom with wildflowers for summer. In a couple years who knows what the boy will choose. He has his mother's eye for art. He has her softness, too. Finally, it will be Richard's turn again, and grizzly bears scooping up salmon and wolves prowling the tundra will guard the leftovers once more.

Anne cusses under her breath and twiddles the knobs of the espresso machine.

"Everything okay?" asks Richard, turning away from the calendar, concerned, noticing the puffiness around her eyes.

"I didn't sleep well. Or at all really. My hip's bothering me again."

"Is it tight? Would you like a massage? Can I get you anything? Breakfast?"

"Just an Advil. Or two. And some orange juice. And an espresso."

"Okay, take a seat, one chef's special coming right up," says Richard. He shakes a couple Advil out of a jar on the counter and pours her an orange juice, then begins to troubleshoot the espresso machine. "Third time this week. You should go to the doctor's today. I'll get the kids after school."

"It's just stiff in the morning," she says, rubbing the offending hip.

Richard raises an eyebrow. "It's not the only thing that's stiff in the morning."

29

She laughs tiredly. "Oh shut it. It'll loosen up as the day goes on. And you don't need to pick them up, they have a ski team meeting and then a team dinner after, remember?"

"Exactly, just testing you."

Sarah waltzes into the kitchen, done up to the nines, with a bubbly, "Good morning, parental units!" She wrenches open the fridge, grabs a yogurt and dumps it into a bowl, then peels a banana and chops it with an unnecessarily sharp knife. She draws the knife deftly away from her body, just like Richard taught her. The makeup-caked teenager devolves—he sees for a moment an eight-year-old with s'more-smudged cheeks learning to whittle, enthralled by the responsibility of a Swiss Army knife, her concentrated expression illuminated by the light of the campfire.

Maybe it's time for another family camping trip. Richard has no problem camping in the snow. Due to the lack of fellow campers, and the muffled silence of a snowy landscape, he almost prefers it.

Sarah sprinkles granola on top of her masterpiece.

"Are your brothers moving?" asks Richard, if only so Anne doesn't have to.

"Am I my brothers' keeper?" asks Sarah, grinning. Her cheeks show blush, her lips are shiny with some potion or another. Like every father when his daughter begins to become a woman, Richard is unnerved. He's an alpha male through and through, and ultra-protective at that. He struggles to refrain from threatening to cut the tongues of her male classmates out with a red-hot butter knife. Not that he needs to. A scowl from Richard is enough to cause an adolescent boy to embrace premarital abstinence quicker than even the most persuasive priest. That said, he knows that if she wants to wear makeup, that's her right. So long as she doesn't use hard drugs, develop an eating disorder, or get pregnant by the time she leaves home for college, he'll be happy. That's all anyone can ask for these days.

"Any plans this weekend? Want to help me change the snow tires tonight? I'll let you use the jack." He says it as if offering a dog a chicken bone or a teenager the keys to the Porsche. "Or we could go on an adventure tomorrow. A fishing trip before the river freezes completely?"

"Sorry, I've got plans," she says with no intonation of apology, shoveling yogurt quickly but carefully into her mouth so as not to disturb her makeup. "I'm going to the mall and the movies with Jess tonight." Before Richard can answer, she squeezes in: "And tomorrow I've got plans, too."

Two years ago, she would've scoffed at going to the mall and instead opted to wake up early and go fishing with her father. But things change.

"Fair enough." Richard tries not to sigh and catches Anne glancing at the oven clock. He throws a heavy hand gently across her shoulder and kisses her frazzled head. "I'll go herd those cats of ours."

Halogen lights cast a mechanical glow about the garage, the high ceilings of which make even Richard's living room seem claustrophobic. A half-eaten extra-large pepperoni pie from Rodolfo's is getting cold, the clamshell box open and resting on top of a snowmachine.

It's been a long day.

Bruce Springsteen's "Born to Run" blasts over surround-sound speakers. The heads of Alaskan beasts—a moose, a caribou and a lynx—decorate the walls. The lifelike taxidermies make it seem as if their bodies are stuck on the other side of the galvanized walls and the animals are receiving medieval punishment, doing time in the stocks. The moose and lynx are decades old, gifted to Richard by an older Alaskan who, spurred by arthritis and cajoled by depression, left Alaska's cold, dark winters for the greener latitudinal pastures of Florida. Richard shot the caribou himself, though he only hunts what his family—and friends—will eat. An industrial freezer in a corner of the garage houses enough wild game to start a butcher shop, and a week before Christmas every year, Richard proudly sends out gift boxes of caribou steaks and sausages to loved ones across the country. For a few days, the garage becomes a meatpacking plant.

To an outsider, the triple-wide garage would seem simply a toy chest for a wealthy Alaskan. But it's so much more than that: It's Richard's respite from work and family life. Four snowmachines are parked in an orderly line. A speedboat takes up the bulk of the space—in the summer, Richard whips the kids around on wakeboards, inner tubes, water skis, and inflatable manta rays. A full woodworking shop wraps around the far corner. Though he's only a hobbyist, Richard's setup would make a professional craftsman jealous. The workshop is replete with tool chests, countertops with vices, every kind of saw you could want, an assortment of power tools, shelves filled with varnishes and lacquers, drawers stocked with nails and screws, plus snowmachine parts and files, wax and scrapers for tuning skis. Then there's Richard's favorite touch, the obligatory mini-fridge completely filled with Alaskan beers.

When he has the time, and even when he doesn't, Richard spends hours in the garage, drinking beer, working with wood, the music blasting at concert volume. He builds shelves and cabinets for the house, coffee tables for the office, that sort of thing. What he's building isn't as important as the fact that he's building it. When the music is on and the smell of sawdust fills his nose, he gets lost in the work.

He cranks at the last of the Suburban's lug nuts. The boys are still out to dinner with the ski team after their meeting, Sarah is doing God knows what at the mall, and Anne is likely half asleep on the couch while her singing competition show squawks in the background. Everything is as it should be.

Finished, he wipes the grime on a dirty rag and trades it for pizza grease. The pizza is cold, and the satisfaction of completing his task is short-lived. Mouth full, he looks around the garage, searching for something else to do, something to captivate his attention, to distract him from everything beyond the tool-laced walls. His eyes settle on his race snowmachine: a Ski-Doo Freeride 850 E-TEC 165, modified with a gas rack on the back, extra storage, a studded track, and countless other odds and ends. His baby.

After his family and football, snowmachining is his third love. He hops into the seat, wipes his hands again, and grabs the rubber grips. He closes his eyes. It's like he's a kid again, back on his bike in Oregon, pedaling to the pier with a playing card in his spokes, pretending his Schwinn is a Ford Mustang. The garage transforms into open tundra—a land without roads, one of infinite possibilities. The world whirs by underneath the spinning tread, the machine kicks up clouds of powder, like dust under the hoof or paw of a mighty beast. Man and machine united, as sacred a union as cowboy and stallion.

He opens his eyes and checks his phone. It's 9:02 p.m. It's late, but he and Jim still need to train for the race. Those miles aren't going to ride themselves. He presses the home button and tells Siri, "Call Jim Sullivan."

The phone rings twice, and Jim picks up.

"Hey, buddy. I was just about to call you. You thinking what I'm thinking?"

"Ride tomorrow?"

"Perfect."

"What time?"

"Let's go early, eh? The snow's starting to fall a bit heavier."

"Really?" Richard rolls up the garage door. Sure enough, the flakes have thickened; a couple inches of fresh snow blankets the driveway. "I'll be damned. What's the forecast for tomorrow?"

"Should get heavier tomorrow evening. But we'll be fine early."

"Okay. Meet me at the diner?"

"Course."

"Six-thirty?"

"Let's say six."

"Done. See you tomorrow."

Richard hangs up. He flips open the hood of the snowmachine, grabs his tool chest, and proceeds to wrench, change the chaincase oil, and clean the engine for another few rotations of the Bruce Springsteen album.

Just before midnight, he puts the last few slices of pizza in the fridge. He loads the snowmachine onto the trailer, the steadily falling snow collecting on his flannel. After locking the trailer onto the Suburban, he pulls out of the driveway, testing the freshly changed snow tires by braking sharply on a loop around the block.

He's in no hurry to get to bed. Sleep, as always the night before a big ride, will evade him.

Chapter 2

Naked and wet after a leisurely bath, Mel Drummond prowls back and forth in her hotel room, a towel twirled around her jet-black hair like a terry turban. Were it not for her attire (or lack thereof), the tumbler of mimosa in hand, and the starchy spotlessness of the Anchorage Marriott, she'd seem a prisoner. Her body language, at least, suggests that she's stuck in cellblock D of San Quentin. Of course, there are no bars on the windows of the hotel, which towers over Anchorage's diminutive downtown, and Mel is free to come and go whenever she pleases. And yet, she's spent the bulk of her vacation locked alone in her room, drinking heavily and ordering room service, the slate gray faux velvet shades drawn.

Her phone plays muffled jazz from a crater in the feathery duvet, while local news anchors flap their gums on the flat-screen, unaware they've been muted. A bottle of vodka, another of Champagne, and a carton of orange juice stand precariously close to the edge of the bedside table. The clock radio, which once shared a perch with Mel's booze, has a new home on the floor. Sleepless as usual and fed up with the glowing reminder, Mel shoved the damn thing into oblivion at exactly 4:13 a.m. If someone were to ask the time now, Mel couldn't say. It's five o'clock somewhere—time to mind your business and fuck off.

Her damp robe hangs on the lampshade, casting a soft orange glow about the room, simultaneously setting the mood and mocking her eternal solitude. Lacking carnal entertainment, Mel settles for the digital variety. She plops onto the king bed, grabs her laptop, and flips it open. A glance at the upper right-hand corner of the screen affirms that it's not quite noon. But before she can navigate to more stimulating corners of the internet, her practiced fingers dive-bomb the keys, bang in her password, and click the email application icon in one fluid movement. She does so not out of desire—she's on vacation, after all—but out of habit, a reflex cultivated by 60-hour work weeks and constant work-related stress.

She stares at the uncooperative screen and furrows her artfully plucked eyebrows. The Wi-Fi is sluggish, and her emails won't load. She scowls at the pulp at the bottom of her empty glass and curses the hotel for the fourth time that morning. She should probably just log out, she thinks, when the emails finally load.

Seventy-two received emails since she checked late last night—or, rather, early this morning.

She quickly scans the unread emails for anything personal, but each seems work related. Much to the chagrin of her therapist, Mel forwards her work email to her personal inbox. She does so under the pretense of efficiency, but the true reason is a stunning lack of social life—going days without meaningful contact from friends or family is depressing beyond measure. What she does measure, though, is the proportion of work-to-personal emails: 22.43-to-1, last time she did the math—quantitative proof that she has no "work-life balance" whatsoever.

Another email blinks blue across her screen. That's seventy-three.

Grumbling, she fixes herself a fresh mimosa, using a Champagne-to-OJ ratio similar to that of her work-to-personal emails—a full glass of bubbly to a dash of juice.

It's noon in Anchorage, which means it's 4 p.m. back on Wall Street. The flow of emails will soon slow to stagnancy, and a stream of overworked, overweight, and largely overpaid stockbrokers will emerge from their office buildings and shuffle out into the weekend. Momentarily, they'll toast to their freedom and good fortune.

They'll self-medicate, spend time and money on vices, and scratch desperately after fulfillment. Saturday morning will blur into Sunday night, and Monday morning they'll knot ties like nooses and catch trains and taxis back to Wall Street. The market will open, and the world will keep on spinning.

Mel is all too familiar with this corporate clockwork. In ten years, this is only her second vacation. Many of her coworkers at Williams, Walker, & Pollard, the boutique brokerage at which she works, take frequent, extravagant vacations—Turks and Caicos to go fishing with their families over Christmas, Florida golf trips with the boys, "business trips" to Europe with the mistress. But Mel has to work three times as hard to be taken seriously. She doesn't use her sick days, arrives early, stays late. She doesn't make jokes, just keeps her head down, does her work—and she does it well.

She is, undeniably, an outcast in her office. Firstly, she's a woman—a rarity in the testosterone-heavy seas of the NYSE—and she's a person of color. In that corporate war zone, similitude is camouflage. Any deviation from the whitewashed, overwhelmingly male pack puts a target on your back. And Mel's had a target on her back since before she was born.

Mel's mother, Diane, came from old, white New York money— she would've fit right in with the Wall Street crowd. Her grandfather, Curt Pierce, founded a famous pharmaceutical company, creatively named Pierce Pharmaceuticals, and Diane's parents' generation took the company public a couple years before Diane was born, making the family a fortune. From birth Diane was guaranteed millions in company stock, all tied up in a trust she'd be able to access upon her twenty-fifth birthday.

Growing up, hers was a fantasy world. Diane spent her summers at a house in the Hamptons and the school year at a sprawling penthouse on the Upper West Side, complete with a view of Central Park. After junior high, she attended an all-girls boarding school in Connecticut, where she played field hockey and snuck out of the dorms to smoke pot, drink and canoodle with the ice hockey players from the all-boys boarding school the next town over. She spent her junior year abroad studying in Toulouse, France, then went to Princeton for college, where, coincidentally, the Pierce Foundation had donated a state-of-the-art science wing. She studied art history and anthropology, and after graduation secured a high-paying, high-status job with a family connection, planning charitable galas and events for New York's high society.

Three summers before Diane was to gain control of her trust fund, she met Mel's father at her yacht club in the Hamptons. Donny Drummond was a year older than she was, a handsome and clever African-American tennis instructor with a brilliant smile, patient disposition, and deadly forehand. Donny had earned a Division I tennis scholarship to St. John's, but his father, a portrait painter who worked boardwalks up and down the East Coast, passed of a heart attack while Donny was a senior in high school. His mother was arthritic—the death of a seamstress—and couldn't work needle and thread with the speed or skill she used to. With several younger siblings looking to Donny to put food on the table, he put his education and tennis dreams on hold. Instead, he worked his ass off at the yacht club, teaching the basics of the sport he loved to the rich.

The Hamptons was only an hour commute by bus from New Suffolk, but it felt worlds away. Donny put on an act for the snooty yacht club patrons, tailoring everything from his speech patterns to his political leanings to their brittle sensibilities—he was there to make tips, not enemies. But he genuinely liked Diane. She wasn't so uppity, and she made him laugh and nearly forget, for the briefest moments, at least, the socioeconomic chasm between them. Plus, she had long blond hair, jogged on the beach in the shortest shorts he'd ever seen, and was drop-dead gorgeous. He knew any breach of yacht club commandment number one—no hanky-panky with members—was a bad idea, but Diane was nothing if not convincing.

At this point, Diane was living under her own roof back in the city, a chic loft in the Village, and she relished the freedom to do what and whom she pleased without the stuffy oversight of her parents. In the Hamptons, though, she stayed at her parents' estate, still their little baby, so she and Donny kept their affair quiet.

For Diane, it was a bit of a game—she liked being promiscuous right under her parents' noses, breaking the unwritten rules of the crushingly white, wealthy Hamptons, although she did worry she would draw ire if found out. Donny was genuinely terrified that, if discovered, he would lose his livelihood. Their fears would prove to be well founded, and their affair, which both Donny and Diane assumed would be a short-lived summer fling, had its consequences—among them the birth of Mel.

Donny was fired just minutes after Mel was conceived. At a yacht club picnic, Diane dragged him into the boathouse gear closet for a quickie.

"I don't think this is the best idea," he hissed, torn between removing Diane's bikini top and removing himself from the situation. She grinned impishly, reached over her shoulder, and yanked a string, making the decision for him.

As they extricated themselves from a makeshift bed of life vests, Donny's boss unlocked the door, whistling cheerfully as he returned a set of croquet mallets. He saw Diane topless, dropped the mallets in a clatter, and did a double take before embarrassment set in. He sputtered unintelligibly about croquet. Once he gathered his wits, and before he gathered the mallets, he sacked Donny on the spot.

Word spread around the yacht club like a virus. The club was essentially a gilded petri dish for upper-class gossip and drama. And a scandal like that? It was the talk of the summer. Diane's father went into a rage.

"Have you learned nothing at Princeton, you dumb slut?" he yelled, spittle flying, his face inches from hers, his flushed cheeks as red as the yacht club's crest on his polo shirt. "My daughter! In a janitor's closet like a whore filming a porno? At my club? You've disgraced our family."

He went from mad to worse, screaming unspeakably racist,

sexist obscenities until his voice grew hoarse. The tirade lasted an eternity. Diane didn't stand up for Donny. She didn't stand up herself. She just teared up and took the abuse. Later, she judged her cowardice one of her biggest regrets in life.

She finally drew a line in the sand when she told her parents that she was pregnant, and her father demanded that she "get the damn thing taken care of." Diane had been on the fence, but her father's orders pushed her over the edge. She decided to keep the child, and his fury turned to harsh denial. As far as he was concerned, he had no daughter—not anymore. Within days he'd canceled her credit cards. Diane's boss reached out, terminating her position, citing a lack of funding. An eviction notice was posted on the door of her loft. Diane tried to find Donny, but the yacht club wouldn't give her an address or a phone number, and she had nowhere to go. Realizing Diane might soon become homeless, her mother stepped in and begged her father to relent. He agreed to send Diane to France, if only to save the family further embarrassment. "The only thing worse than a whore is a hobo," he said—the last words Diane ever heard her father say.

She gave birth to Mel in a French hospital surrounded by strange doctors. They lived together modestly in a small flat in Toulouse. Mel, a precocious and lovely child, was nearly three when she first set foot in the United States.

Diane made the trip home for two reasons: to introduce Donny to his daughter and to finally access her trust. But her return to New York was far from triumphant.

Diane first visited her family's bank expecting no trouble. She had been living frugally in France on a paltry allowance, eagerly anticipating this moment—she would soon have enough money to set her and Mel up for the rest of their lives.

But the bank made it clear that the funds were inaccessible. When she asked why, the bank manager brusquely kicked her out of his office. It turned out that, in her absence, her father had done everything in his power to tie up the trust in legal red tape, even going so far as to liquidate certain assets and move money around. Diane didn't understand the specifics, but it hardly seemed legal. Still, few Manhattan law firms would even take a meeting with her—to do so would upset one of the city's most powerful families. Besides, Diane had no money of her own to speak of.

She eventually found a sharp albeit greaseball attorney, a Mr. Thomas Pittman, from Long Island, who was game to take her case for free on the condition that if he gained access to her fortune, he'd receive thirty percent. It was a crap deal, but Diane had little choice.

Once Pittman had the case in motion, Diane sought out Donny. She tracked him down selling medical equipment in Newark, where he had a wife and one-year-old daughter of his own.

It was as if Donny had been waiting years to speak his mind. In the front yard of his suburban home, he told her that their relationship, if it could be called that at all, had been one-sided: Diane had been concerned only with her own pleasure, her own upper-class family dynamics. "It was a sport to you," he said. "But it was my life you were playing with." She had known he was living paycheck to paycheck, supporting his aging mother and younger siblings, and still she was so cavalier. That mistreatment alone was cause for anger; but carrying his seed all the while? Without so much as a letter?

"I'm sorry. I'm so sorry. I tried to find you," wept Diane.

"Did you come to New Suffolk? Ask for the Drummonds? Look in a phone book? No? I didn't think so."

As Donny's initial shock and ire lessened, he explained that, past aside, his wife, a night nurse, was a protective woman worn thin by raising their own daughter. They would need time to digest this development before Mel could become a part of their life.

"I understand," said Diane, crestfallen.

Pittman eventually got Diane access to her fund, but the millions she was expecting had dwindled to just over six hundred thousand dollars. Still a boon, but not enough to live off for the rest of her life. After Pittman's cut, she had enough to buy a townhouse in a middle-class suburb outside of Boston, where she tutored students at a local community college. With the leftover cash, she pursued a master's degree in social work—Donny's barbed reproach had cut deep, and she wanted to spend her days contributing to society.

Mel never met any of her family on her mother's side growing up. Diane never spoke about them and had asked Donny to do the same. Diane changed her last name to Rose, rarely dated and never married. The Drummond family, though, was warm and welcoming. Donny's wife, Layla, eventually got used to the idea of having another daughter. Mel spent her summers and school vacations with the Drummonds, where she shared a bunk bed with her half-sister, Shawna, who became one of her closest friends. Her cousins and aunts and uncles and grandparents couldn't get enough of her visits, and took her to baseball games, barbecues, museums and concerts. Her father taught her to play tennis. The Drummonds made her feel like she was home, despite the lightness of her skin in comparison to their own. Although she loved her mother dearly, she was always sad to leave Newark and head back to Boston.

High school was challenging for Mel. Academics came easily but navigating the ruthless public school system was aggravating to the point that it caused her serious anxiety. She bit her nails, slept poorly, and grew moody. She was, as rapper Earl Sweatshirt would pen many years later, "too Black for the white kids and too white for the Blacks." Fitting in was an everyday struggle. She saw a therapist, who recommended she see a psychiatrist, who prescribed her the first of many antidepressants. The pills didn't help much at first, namely because Mel took them irregularly and preferred to self-medicate with booze and weed.

Her grades suffered. When Mel turned sixteen, Diane, only semi-cognizant of her daughter's inner strife due to her extremely demanding work schedule, finally opened up about her fall from grace. She told Mel about the Pierce family's fortune, her birth and early years in France, the legal fallout upon their return, how she hadn't spoken to her parents in over a decade. After keeping the truth bottled up for so long, Diane held nothing back.

Mel researched the Pierce family obsessively and saw pictures of opulence she could scarcely fathom. Cousins her age attended posh private schools, drove Range Rovers, and wormed their way into tabloid pages. Had her mother decided to fall for a blond-haired, blue-eyed tennis instructor, Mel would probably be driving a BMW to school every day and skiing in the Alps over winter break. The prejudice was infuriating. It ate at Mel that her very existence could cause such a rift in the family. She blamed herself for her mother's and father's hardships. If anything, the knowledge made her anxiety even worse. But the revelation, as much as it pained her, was a wakeup call.

There were people out there who hated the very idea of her existence. And they wanted her to fail. Hell, they expected her to.

With her father's blessing, she changed her last name from Rose to Drummond, and vowed to become a self-made success. She went to therapy diligently, smoked less, took her pills regularly. She still drank, more than she ought to, but she hit the books, squeaked into Columbia University, and graduated from high school with top honors. She kept it up in college, interning at a respected firm and eventually becoming a licensed stockbroker. Revenge, in her mind, would be supporting her parents financially, being a self-made success. Helping her parents retire early. Making them proud.

Mel carries this past with her—an invisible burden that no one knows aside from her parents and, to a much greater extent, Dr. Meyer, her current psychologist (her fourth since moving to New York). Mel can't walk through a pharmacy without seeing the Pierce name plastered on pill bottles, and she finds herself in pharmacies all too often. Picking up her anxiety medication is, ironically enough, an enormous source of anxiety.

During one of Mel's first sessions with Dr. Meyer, when she was in bad shape but hesitant to get back on medication, the psychologist described her anxiety as a stove, and her well-being as a pot of rice.

"If left to its own devices, your flame likes to burn hot and high, and your pot will quickly overflow," she said. "But medication—the right medication—allows you to control the flame. You let the flame simmer, and the rice is cooked to perfection."

Dr. Meyer recommended she try a new antidepressant—a fresh start. Mel relented, so long as it wasn't anything produced by Pierce Pharmaceuticals. Dr. Meyer set her up with a psychiatrist, who prescribed her a fifty-milligram starter dose of sertraline, also known as Zoloft.

A couple weeks into the new medication, Mel was feeling no better, and she broke down in her weekly appointment with Dr. Meyer.

"I feel like I'm one snap away from a panic attack every day," Mel cried, exasperated, exhausted. She bottled up her stress all week at work, but curled up on the couch, her muscles clenched, her fingernails digging into her palms, she gave herself the rare permission to let go. Dr. Meyer nodded and scribbled a note on her pad.

"I'm so close to boiling over. Shouldn't the rice be simmering right now?"

At that, Dr. Meyer smiled sadly. "The medication takes a while to kick in—we have to give it time. If we don't notice results soon, we can bump up the dose if need be. For some of us, it's a lifelong pursuit to balance the flame. But that's why you come here. In our sessions, if you're boiling over, we can lift the lid and let the steam escape for a moment."

"Doesn't that ruin rice?"

Dr. Meyer laughed. "Not this rice."

Mel's angst doesn't end at the pharmacy. She can't see a boat or a tennis racket without thinking of her parents, young and in lust and oblivious of the future. She can't see so much as a croissant or a jar of Dijon mustard without thinking of France. She doesn't remember much from her time in Toulouse, only flashes of a cathedral spire against blue sky, the smell of strawberries and cream from their neighborhood crêpe stand, looking down at a pair of tiny pink shoes on a cobblestone street.

Even more so than the pills, New York is the cure for her anxiety. She loves the city—it's the only place she doesn't feel like an outsider. After growing up in largely white spaces, it's a relief to get lost in the city's infinite hues, to be just another face in the crowd. But while Mel belongs in the city, she's never felt like she belongs on Wall Street, and that's only made her grind harder. She sees herself as an infiltrator, every dollar earned as a vitriolic and triumphant loogie hawked in the face of the Pierce family and the socioeconomic system they represent.

Dr. Meyer was right. She needs a vacation.

Mel has one more day in Anchorage, and then she's heading north, to a luxurious boutique winter lodge. She'll stay there for a few nights, snowshoeing, embarking on sleigh rides, and hoping for a glimpse of the northern lights. That was the real reason she came to Alaska—to see those green lights. She's never believed in God, especially not since she found out the truth about her past, but if there's one thing on earth that could make this skeptic believe in something bigger, it's garlands of green flickering in the night sky.

She removes the towel from her hair. Coiled curls, still wet, tumble down her shoulders. She knows she shouldn't, because she's on vacation, but she turns back to her computer and scrolls through her full inbox like a stoned teenager flicking through TV channels. Eyeing the screen with both distaste and vague interest, Mel marks emails as "read" despite only scanning the subject lines. Taking it one step further, she imagines how she'd respond if there were no consequences for her actions.

Subject Line: Important—Updated Office Fridge Policy
From: Ed Newman

How about this for a fridge policy, Ed: Steal my roasted red pepper wrap once, shame on you. You dick. Steal my roasted red pepper wrap twice, and I'll momentarily forget the twelve years I've spent dedicated to a plant-based diet, gut you with a dull letter opener, start a fire in the break room, and roast your floppy loins over it on a spit. I will then bait the office with an email that reads: "Pulled pork in the break room!"

She marks it as "read."

Subject Line: Portfolio Update?
From: Jerry Dickinson

You'll get an update at the end of the month like everyone else, Jerry, you pompous dung beetle. You're making money hand over fist—thanks to me—yet you assume that because I'm a woman I need some superior blessed with both X and Y chromosomes pulling my strings.

Nope. Your privileged ass is set to make twenty-nine percent this year thanks to my Russian oil plays last month. All while your understanding of stocks is weaker and thinner than borscht during a famine in Moscow.

So, much like when that young-enough-to-be-your-daughter, tits-faker-than-the-moon-landing piece of post-divorce ass of yours gargles your wrinkled ball sack and sticks a manicured pinky up your jaundiced starfish, don't ask me to explain to you what I'm doing—just sit back, shut the fuck up, and be thankful.

She marks it as "read."

Subject Line: New York City Singles—Matches of the Week
From: OkCupid

Dear all:

If "dating in New York" and the sixth ring of Dante's Inferno were the two circles of a Venn diagram, they would layer up almost entirely, like the sun and moon during an eclipse. If you did not understand the particulars of this astute and hilarious observation, you are part of the problem.

Quit calling your Brooklyn closet a "loft." Stop trying on feminism like a jacket to get yourself laid. That jacket doesn't fit you. Also, your actual jacket doesn't fit you. And whatever you do, please, please don't feel obligated to shuck out your shekels for my glass of wine. Why? Because:

a) Chivalry is dead. Decomposed, rotting-corpse, embalmed-mummy, muskrat-pancaked-on-the-highway dead.

b) I likely make more money than you.

c) Insisting minimizes the already slim chances of converting this encounter into anything erotic. Split the bill, and there's a small chance I'll invite you to split me in half (a wistful thought).

Marking it as "read" doesn't seem to be a strong enough punishment for this digital dispatch from OkCupid. No, Mel dumps this email into the trash. She doesn't need to click on it to see the rows of smiling faces, their names, likes and dislikes, the potential for time wasted. How many times has she had her high hopes dashed against a subway grate?

For a moment, she's happy to be in Anchorage, happy to be on vacation, far away from New York and the squadrons of single males marching up and down the avenues, holding condoms like hungry deli-goers clutching tickets and waiting for a pastrami on rye. The thought of courtship—i.e., the prolonged, political prelude to fucking—makes Mel exhausted.

Lesbianism isn't a choice, obviously. Mel would've picked it by now.

Thankfully for her, there's a reliable subsection of the robot community that doesn't speak so much as hum, whose sole purpose in life is the dogged pursuit of the female orgasm. Yes, the phallic pinnacle of modern invention, a discovery responsible for contributing more to global serotonin release than MDMA, roller coasters, vinyl records and candied bacon combined: the mother-diddling vibrator.

She's on the verge of exiting her email to employ the services of Astrid Double-Time. Astrid is Mel's purple, dual-pronged silicone travel companion, upon whom Mel has bestowed the character of a 1920s jazz singer renowned for her ability to bebop and scat at speed. But before Mel can quit the application and Astrid can kick off her performance, another email blinks on the screen. And this time, the subject line actually piques Mel's interest:

Subject Line: Re: Snowmobile tour tomorrow?
From: Anchorage Alaskan Adventures

Careful not to spill on her keyboard, Mel takes an aggressive chug of mimosa, one more appropriate for keg beer than sixty-dollar-a-bottle Champagne. She belches loudly and finds herself strangely satisfied at both the reverberations and the acrid reminder of her eggs Benedict. Though the taste itself is foul and fermented, there's something inexplicably delectable about the contradiction of acting like an animal in such an elegant setting.

After reading the short and borderline-incoherent email—is spell-check an adventure these Alaskans have never embarked upon?—she picks up the hotel phone and dials.

It rings twice and sends her to voicemail. How efficient.

"Hello, this is Anchorage Alaskan Adventures—a.k.a. Triple-A! Our office is generally chuggin' from 7 a.m. to 7 p.m. Monday through Saturday, and Sunday from 10 a.m. to 5 p.m. If you've reached us during these office hours, well, we're probably out on an Alaskan Adventure!"

Yuck. Mel is dangerously close to hanging up. Were it not for the mimosas, she'd likely have immediately bailed after the gleeful "a.k.a. Triple-A!" As cynical as she is bright, Mel is a dedicated pessimist, borderline allergic to positivity. By default, she shits in the punchbowl. The voice on the phone is dripping with optimism, soaked in sunshine and sobriety, likely belonging to precisely the kind of upbeat chatterbox she wouldn't want to sit next to on a plane.

But she decides not to hang up.

"If you're calling to see what trips we offer, please go to our website. If you want to set up a tour or inquire further about a trip, please leave your name and number, and we'll wrangle you up just as soon as we can."

Wrangle? Will they be coming with lassos?

"Thanks so much for picking Anchorage Alaskan Adventures for all your adventurous needs!"

Mel's almost surprised by the beep. "Hi, uh, yes, hello. My name is Mel, Mel Drummond, and I just got an email back from one of your associates, I believe his name was Marvin, or Murphy, sorry, I can't recall, but anyway, I was hoping to get on the snowmobile tour tomorrow. Is there still—"

Someone picks up the phone.

"Hey, hey, Mel, this is Marty! Neither Marvin nor Murphy, but you were right on the money with the first letter and number of syllables. Thanks for getting back to us."

"Ah, yes. Thank you. So there's still availability on the snowmobile tour tomorrow?"

"There is indeed! Also, just so you know, in Alaska, we call snowmobiles 'snowmachines'—they're the same thing. How many in your party?"

Asshole.

"Just me."

"Okay, we've got a group going out tomorrow, if that works. We could set you up with a private tour, but that's three times the cost."

A snow jacket and pants, unworn, tags on, are draped over the back of an upholstered chair, goading her. Her colleagues would likely be less surprised to see her naked and two-stepping through the office than bundled up in that atrocity and speeding on a snowmachine through the Alaskan wilderness.

"Fu—, what the hell, sign me up, Marty. The group is fine. I can't imagine we'll be doing much socializing on the snowmachines."

The man laughs. "All righty! Now whereabouts are you staying? We'll send a shuttle to come to pick you up tomorrow morning at around seven."

"I'm at the Marriott."

"Fancy," he says. She hears him shuffling papers. "Let me just pull together some paperwork and we'll get you dialed."

She imagines him alone in a cramped office akin to a high school football coach's, the smell of cheap coffee only barely blocking that of unwashed jockstraps.

The weatherman is miming away on the TV. Waving the remote like a magic wand, Mel grants him speech.

"Big storm coming our way, storm fronts currently out to sea, but we see the start of the storm, just the fringes of it dropping an inch already."

Intrigued, Mel, swings off the bed, pads to the window, and opens the curtains. Sure enough, snow has started to fall.

"Hey, Marty," she says, "you there?"

"Yes, ma'am."

"You're not concerned about this storm at all?"

Marty laughs. "Where you from, Mel?"

"New York."

"New York City?"

"Yeah. New York."

"Well, correct me if I'm wrong, but what's a debilitating snowstorm in New York, here in Alaska is just daily life." He manages to say it without being condescending; still, watching the snowfall outside her window, she feels vaguely uneasy.

But it wouldn't do to stay put in the hotel for a week straight. Anchorage feels more like a town than a city, like New York's runt of a cousin who was sent away to work in the gulags. No, you don't come to Alaska for the Marriott. You come for the mountains, for the sea, for the tundra, for the night sky. At least that's what National Geographic says. She wants to get out, to feel something, anything, to experience the power of nature she's read about more often than felt herself—the way someone from a small town hears tales of New York and wants to stand on the sidewalk and break their neck staring up at the skyscrapers.

"We've got our eye on the storm, don't you worry," says Marty. "We'll go for an hour or two tour tomorrow and be back by noon. Storm won't pick up until the evening."

The forecaster continues as if privy to their conversation.

"The storm should pick up in the morning, but it won't really get going full speed until tomorrow afternoon. Then, starting in earnest tomorrow night, we're looking at storm totals well over two feet, with more in the mountains. But, as I mentioned, most of this will take place tomorrow night into Sunday night, with Monday slowing slightly. Then another heavy front comes in shortly after—looks like it's shaping up to be a stormy month…"

Mel listens with her forehead pressed up against the cool glass, gazing down into the empty streets, wondering if anyone's looking up at the seventh floor and can see her naked body through the lightly falling snow.

"As I said, Thursday we'll be back to a sunny day in the city—excellent skiing conditions—and then accumulation continues through the weekend and into next week. In the meantime, stock up on necessities, grab a frozen pizza or five, and try to minimize your driving—expect roads to be a mess by tomorrow at 7 p.m."

Mel doesn't drive. She hasn't since high school. Like many New Yorkers, she bounces between taxicabs and subways—the last time she drove, it was a bumper car at the fair, and she left with a sore ass and a bloody lip. She has no desire to drive a vehicle on some snow-caked Alaskan highway, but a snowmachine? That could be precisely the kind of adrenaline rush she needs to clear her head.

"All right, Mur—Marty," she says.

"Don't worry," he says, sensing her trepidation. "We've been doing this for fifteen years, never lost a soul," he laughs, then, more somberly: "Knock on wood."

She gives him her credit card details and hangs up.

The weatherman is gone, replaced by a couple news anchors with plastic smiles discussing a local factory accused of poisoning the Turnagain Arm.

She mutes the TV and shuts her laptop, unsure of what to do next. That settles tomorrow, but what about today?

Fuck it. She's on vacation.

She tops off her mimosa with more Champagne, reaches for the landline, and dials room service.

Chapter 3

James Connelly removes a hand-sewn rabbit-fur mitten with his teeth and stretches out a bare, rough-skinned hand. Snowflakes drift into his palm. The forest is quiet. Not dead quiet—no, James has long rejected that turn of phrase. This is a living quiet. The first breath of a storm whispers across the range, a slowly building exhale blown in from the Aleutians. James feels the bite of winter on his exposed cheeks and quickens his pace, pleased. He revels in the cold. Snow, if nothing else, further stifles the outside world.

When the sun will peek out again is the weatherman's guess. Sometimes, James sits by the fire and listens to the meteorologist's monotonic speculations over the staticky radio. He does so mainly to hear another voice—it's the only channel he gets. The forecast itself is rarely useful. The Glacier Range is a remote and expansive string of mountains that's mostly uninhabited, and any mention of the range is usually brief, general and completely wrong. Either way, it doesn't much matter. He doesn't need a meteorologist to tell him that a storm is coming.

James' heavy-soled, fur-lined boots crunch into crusty snow. His respiration is steady. Lanka, his two-year-old husky, pads obediently a half-step behind him. The occasional caw of a raven ruptures the rhythm of their footsteps—a haunting horn over a simple drumbeat. He trudges on until silver frost ornaments his long, brown beard. The paths of summer are buried feet below him. In their place are frozen impressions of boots and paws and sled runners, a temporary trail he's trekked four times since the last storm exited the range two weeks ago. With fresh snow on its way, those tracks will soon fill in and disappear. The landscape will smooth, swell, warble, transform. Walking anywhere like this will be impossible—he'll have to take snowshoes or the dogsled—which is why he happily hikes along now, savoring the movement, his slightly elevated heart rate, the sweat that dampens his lower back.

This coming storm, James bets, will be measured in feet, not inches. He doesn't make this assumption based on weather maps or Doppler radar or even the weatherman's monologues, but the intensifying ache in his knee. The dull pain always sharpens before a storm. And right now, the cold might as well be swinging a scimitar at his joint. Nonetheless, he limps on. He's long since relinquished the crutch of painkillers and learned to walk—if not perfectly straight—on his own.

He's been clean for nearly fourteen years. Life in the bush, as it turns out, demands sobriety, at least to a certain extent. To persevere through winter, alone and with his cursed limp, James could not afford to be wrapped up in the foggy lethargy of opiates. A clear head is the only thing that's kept him alive out here. It's been fifteen winters now—a feat that any backwoods Alaskan would respect.

So his habit dissolved in circumstance like Oxy in the bloodstream. That said, when the pain gets bad and his knee stiffens up, he craves the caress of painkillers. Longing laps at his resolve like tidewaters against a pier. Luckily, temptation's a two-day trip away—a trip he can't afford to take. Still, he's no teetotaler. A generous pour of whiskey is a welcome escape these days.

He limps efficiently forward. James knows this forest well. After years of establishing, tweaking, and running this trapline, he recognizes subtleties in the landscape—the crisscrossing boughs of a cottonwood, a creek buried beneath the snow. He passes the remnants of a trapping cabin. Only a dilapidated corner of the simple structure survives. Bishop had reckoned it was from the late

1800s. Aside from a few distinguishing features like the cabin, this stretch of forest is a maze, with tree tunnels so hauntingly similar that getting lost is all but guaranteed. At first, getting lost was all James did.

That initial winter, after he murdered Bishop, James ventured from the cabin tentatively, moving slowly but losing his way regardless. It didn't help that he was bogged down by a backpack stuffed with survival gear. Petrified of spending a night out in the woods, he crammed gizmos and gadgets and spare equipment into his pack until it eventually burst at the seams. With time, his confidence grew and his packing list shrank. James sewed the first pack back together three times, and then, when he no longer needed the volume, bought a smaller one.

He shifts the newer pack now—an aluminum-frame REI sixty-liter that's seen twelve years of heavy use. He stretches his shoulders and tightens the hip belt, notices the pack's weight, its center of gravity. He chuckles to himself ruefully, remembering those days of hauling shit he didn't need.

Now, he packs light and moves quickly—well, as quickly as a man with a sliver of a bullet buried in his knee cartilage can. He feels the familiar weight of the hunting rifle over his shoulder. It's the same Winchester Model 70 Alaskan that Bishop helped pick out so many years ago, and at this point the weapon feels like an extension of his arm, an intrinsic part of his being. Between the pack and that trusty firearm, James feels well prepared for whatever comes his way. He intends to be back by nightfall, but if he needs to spend a night out, it's no problem. He's done it before, and he'll do it again.

Sure enough, the clouds roll in, obscuring the surrounding peaks. Navigating is much more manageable when the sky is clear—foothills rise at the edges of the river valley and the towering mountains beyond guide the trapper like constellations led seafaring explorers. The peaks look deceptively close, but traveling from the river to the base of the nearest mountains takes several hours on foot.

Cleaving through the valley is the Hope, the longest river in Alaska. Mighty tributaries flow into it, and in spring it becomes dangerously swollen with snowmelt. Follow the river downstream, as survival texts suggest, and eventually it'll send you south to civilization. On the way, though, you'll encounter tricky river crossings, impassable waterfalls, and, depending on the season, grizzlies hunting for salmon.

Without a bush plane, the only way out in winter is to take a snowmachine or dogsled down the frozen banks. The forest, though a more direct route, is too difficult to navigate. Either way, walking, especially for James, would be a death march.

No, James relies on a team of sled dogs. So he leaves only twice a year to buy supplies: once, a month or so after the snow starts to stick, and again a few weeks before it melts. As far as James is concerned, when the snowline recedes, he's stuck.

Civilization. He looks forward to his visits, yet also dreads them.

James sleds to a ranch outside of Timber—a journey that generally takes two full days, conditions dependent—where he trades a stack of pelts to board the dogs for a few days. The owner of the ranch, a solitary fellow who seems to feel kinship with James, keeps James' old truck in a barn during winter and starts it every month or so. It costs James a few more pelts, but it's worth it. Assuming the truck starts, James makes the three-hour drive southwest to Anchorage and beelines it to the nearest cheeseburger joint. Then he books a motel, delivers the rest of his pelts to Ray's Trapper Co., and Ray buys them—cash, no permits, no questions asked, for a discount, of course. James hits the storage unit where he keeps nothing but a duffel bag full of money and spare hunting gear. Flush with cash, he visits the outdoor store, the grocery store and the hardware store. Carefully, he follows the lists he's written in his ledger and stocks up for the months ahead.

With time he's gotten much better at figuring out what he needs, what he doesn't. He religiously measures the rate at which he consumes everything, from grains and spices to toilet paper and novels. When you're as many as seven months between trips to the store, running out of food might be a death sentence—running out of toilet paper or reading material, however, is a less-fatal but potentially worse fate. One winter long ago, he ran out of toilet paper first, and his reading material came in handy. His least favorite books found a new home in the outhouse, their uninspiring pages serving a newfound purpose.

Without fail, James visits the bookstore, Tundra Titles, last. A reward. He takes his time in the used section. He's both discerningly picky and open-minded—he'll read fiction or nonfiction, anything from cheap-thrill sci-fi to American classics and ancient philosophy—so long as it's captivating. A stack of thirty to thirty-five books does the trick for six months. He keeps the great ones in the cabin to reread in years to come and returns subpar titles—those that escape the outhouse, at least—in exchange for a discount.

The middle-aged hippie who owns the shop, Jane, wears wire-rimmed glasses and her shawls change color with the seasons. On his second or third visit, over a decade ago now, she was curious about his tottering stack of novels, and they started talking about books—which ones he liked, which ones he didn't, and why. These days, he buys her a sandwich at the deli next door and surprises her for lunch.

"You again? Thought this winter would've snatched you up. What do you got for me today?"

"Veggies and hummus. Wasn't sure if you're a vegetarian these days."

"You dog! Okay, break out those sandwiches, give me half of both—I smell that pastrami. Now lay it on me. What did you hate this winter? Then we'll get to the ones you liked."

Without fail, she asks him about life in the wilderness, and he answers less gruffly than usual. She boils the news of the world down into fifteen minutes of liberal politics. He doesn't agree with her perspectives completely, but thoroughly enjoys listening to her passionate complaints. He asks teasing questions, if only to get her riled up. Once, she asked him if he voted and he laughed out loud. "I don't have so much as an ID, sweetheart," he said. After she helps him pick out new books, he packs up his purchases, says goodbye, and goes back to his motel room.

She calls him Stephen.

Closest thing to a friend he has in this world, and she doesn't know his real name. He's considered asking her out on a date many times, and thinks of her on the loneliest, longest nights, but never once mustered the courage.

Aside from these logistical errands, he gives in to his baser instincts, and binges accordingly. He goes out to Chinese restaurants and gorges himself on fried food. He drinks too much at the bars. He buys nudie mags and fucks whores, who inevitably comment on the piles of groceries and gear carefully stacked in the motel room.

"You're not preparing for the apocalypse or something are you, honey?" asked one, smirking through rouge.

He answered her question with a question.

"How much to gag you?"

In a snap, he's sick of the city, sick of humans—whores and otherwise. He can't stand cars, hates using money, cringes at the sound of his voice, and, like a wild animal, retreats to the mountains. The relief upon picking up his dogs, sledding back into the bush, and finally arriving back at the cabin is better than any drug, the sweetest respite, like walking from vision-blurring desert heat into an air-conditioned room.

Just thinking about Anchorage, James grimaces. He won't be going back to the city for at least another five months, and by then he'll probably be excited about it. In the meantime, he's suddenly grateful for the little details around him: the dense woods, the frozen footprints, the gently falling snow. He can no longer see the mountains, but, like a faithful man who cannot see God but knows him to be true, senses their lofty presence.

This is home. He can't imagine returning to New York

now. These are the corridors of his castle. This is his borderless kingdom—a tenure not granted by birthright but seized with a well-placed blow from a tin coffee mug.

It was the right thing to do—not morally, but strategically. Rusty just never understood that.

"Life is like chess," James told him. "Sometimes, you have to sacrifice a bishop to protect the king."

How long ago that was. James imagined himself then a hard man, a killer, but he was, in reality, soft, his hands free of calluses, his mind untested by winter. If the James from fifteen years ago could meet the James of today, neither would recognize the other. No longer is he that weak outsider—he's hard-edged, adapted, a fixture here, a part of the landscape, same as the branches bending under heavy snow, the river rapids freezing and thawing season by season, the pine needles quaking in the howling winds. He's acclimatized, as at home as the snuffling grizzlies, the spawning salmon, the prowling wolves. He may still be a criminal in the eyes of the law, but he's more than that now—a trapper, a hunter, a fisherman, intimately entwined in the ecosystem of this great wilderness. He is a predator.

In James' view, the outdoorsman who focuses on self-imposed objectives, like scaling a peak or traversing a range for the sake of recreation and personal achievement, fails to attain the depth of connection felt by the hunter who engages in the ancient dance of man and beast. The kayaker passes through the river, the river passes through the fisherman. The hiker passes through the forest, while the forest passes through the hunter. Furthermore, James believes that it isn't until you become reliant on hunting and fishing, when you pursue game not out of joy but out of dependence, when you don't live to hunt but hunt to live, that you can begin to understand the profundity of man's relationship with wilderness.

At the end of that first winter, rations got low and tensions between him and Rusty intensified. James had the pioneer's epiphany: Survival was not guaranteed. In Alaska, odds were always on demise. Daily, he squared up with the reaper, as the weight of self-sustenance fell upon his shoulders. He hunted with desperation, fished until he had frost-nipped fingers, trekked through waist-high snow to check his traps.

Only then had he started to understand.

He does not expect those who live in Anchorage, much less New York, to comprehend the connection he feels for his rifle: a primitive trust, bordering on love, that of soldier and sword, brave and bow, caveman and spear. Like the forest itself, his gun is both life-giver and life-taker.

The husky sniffs, whines and yelps sharply, shaking him from his thoughts—her superior senses noting something he cannot.

"Easy, Lanka," he says, calming her. "Shh."

She's young, yet to be fully trained—a more mature dog, like her mother, would stiffen and point out the source of agitation silently, so as not to give away the party's position.

All in due time. She will learn to live in this wilderness, just as James has.

James slows his steps, puts an open palm in front of the husky's nose and Lanka stops. Deftly, he rotates the rifle across his chest and aims it at the zigzagging path of their past boot and paw prints ahead, which bends through a shadowy tunnel of spruce. He reckons most grizzlies are hibernating for the season, but that's not exactly something you want to gamble on.

They're nearing the third trap in his trapline of ten. The first two traps were empty but given Lanka's escaped emotion—her silvery hair standing as if rubbed with a balloon, lips pulled back, ears pricked up—he's guessing that the third has struck pay dirt.

He rounds the corner and steps into the clearing. Sure enough, in the jaws of the Conibear—a body-gripping steel trap triggered by a hidden wire—is a dead marten, its spinal column snapped like a cheap chopstick. A gray wolf stands over the trap and looks up from its meal. The marten has been mauled into pulp. The pelt, obviously, is unsellable.

Not quite full grown, the wolf is likely a lone adolescent. He looks directly at James, seeming almost embarrassed to stoop to the level of eating something he didn't hunt for himself. Caught red-pawed, so to speak.

From thirty yards away, James has a clean shot. Lanka growls, her lips pulling back even further. James grins—she's got heart—but that red-lipped wolf would rip her to shreds. James doesn't aim to let that happen, and peers through the scope.

The wolf licks its teeth and takes two steps toward them. Lanka tenses, quivering.

"Hush, now, girl." James remains calm, though his heart thumps double-time and hot blood rages through his veins like the Hope River during the spring melt.

Thank God for sobriety. He wouldn't want to face a wolf wobbling off an Oxy high. Steadfast, he will dispatch the beast with one pull of the Winchester's well-oiled trigger.

Through the scope, he gets a better glimpse: the sinewy stateliness of its back, the eerie intelligence of its eyes, yellow as larch leaves come fall.

It takes another step forward.

Lanka is conflicted. Fear says retreat, pride says fight, training says wait for a command. James, in tune with his companion, aware of her twitching muscles, lets the wolf take another step, and then another. As soon as it makes a move, he'll kill it before it can entangle with Lanka—if they grapple, a clean shot will be impossible, and the husky's death likely.

In the meantime, this is the real-world training a dog needs to survive out here.

"Patience, Lanka," he whispers. "Easy, girl."

At fifteen yards, James realizes the wolf has a gash across its muzzle, and the blood on its fur is not only that of the marten. Its coat is patchy at the shoulders. The loner has likely been kicked out of its pack—and it's ridden with lice to boot.

Its mangy pelt is worthless, just like that of the marten. And the meat of a free-ranging wolf isn't exactly choice, either. It'll serve for the dogs, though. With ten hungry mouths to feed, he needs all the meat he can get in winter.

Ten yards away, the wolf stops.

Three predators, in a quiet clearing, almost peacefully poised. One word and Lanka will throw herself against an adversary that outsizes her. She will walk straight into the scythe if he asks her to—is that not the highest loyalty a man can hope for?

One jerk of his finger and wolf blood will drip red into the snow.

The marten, inauspiciously crushed in the steel jaws of the Conibear, lolls broken in the background.

The three stand still, taut with anticipation.

Snow drifts down between the trees.

And then, the wolf turns and walks back toward the marten. It sniffs the carcass, looks over its shoulder at James and Lanka, and slips into the woods at the far end of the clearing.

Lanka relaxes in the anticlimax and looks up at James, quizzically.

"I didn't want to shoot him," he explains, shrugging. "Didn't see no reason to. Especially when I have you to protect me."

He reaches into his jacket pocket and pulls out a piece of home-smoked moose jerky. He takes a knee. The cold presses against his leg through his patched Gore-Tex snow pants. He gnaws at one side of the jerky and lets Lanka bite the second half out of his mouth. As she chews, he scratches behind her ears.

"Good girl. You held fast, didn't you? You held fast for me." The eyes of the scrawny wolf flash through his thoughts. He looks up, half expecting to see it silently charging across the clearing. But the forest is empty and quiet.

"Hold fast. That's what we do out here."

James stands, dusting snow from his knees. Lanka eyes him expectantly.

"All righty," he says, as much to himself as to the dog. "Let's go see if we can salvage this marten, eh, girl?"

There was a chance that wolf was a scout, that it will be back soon with a pack. But James got the feeling that the wolf was out on his own—a castaway, an outcast.

It takes one to know one.

Chapter 4

Four strips of bacon. Three eggs, over easy. Quadruple stack of sourdough toast, butter, no jam. Half order of hash browns, half order of home fries. Grilled tomatoes on the side.

This is Richard's "Usual."

That, plus a never-ending waterfall of black coffee.

Speaking of which, Richard examines his mug. It's nearly half full. Richard waited tables at a diner back in college, and by decree of his tyrannical manager, a mug was to be considered empty when half full. "They don't buy our coffee for the taste," he'd claim, jabbing a penny-pinching thumb at the neon promise of "Free Coffee Refills" blinking in the window. To this day, no doubt a remnant of those traumatic and formative years spent slinging Usuals himself, Richard believes speed of coffee refills to be one of three telltale indicators of diner quality, the others being pie selection and hash brown execution. Donna's doesn't score particularly high in any category, but rather is consistent across the board. And consistency counts for something in Richard's book.

Not too many folks can claim a true Usual. You've got to be a restaurant fixture, as fundamental to the joint as the pictures on the walls and the cooks in the kitchen. Richard's name isn't carved into a barstool, but an imprint of his ass may as well be formed in the red vinyl of the corner booth. He can tell when Susan, waitress and single mother of three, attended night school the previous evening by the rings under her eyes. He's seen the chef, Joaquin, out of his grease-stained whites and in a rented tux, having attended two of Joaquin's three weddings. And he's sent the entire staff of Donna's boxes of steaks and sausages every Christmas for nearly a decade. If eating were a sport and Donna's Diner a stadium, Richard would be on track to have his jersey retired. His prolonged absence wouldn't just be noticed, it would be cause for concern.

It's still dark outside. Richard works methodically through his usual. He scoops runny eggs onto golden toast, crunches up the bacon in his hands and sprinkles it on top—a slice of tomato, a dash of hot sauce, and a squirt of ketchup tie it all together. Across the booth, Jim, a post-divorce vegetarian, shovels down granola and yogurt. Diet is one of the few things Richard and Jim disagree on— and they rag on each other's preferences with enthusiasm.

Over Jim's shoulder, Richard surveys Donna's: the polished white countertops, chrome details, red vinyl booths and swivel stools. The restaurant is empty, save for a few tired truckers sipping coffee at the counter. It's as archetypal an establishment to America as the gladiator's fighting pits were to Rome—and with few regular customers and an unreliable dribble of new business, Richard fears Donna's may soon be a dust-covered ruin as well.

He once voiced this concern to Katherine, Donna's middle-aged daughter and the matriarch tasked with keeping the train on track since her mother passed.

"Don't you worry about that, Richie," she scoffed. "Donna's will be here long after you and I stop kicking."

Katherine's a funny woman, old-fashioned almost to a fault. There are hand-painted signs on the wall that read: "Hash browns, no hashtags!" and "Eat your food, don't take pictures of it."

"We're a diner, honey," she said to him once when he asked why she so adamantly disliked digital marketing and social media. "We rely on word of mouth. If you like what we put in your mouth, by all means use that mouth, tell your friends, bring your families. But, and don't pardon my French because I mean this with all my heart, fuck a Yelp review."

Richard chuckles at the memory, causing Jim to look up from his granola. "What're you laughing about?"

"Nothing," says Richard, shaking his head. "Well, hashtags, I guess." He gestures at Katherine's signs. "You know, the pound sign."

"I know what hashtags are, Richard. I use the internet," says Jim, grinning. "The question is, do you?"

Richard grunts. He does use the internet. More than he'd like to. He spends his workday on the computer, sending emails, checking in on finances, managing the shipping software. And he has a vague comprehension of hashtags, too, thanks to Sarah. His teenage daughter serves as both tech support and his main pipeline to popular culture. When Sarah saw Katherine's sign, she said, "It's cool to post pictures of your food, Dad."

"I'd sooner take a picture of my poop," he responded to his cringing daughter. "At least I play a part in making it."

He is, in Sarah's words, a "technology T. rex."

A fossil from the Jurassic Era of floppy disks.

His coffee is now lukewarm, the mug dangerously close to a quarter full. He watches snow fall, slow and steady, out the window. In the reflection, he sees Susan hustle over with a steaming pot. "Here you go, Richie. Sorry for the wait."

"No problem, Susan. Keep it comin'. Thank you kindly."

"You boys going for a ride this morning?" She nods at their trucks and trailers parked outside.

"Yes, ma'am," says Jim, in between mouthfuls.

"Be careful out there," she says. "Storm's comin' already."

"With a breakfast like this under our belts, we'll be all but invincible," says Richard.

"Well, I will be," says Jim, scraping his bowl. "This bacon-guzzling son of a gun is dangerously close to a heart attack."

Laughing, Richard chokes on a forkful of egg, hash browns and bacon. He sputters then takes a sip of scalding coffee to wash it down.

"See, would you look at this, Susan? He's dying already," chuckles Jim. "The pig will kill him—one way or another."

"Oh, quiet," says Richard once he regains his breath. "There's only a syllable difference between lettuce-eater and lotus-eater, you know." Jim scoffs, and Richard looks at Susan, who doesn't get the joke. "Ever since he became a totalitarian—I mean a vegetarian—he thinks he's Gandhi."

"I'm a practitioner of naan-violence," says Jim, drawing out "naan" to ensure that his pun comes through.

"Well said," says Richard.

"A thigh for a thigh leaves the whole world obese," says Jim, grinning.

Susan shakes her head, lost. "I don't have time to waste talking nonsense with you two."

She walks off to tend to the truckers, and Jim watches her go. "What do you think?" he asks.

"About what?"

"Sue."

"As a waitress?"

"You know what I mean."

Richard suddenly gets serious.

"If you screw Sue, and screw up this diner for me, I will personally force-feed you pork products until you die of a coronary."

This threat is only mildly hyperbolic, and Jim knows it.

Jim watches Sue lean over the truckers' table to top off their coffees, then shrugs. "Might be worth it. I don't think I've ever been with a waitress. There's an allure to them, a nostalgia, ya know? Same thing goes for stewardesses. And teachers. What do you think?"

"I think you've been watching too much porn."

"You're not wrong, my friend," says Jim, smiling. "Ready to hit the road?"

Richard answers by crumbling his last strip of bacon onto a piece of yolk-drenched toast and devouring it in a single bite. He throws a couple twenties on the table. Jim pulls out his wallet in protest.

"C'mon, Jim, that granola is cheaper than the dirt it tastes like," laughs Richard. "You grab the next one."

"That's two Saturdays in a row. I'm up this week and next."

"Sure," says Richard, not a doubt in his mind that next weekend he'll be back in this booth, talking shit before a ride with Jim.

At 6:35 a.m. they caravan from Glacier Point toward Glennallen. They hit seventy mph and tear by slow-moving SUVs with out-of-state plates. The snowfall isn't too heavy. Not yet, anyway.

Richard shuffles through a classic-rock playlist. He's humming along to Tom Petty when Jim radios on the walkie-talkie.

"Lone Ranger requesting relief. Over."

Richard clucks. Jim pisses more than a ninety-year-old woman in a nursing home.

"We're going to have to get you a catheter for the race, Lone Ranger. Over."

"Anne's already custom-fit one for me. Didn't she tell you? It's huge. Over."

Richard chuckles as he pulls over the rig and watches Jim exit his truck cab, stick his tongue out, and wave through the falling flakes.

He rolls down the window, shouts into the wind, "Don't let that little icicle of yours freeze off!" then rolls it up before Jim can respond, miming deafness. Jim responds with typical melodrama, flailing as he pisses his piddly three-letter name into the snow.

If anyone else talked about Anne like that, Richard would knock their fucking teeth out. But Jim was his backup in high school brawls, best man at his wedding. He's the godfather to Richard's children. He can get away with anything, and he knows it. But while Jim plays the jester, when it comes down to it, there's no one Richard would rather have at his back.

These sentiments are momentarily forgotten when Jim turns, shakes his cock obscenely in Richard's direction, zips it up in his jeans, winks and skips to his truck.

Sometimes that motherfucker does take it too far.

Richard's watch reads nine-fifty when they park at the trailhead. The sun's just risen. A later start than anticipated, thanks to Jim's pit stops, but plenty of time to log some miles.

In unison, like synchronized swimmers, they shimmy into thick snow pants and insulated jackets in their trucks, then venture out into the swirling snow, crack open trailer doors, drop ramps, and guide the sleds out into the parking lot, working silently in the chill.

Both sleds are in pristine condition—racing sleds of the top caliber, last year's models, with upgraded suspension and customized racks. The Iron Dog, the snowmachiner's version of the Iditarod, requires as much. Two thousand thirty-one ungroomed miles across the Alaskan wilderness. Frostbite, one-hundred-mph crashes, machine failures, dehydration, all have the potential to throw a team out of the race—not to mention kill a rider. It's a miracle no one's passed away in the years they've put on the race. A few broken bones and the occasional bout with hypothermia, but no casualties. Richard isn't sure if that's a matter of chance and that statistic is bound to change, or it's merely a result of old-fashioned Alaskan preparedness. Probably both.

Last year was the third year Richard and Jim entered the race, and the first time they finished. Dehydration kicked Richard's ass the first year, causing him to get dizzy, lose vision and faint. Jim irreparably smashed his sled hauling through a five-mile section of corridor-tight trees known as "the Tunnel" the second year, and they had to ride tandem to the next checkpoint. Last year, they narrowed their sleds, bringing in the width of the skis to make throttling through the Tunnel easier. They stepped up their training regimen from five thousand miles before the race to ten thousand. And Richard chugged so much Gatorade he wouldn't have minded a catheter himself.

Tearing across that finish line, nearly delirious, was a triumph so hard-earned, so rare, so fulfilling that just days after they finished the race, despite agreeing that they'd "never do anything like that again," Richard reapplied.

He called Jim on the phone.

"How're the toes?"

"Thawing."

"Mine too. Whiskey helps."

"What's up?"

Richard paused.

"I reapplied."

"What?"

"For the race. For next year."

"Oh. Yeah. Cool."

And that was it.

"Ready to rock?" asks Jim, helmet in hand.

"Yessir," says Richard.

They hop into the cab of Richard's truck, which has been running for this specific moment—the last few minutes of warmth before they rev into winter.

Removing his gloves, Jim unfolds a topographic map on the dash.

"It's almost ten-twenty, yeah?"

"Uh-huh," says Richard. He knows what's coming. "You thinking we should cut it short?"

He eyes the four-hundred-mile loop they'd initially planned. It should take less than five hours, six at a slower pace with a stop for lunch.

The snow's falling a little heavier now—not that that's a bad thing. After all, the race is wild, the trails ungroomed—they need to hone navigational skills and improve their cold-weather endurance. Better now than in the thick of the race.

"Given the time…" Jim's voice trails off as he glances out the window.

"My vote is we go for it," says Richard carefully, "but I won't be pissed if you pull the veto."

Jim nods. "I hate to do it, but I think I should." He traces out a straightforward two-hundred-fifty-mile out-and-back ride, one they've done five or six times before. "Let's just do the first bit, follow the river to Big Hope Pass, go up toward the pass a ways, then head home."

"A quickie then."

"Storm's rolling in thicker than we thought, no?"

"Sure," says Richard, masking disappointment as he grabs a roll of duct tape off the dash. He rips off two small strips and carefully sticks them to his cheeks—at the speed they're going, any exposed flesh between his goggles and balaclava will succumb to frostbite in a matter of miles.

Fewer miles, fewer minutes—that seems to be the trend. This year, they decided to cut the training regimen back to five thousand miles, and this is only their second ride. Jim's got his hands full with the divorce, and Richard doesn't exactly have time to spare either, dealing with the merger at work and the kids at home. Both men agreed it was necessary, at least this year, to prioritize other responsibilities.

Not that Richard doesn't feel prepared for the race—after last year's success, he knows they'll get away with less training. He just wishes he had the capacity to ride more. At times like these, it's the only thing that keeps him sane.

He hands the tape to Jim, and after he goes through the same ritual, Richard turns off the truck. As always, he takes the key and places it on top of the rear tire.

A thin film of snow cloaks the snowmachines in white. Perhaps Jim's right. Always better to be safe than sorry. And besides, with the chaos of the merger, it's a blessing just to get away for a day.

They speed out of the parking lot, following the riverbank toward the Hope Mountains. There's not a feeling in the world that Richard can compare it to.

Snowflakes bounce off his goggles and whip into the ether.

He savors the g-forces of a banked turn.

The stomach drop of catching air.

The whump of suspension absorbing the impact.

No feeling, none at all. Not drugs, not sex. Not riding a motorbike in the summer or skiing in winter, not surfing big waves in Hawaii like he did for a couple years after college. For Richard, the snowmachine delivers adrenal nirvana—it turns the helpless, frail, and under-adapted human into a master of winter.

The visibility is steadily dropping.

They follow the river valley, speeding eighty-five mph across the valley floor, keeping a careful distance from the river and maintaining contrast by hugging the trees.

After cruising for an hour or so down-valley, almost at Big Hope Pass, Jim pulls up alongside Richard and signals to stop.

They pull out of the wind and shut off their engines.

"What, you gotta pee again?!"

"Nope. Better. Coffee!" says Jim, reaching under his snowmachine seat and pulling out two Thermoses. "Nicaraguan fair trade for me," he says, shaking one thermos and chucking the other to Richard. "Dunkin' Donuts' shitwater for the prince with the peasant's palette."

Richard grins gratefully beneath his frozen balaclava. Jim knows him all too well.

"I've got the perfect thing to go with it," says Richard.

He reaches into his jacket pocket. Kept from freezing solid by his body heat are two macadamia nut bars topped with coconut flakes and eggless chocolate fudge. He hands one to Jim.

"Don't worry. No meat, no gluten, no fun."

"Good lord. That wife of yours," Jim says, eyes closed, relishing his first bite, "could make a—"

"Careful, my daughter made these."

"Ah, well, my compliments to the teenage Martha Stewart. May she live long and prosper."

"What is she, a Klingon?"

"You better hope she clings on for a while longer. How is little

Miss Sophomore these days?"

"Sophomoric," says Richard. "At least in some regards. And simultaneously more and more mature, like her mother."

"Not a bad thing."

They munch their macadamia nut bars, savoring them as one does in the woods, where the simple act of eating something delicious seems out of place and therefore a minor miracle.

"The boys," says Richard, losing a crumb of coconut amongst the snowflakes gathering in his lap and searching for it absentmindedly. "They're just easy. I was one, you know? I've been there. I remember that. Girls, on the other hand, completely foreign to me. Granted, Caleb's a bit tricky sometimes, too. He's much artsier than I was. Takes after his mother. Thank God for Anne, I tell you. We could trade places and she'd be fine, she'd run my business like she does the house; but me, I'd be lost in her shoes."

"I don't think you'd fit in her shoes," says Jim. "What does she wear, sevens?"

Richard laughs. Leaning against the saddle of his snowmachine, a hundred miles from the nearest road, this is as close as he gets to the therapist's couch. He claps his hands, brushes the snow off his lap, having given up on the coconut morsel, and stands up.

"Should we get a move on?"

"Sure thing, let me just check the satellite phone."

Richard stomps his feet and windmills his arms to stay warm.

"Oh, shit," says Jim, looking down at the screen. "Oh, shit. Shit."

"What is it? Everything okay?"

"Jess."

The epitome of all things evil in Jim's life—his ex-wife and the former fourth wheel that slowed them down like a perpetual flat tire.

"What now? She ask for the rights to one of your kidneys?"

"Very funny. No, she's in town this evening, she's going through the place one last time with that fucking lawyer."

"Is she surprising you?"

Jim looks up from the sat phone, sheepish. "No, no. This one's on me. I totally forgot, she told me last week. There's just, you know, been so much going on."

"Don't worry about it."

"Fuck." Jim checks his watch, dejected. "I've gotta turn around."

"Now? Just fifty more miles and we're halfway there."

"If that vampire's in the house without me, she'll rob me blind and likely wipe my toothbrush across her foul, lawyer-licked bleached asshole."

"Yeesh," says Richard.

"You don't know the half of it. Well, the bleached asshole's not so bad."

Richard suddenly feels ashamed for hashing out the details of his own relatively minuscule issues. He has a loving wife, beautiful kids, a family, a successful business, a purpose to his being. Jim's dealing with a soon-to-be ex-wife who's currently fucking her divorce lawyer.

At the same time, though, Richard feels uncharacteristically selfish and frustrated. They've already cut their ride in half. Now to cut that short? No, he needs this. These are the few hours of tranquility he has each week, the moments that replenish his drive and keep him slogging through the trenches.

Richard hears himself say, "You go on home. I'm going to finish the ride."

"What? No, c'mon man. Rule number one."

Stick together.

Richard persists. "I'll just bust out the last fifty and turn around. I'll be an hour behind you. Hell, the way you drive, I may beat you back home."

"Rich…"

"It's fine, Jim. I've got a sat phone." Richard pats the satellite phone he keeps warm in his chest pocket. "And I've got a sleeping bag and enough emergency rations to make it through a week out here, not that that's going to happen."

"I can't let you do that," says Jim firmly.

"I need this," says Richard, even more so.

There's a strained silence. Jim's distant expression gives off the impression that he's no longer here anyway, but back in the halls of his almost empty home, squabbling with his ex and her law-practicing lover over furniture and paintings and silverware.

"Go," says Richard kindly. He claps a glove on his friend's shoulder. "I'll give you a ring when I'm out, and I'll stop by tonight to give you some backup with Jess."

Jim nods slowly. "Be careful."

"I'm still going on this coffee, mind if I bring it back tonight?"

"Tonight. Fine."

Richard watches as Jim mounts his machine and disappears, retracing their tracks, which are now just barely visible.

Alone. Richard is completely alone.

There's a tinge of fear, an electric excitement to that solitude and silence.

No one to take care of you. No one but the wind and the wolves.

Richard takes a final swig of coffee. He starts his machine and mounts the beloved, well-maintained 850. He pats the side like a cowboy encouraging a loyal mustang.

All right, Rich. Just you and the storm now. This is what you wanted, right?

He hits the throttle.

Snowflakes bounce off his goggles and the landscape unfurls ahead of him like a frozen scroll.

Chapter 5

Mel makes a list in her head. Over and over again.

Netflix. Italian wedding soup like Mom used to make—rich chicken-broth base, squishy dumplings, topped with chopped parsley. A steam shower, scalding to the point of masochism. Plush comforters. A couple rounds with Astrid—maybe even the touch of a gentleman caller. Matter of fact, make that a tropical beach and a swinging hammock. And some brawny, bronzed local, obviously shirtless, expertly wielding a machete, sweat trickling down his pectorals, hacking at a coconut with precise, practiced strokes, then offering it to her with a wink bawdy enough to make a nun forget her vows.

Things she wants. Things she'd rather be doing. Places she'd rather be.

Right now, she'd take the office break room back in New York. And that's saying something.

Snowmobiling, snowmachining—who gives a shit what it's called—was supposed to be fun. According to Marty, at least, and the pamphlets that hawked Triple A's introductory tours. But she's not having fun at all. Her neck and shoulders are sore from the unfamiliar posture, her thumb aches from clenching the throttle, her groin is tight from straddling this cursed machine. The tiniest crescent of her right cheek is exposed, unprotected by the peeling duct tape. It hurt at first, as if lashed again and again by a whip made of icy nettles. Now, it's numb to the point of concern. Maybe the first sign of frostbite? Mel has no fucking clue. This is all foreign to her.

Ever analytical, even in anger, Mel is aware of a reciprocal relationship between her physical and mental temperatures. The colder she gets, the fierier her wrath. As she loses feeling in her fingers, toes, and face, her internal furnace burns hotter and hotter. Alaska, she decides, is a dreadful place. Maybe she'll skip the fancy lodge and the aurora borealis and just catch a flight home this evening. That is, if planes are still flying in this storm. JFK and LaGuardia have shut down over less.

Follow the lights, Marty said. Follow the lights. Mel repeats it like a mantra, watching a line of taillights bob ahead of her in the blizzard.

Keep them in range, he said. Stay at fifty yards, no more, no less. So you can see the person ahead but won't smack into them if they crash or slow down.

Follow the lights.

The snow drops down in drapes, so much so that fifty yards is impossible to gauge. She squints through the spiraling snow, depth perception a cruel joke. She can barely see anything speeding across this godforsaken tundra. It's like looking through her nearsighted grandmother's Coke-bottle bifocals while squadrons of frozen gnats kamikaze into the lenses.

She can't believe it, but she'd prefer to be bored out of her mind in a cubicle. The grass is always greener, she thinks—especially in Alaska, where there's no grass in sight because it's buried under the fucking snow.

Marty was helpful enough. The cheery giant's over-the-phone disposition proved even sunnier in person. He was the bearded cliché she imagined him to be, broad shoulders under a red flannel, crow's-feet splaying off bright eyes. He picked her up from the Marriott in a white four-by-four Sprinter van.

"And you must be Mel. C'mon in! What a joy to meet you in

person. You've got plenty of warm clothes? Gloves? Long underwear? Jacket and pants? Winter boots?"

She nodded blearily.

"Great! We're going to have the most fun today. Mel, meet the Slater family, from Oklahoma. Slaters, this is Mel, from New York City."

The Slaters all grinned the same big Oklahoma grin. Someone shook her hand. Mel scrunched through a tunnel of jabbering Slaters and made it to a seat next to the window in the empty back row. She wondered, for the second time that morning, what the fuck she'd gotten herself into. The first had been when she dispatched her 6:15 a.m. alarm with a violent thrash, knocking over a soon-to-be-empty bottle of Champagne and clambering for ibuprofen in one pathetic, primordial, hungover movement.

The Slaters politely asked what she did for a living (banking) and if she had a husband (no). Then she put her headphones in, though she didn't play any music. An old trick. Just like she used to do, burying her nose in a book on the bus to school, not reading a word, just eavesdropping on the popular kids. Capable of comprehending basic social cues, the Slaters began to ignore her just as the van rolled onto the freeway.

Left to her own devices, Mel counted the Slater children. There were only four—an underwhelming total given the frenzied vibe in the van, which at first felt like a bus transporting problem primates from zoo to ape asylum. She watched them from behind tinted designer shades like a haughty Jane Goodall.

The oldest was a sullen teenage boy, probably already applying to colleges and smoking pot. He slouched against the window in the middle row, glowering, likely texting his girlfriend about how shitty his family vacation was and how he eagerly awaited another hand job. Two squawking preteens, clearly twins, poked and prodded each other next to him. More like hyenas than monkeys, she thought. The youngest sister, maybe nine or ten, sat sniveling in the front row between her parents, apparently having been the victim of some sibling torment of one kind or another.

While the kids and parents joked and laughed and whined and fought, Grandfather Slater sat silently in the front seat. His eyes met hers briefly in the rearview mirror. He looked lonely. Mel wondered why. Maybe his wife had passed. She could read sorrow etched into his face the way she could sense the happiness emanating from Marty's. Or maybe Mel was entirely off-base and the old crone was still alive, just smarter than the rest of them, opting for a spa day over the snowmachine tour.

She wondered about the Slaters, who they were, what their family story was—just not enough to ask. She wondered what they thought of her, a mid-thirties stockbroker all alone in Alaska. She wondered whether they could sniff last night's Champagne in her sweat or this morning's bloody Mary on her breath. Most of all, for the third time that morning, she wondered what the fuck she had gotten herself into.

Mother Slater turned around to separate the twins from a tussle that was rapidly approaching mortal combat, a cross swinging from her dainty neck. She mouthed "I'm so sorry" to Mel, who waved her off as if to say, "No problem, I get it." With this new data on hand, Mel pegged the Slaters as a devout Catholic family who frowned upon contraception. It was the only way to explain four kids these days. Mel winced. She had many fears, among them an irrational fear of sharks—she refused to swim in the ocean, so unless great whites started prowling the subway or got punch passes to her local YMCA, she ought to be fine—and much more rational fears like cops, cancer, people driving while texting and recessions. But her deepest fear of all was pregnancy. She'd rather chop up a handful of Plan B's with a razor blade, roll up a hundred-dollar bill, and get her Scarface on than have a baby, thank you very much.

Kids disgusted her. Not in the sense that they were gross and pink and fleshy and shit themselves—though all of those things were disgusting, too. Instead, they disgusted her with their greedy little needs. She saw them as black holes for hopes and dreams, suckling at bank accounts long after they stopped suckling at the teat. And besides, who could justify bringing a kid—much less four—into a world of climate change and social media and bullying and systemic inequality and political divides so deep every election felt a single gunshot away from all-out war? A post-apocalyptic future seemed increasingly likely, and she's read Cormac McCarthy's The Road. When the world catches fire, or the food runs out, or the zombies come, a kid is a burden, plain and simple.

These are the arguments Mel put forth whenever friends, family, colleagues and potential partners asked her if she was interested in having children—although the points about the apocalypse didn't typically spill out until drink four gave way to five and six. The base of her disdain, though, at least according to Dr. Meyer, was that Mel was haunted by the traumatic repercussions of her own birth daily.

Regardless, there was no maternal twinge deep in her biology. Her female friends spoke about getting hit with an uncontrollable urge to procreate in their late twenties and early thirties, that it came screeching into their lives like a hormonal freight train. When Mel saw children, however, her primary thought was that she'd rather be hit by a freight train than have one. If there were some sort of biological clock ticking away in her ovaries, she'd smashed the snooze button so many times that it was broken. Menopause didn't sound so bad, to be honest. She'd save a fortune on condoms and tampons.

Eventually, the kids quieted down, and Marty turned on the radio to some Anchorage sports talk show. This was Mel's cue to turn on her music. She had grown bored people-watching, anyway.

The trailhead parking lot was empty, save for a few trucks with trailers. When the van rolled through, the tires left trenches in the powdery snow. She shivered; it looked like the inside of a freezer outside.

A young man with a dark beard in a puffy black jacket was unloading snowmachines from a massive trailer with "Anchorage

Alaskan Adventures" emblazoned on the side. Marty waved at him like a soccer mom pulling up to practice.

"Okay, everybody," said Marty. "It's showtime! Me and Davey are going to set up the snowmachines. In the meantime, get all your clothes on, you're going to want to put on those extra puffy jackets and balaclavas I brought. Windchill is a primary concern. Also, you see this duct tape? Lay a little piece of it on your cheeks, okay? This will protect the gap between your goggles and your balaclava. Beyond that, we've got hot tea, water, food and all the emergency supplies. So no need to bring anything except your clothes, a camera if you want it, one walkie-talkie per snowmachine and a thumb for the throttle, all right? It's snowing a little harder than we thought, so we'll make it a quick loop, but no need to worry. Any questions?"

The kids squirmed and the Slater parents grinned at each other. Someone cracked a joke, but no one asked anything. Marty shook hands with Davey and the two of them methodically prepped snowmachines. Clearly, they'd done this before. She trusted him. They'd never lost anyone before. Knock on wood.

Still, was she the only one who thought that taking this group of incompetent nincompoops—herself included in that assessment—into that swirling white oblivion was an untenable, idiotic idea on par with polygamy or the electoral college?

With her Goodall goggles on, she watched the family decide how to pair up on the snowmachines: the grandfather and the youngest daughter, the mom and dad each took a preteen, and the teenager proudly went by himself. Mel had her own sled, too—she didn't come here to be a passenger.

Although perhaps, just maybe, she'd partner up with Marty later. There was a ruggedness about him that was a welcome change of pace from her usual metropolitan matches. He and Davey moved the snowmachines like Tetris blocks, deftly backing them up, adjusting them until their two larger sleds sat tip-to-tail in front of a line of five smaller ones, parked like students' desks in front of a teacher's. They led the group through the motions for over half an hour, pointing out different parts of the sled, covering everything: how to start it, how to hit the throttle, how to engage the brake, how to position the body when initiating a turn.

"We're not going to go off-road today," said Marty. "We're going on a plowed road that's got maybe four to eight inches of snow on it, a bit more in wind-affected areas, so you'll have some fun with the fresh snow, but you don't need to worry about going off the trail. It's very wide and easy to follow, so long as you pay attention and follow the lights of the snowmachine ahead of you. Remember, always keep the snowmachine ahead of you within fifty yards. We'll go pretty slow today, no more than forty-five mph. We're just going to have a good time. And remember - follow the lights. That's rule number one."

He scanned the team for questions.

No one asked anything. And no one joked this time.

"Okay, great. Davey will lead the way, I'll be in the back. We've all got radios, so just give us a buzz if anything happens. Channel five."

Mel reached instinctively for her chest pocket, just to make sure the radio was still there.

Then they took off. For Mel, whose driving experience over the last decade didn't extend much further than bumper cars, it was exhilarating—going forty-five miles an hour into the stinging snow, following the lights, her heart thumping like she was on drugs.

Forty-five miles per hour apparently wasn't that fast, according to Marty, but she couldn't imagine going much faster.

Yet after thirty minutes, the allure wore off. She grew cold. The wind hurled snowflakes like tiny javelins; they tore at her coat and nipped at the duct tape on her cheeks, which eventually started to peel. Cold spots grew at her knees, where the fabric of her snow pants was stretched taut, and frost crept in between the microscopic gaps in the thread. The hangover from the previous day's mimosa marathon began to catch up with her.

The engines droned on, and she decided to make a list.

Netflix. Italian wedding soup. Marriott comforters. Astrid. Tropical beach. Hell, New York.

She makes a list again, and again, and again.

She wonders for the fifty-second time what the fuck she has gotten herself into.

They stop for tea and coffee. Mel is relieved to note that the spirits of the Slaters seem as low as her own. Davey is a deaf-mute. Only Marty has managed to retain an air of positivity.

He hands her a Thermos of tea, which she gratefully accepts.

"How you doing, Mel? Feeling good? You're looking great on that sled!"

She grunts, wanting to answer him like one of those imaginary emails.

Dear Marty,

Not all of us are meant to straddle these ungainly robotic horses and penetrate these inhospitable lands like some wannabe explorers.

First off, why would anyone want to explore this area? It sucks. Secondly, you say snowmobiling—or, rather, snowmachining—is fun. This argument is fundamentally fucked. You said much of the fun is about the views, but I can't see a damn thing! Thirdly, why the hell are you smiling? Perhaps you were dropped on your head as a baby and you damaged the part of your brain responsible for maintaining a healthy perspective. There is only a small difference between pessimism and realism, both of which you are lacking and I have in spades.

No, Marty, I'm not good. I'm not happy. I'm not warm. And I'm going to write all this on a Tripadvisor review unless we turn the fuck around.

Sincerely,
Mel

Falling snow hides the horizon. The engines are shut off, the children aren't yelling. In the lull of conversation, the silence is total.

Deafening, even. An oxymoron that makes complete sense in the Alaskan wild.

Mel doesn't say anything about Marty's presumed head injury, nor does she mention the overwhelming silence that strikes her so. She rarely says what she's thinking. She wouldn't be where she is today if she did.

She settles for, "Can't say I'm not cold."

"Hmm," he says, concerned. "Do you have glove warmers?"

"What are glove warmers?" she asks, feeling foolish.

Marty reaches into his backpack and pulls out a small plastic packet. He rips off the corner with his teeth, yellow against the white snow—likely stained from tobacco and coffee and a lifetime without dental care—and hands her two small, pillow-shaped hand warmers.

"They're activated by the air, so just shake 'em up, put them in your gloves," he says. "It'll warm you right up."

Touched by his best intentions, Mel has trouble hating Marty as much as she ought to.

"Thanks."

"We're nearly halfway through the loop," he says, patting her shoulder with a heavy, gloved hand that feels like a caveman's club. And then, lowering his voice to just above a whisper: "Almost in the homestretch. You're doing great, Mel."

Following Marty's lead, the group gets back on the snowmachines and charges into the blizzard.

Maybe it's just Mel's salacious mind, but his intonation is borderline unprofessional.

Well, thinks Mel, she might just have to add a postscript to that angry email.

P.S.

Please forgive the above note. I'm just really fucking cold and completely out of my element. Just get me home safe and sound, and you can come up to my room in the Marriott. I'll give you something to be positive about. A reason to show those yellow teeth of yours.

The list has changed.

Hold the Netflix, the soup, and Astrid. Keep the Marriott comforters. Add some spiked hot cocoa. Scented massage oil. And—fuck it—swap Marty in for the tropical suitor with the machete.

When in Rome, right?

She's waist-deep in those Marriott comforters, wondering:

A) How best to proposition Marty into enacting a lumberjack fantasy.

B) If the man has an ax (she's sure he does).

When she realizes that she can no longer see the lights ahead of her.

Fuck.

The snow is falling forcefully now, pinging against her goggles, relentless as telemarketers.

She hits the throttle and speeds up, hoping to see red and yellow lights appear out of the billowing gray walls of snow.

The speedometer hits fifty, sixty, seventy mph.

Her heart pounds under the heavy winter coat.

Her throat tightens in fear.

Don't hyperventilate.

Breathe.

At least she's not cold now. Fear keeps her warm.

After approximately ten minutes, she slows down, second-guessing her decision to speed up.

Rightfully so. It was dumb.

She stops the snowmachine, peering ahead with squinty eyes.

In front of her is endless, featureless white. Behind her is the same. The only difference is the track that runs from the rear of the snowmachine - a faint line drawn across a white page until it fades into the infinite beyond.

Mentally, she kicks herself. Going forward was a stupid move, following what she imagined to be the river valley. At those speeds, she couldn't tell whether she was on the trail to begin with. She forgot rule number one.

"Follow the lights," Marty had said.

Fuck.

Hold on. When shit hits the fan in stockbroking, it doesn't pay to panic. You drown more quickly if you fight quicksand. Moving fast can be a good thing, but it can also be fatal without proper strategy.

She acted rashly.

That doesn't mean she needs to continue to do so.

Mel takes a breath. Slows it down. Counts to ten. Evaluates her situation.

It's a simple math problem. Assuming she was going seventy miles per hour for approximately ten minutes, and the group has yet to realize she's gotten lost—how could they figure that out in these conditions?—and they've been riding for as many as fifteen minutes at forty mph, they could be as far as seventeen miles away.

And that distance is getting larger.

And larger.

And larger.

Fuck.

She has half a Thermos of tea and a water bottle that's frozen solid.

She has her cell phone and the radio.

If her cell phone has service out here, she'll make a shrine to Steve Jobs as soon as she gets back to New York.

She fumbles with her gloves to remove her phone from her pocket. One of the hand warmers that Marty gave her spills out into the snow. It steams in the powdery crystals, sinking low, momentarily fighting the cold around it, the definition of a hot second.

She turns on her phone.

Seventy-three percent battery.

But no service.

She turns it off, puts it carefully back in her pocket, then retrieves the radio.

She shivers, her hand trembling as she presses the talk button.

"Hello. This is Mel. Melissa Drummond. I'm lost on my snowmobile. Shit! I mean snowmachine. I'm on a tour with Anchorage Alaskan Adventures. Over."

She listens. For a click. For static. For Marty's optimistic voice. Don't worry, Mel, we'll come wrangle you.

But there's nothing. No sound. Just her own breathing. And the sound of the wind.

"Come in. This is Mel Drummond. I'm lost. Over."

Click.

Wait.

Nothing.

"Hello! This is Mel Drummond. I'm lost! I'm fucking lost! Do you hear me? Fuck!"

Click.

Wait.

Nothing.

Tears begin to flow, though she can't feel them on her numb cheeks. She wants to throw the radio into the storm. But if she freaks out, she'll meet a fate like that hand warmer, steaming only to freeze, gone in a hot second.

She shoves the radio back into her jacket pocket, then goes through her options. All of them are bleak. She can press onward blindly up the river valley. No point in that. Better to return from where she came. Follow her tracks back to the parking lot. And then there's a third option: stay put. Have faith that rescuers will come for her. But in this storm? How soon would they find her? Could she make it through a night out here alone?

Fuck that, she thinks. Retrace her steps. It's the only thing that makes sense.

She gets back on the snowmachine and starts the engine. She hits the throttle, but the machine won't move. The tread is spinning, but it doesn't gain traction. She remembers Marty saying something about how the snowmachine can sink into the snow and get stuck.

Don't freak out. Freaking out is the last thing she'll ever do. Freaking out is death.

She remembers there's a shovel in the seat. She retrieves it, assembles it, and begins to dig.

It takes her half an hour to dig out the snowmachine. But she gets it done. She's sweating inside her jacket now. Mel doesn't know much about surviving in the snow, but she does know that if she slows down, the sweat will cool, and hypothermia could become a serious threat.

She looks behind her.

That line, that holy line, the track that showed where she came from, it's gone. Disappeared.

Falling snow slashes sideways. Gusts whip and roll over the swelling landscape.

The storm has erased her tracks. And with it, all hope.

Stay put? Or flip a coin, pick a direction, and go?

She won't die staying put. No fucking way.

"Fuck you!"

She flips off the sky with both gloved hands, voice cracking as it splits the ambivalent, omnipotent silence.

She bites down and sets her jaw, terrified but resolute. Praying she doesn't get stuck again, Mel starts the engine and hits the throttle. The snowmachine jumps forward. Wrenching the handlebars, she executes a careful U-turn and guns it into the gray.

The sky is indistinguishable from the sea of snow, melded together by the storm. The same is true for Mel and the snowmachine. She can feel the engine vibrating up through her gloved hands and her aching wrists and tensed forearms, up through her thick winter boots and screaming quads, the machine a part of her, or she a part of it. Melded together by fear, her irrepressible will to survive.

A line of trees materializes on her right. She hugs them at forty-five mph, grateful for the improved visibility.

Don't get cold. Don't stop moving. The shivering intensifies. She flexes her calves, her hamstrings, stands and sits and stands

Chapter 6

Richard feels sick to his stomach. He promised Jim he'd finish the out-and-back, then go home. But when he got to Big Hope Pass, he didn't feel like stopping. Impulsively, he embarked on a modified version of their initial four-hundred-mile loop. He climbed up and over the pass, descended through Cascade Valley, rounded the south ridge of Mt. Augustine and several unnamed but equally impressive peaks, then followed Pine Creek back to the main fork of the mighty Hope River. The route was no picnic under normal circumstances, and it was more stupid than brave to tackle it alone, especially during a blizzard.

Richard knew better. He can't forgive himself. The lie eats at him, from the inside out, like a parasite of his own creation. Jim is his best friend, teammate, godfather to his children. His brother. Sure, Richard got what he wanted—the throttle under his thumb as he speeds through the storm for a few more miles—but was it worth it?

A violent snort escapes his balaclava—an uncontrollable tic that flares up at times of great frustration. Now isn't the moment to mull over his dishonesty, no matter how egregious. Visibility is abysmal, and any distraction could prove deadly in this blizzard. Concerned that atonement has made him uncharacteristically absentminded and he's drifted off course, Richard slows to a halt and kills the engine.

"If I die out here, they'll never find me—or forgive me," he says aloud, confessing his sins to the wind, the storm clouds arching overhead like the vaulted ceiling of a cathedral. The mountains have always been his church, and he can't help but feel like he's desecrated the sacrosanct.

"Pull it together man," he barks, shaking his head.

He retrieves his phone from his backpack and checks the offline GPS app. Sure enough, he's a mile or two east of his intended route, on the flank of a long, narrow body of water called Crow Lake, which feeds into the Hope. Richard's glad he checked. He can easily correct his course before the small error snowballs into a more significant one. According to the app, he's two hundred and twenty miles in, just over halfway through his ride, and the toughest navigation is all behind him. So long as he hugs the Hope as he heads downriver, he'll be home in time for dinner.

He returns the phone to his backpack and prepares to set out once more. The storm growls across the range. The whining pitch of the wind grows louder and louder. This strikes Richard as odd, because he feels no severe gusts—instead, he notices a lull as the sheets of falling snow momentarily thin, and a wall of trees on the far shore of the lake dances into view. Suddenly, he realizes that it's not the wind he hears after all. It's a snowmachine engine.

At first he worries that Jim's returned to catch him red-handed. But that's ridiculous. Jim turned around ages ago—he's back at the truck by now, if not already back on the road.

Another snort. Richard is drowning in that cursed lie. If Richard were even remotely capable of duplicity, Jim always joked, he'd have a decent shot at being a billionaire. "The price of morals," Jim called it.

The motor grows louder and louder, and a snowmachine careens out of the squall.

They'll pass him, Richard thinks, he won't even have to wave hello. But the driver wrenches the handlebars and turns straight toward him.

Richard knows what will happen before the driver does. The skis will slip on the ice. The tread will lose traction.

He almost shouts out a warning, but they won't hear him over the engine. And it's too late.

The skis lose purchase, and the driver loses control. Richard watches the machine spin like a puck on an air hockey table, rotating until it catches and flips. The butt of the handlebar digs into the ice and drags across the lake like the pick of a mountaineer's ice ax.

Richard takes off, running across the frozen lake, doing his best not to slip himself and go sprawling.

They probably don't know it, and they certainly don't feel it right now, but they're lucky. Lucky the crash had a witness.

If they're injured, or their sled won't start, Richard can bring them out, no problem. But a few hundred yards farther away and veils of snow might've hidden them from view. The sound of the motor would've been a fleeting curiosity, nothing more.

Halfway to the pinned driver, Richard watches the worst-case scenario manifest. Spiderwebbing cracks rip through the ice, like an earthquake splitting asphalt. The driver lets loose an anguished howl and writhes furiously, pinned underneath the machine.

Adrenaline spikes. He sprints faster.

That recent warm spell must have thawed the lake, and it's still early season. It might be only an inch or two thick in the middle—enough to hold a human's weight no problem, but a cross-country snowmachine the size of a small sedan getting whipped into it at speed?

No way. It's going under.

The cracks expand, forming a widening hole. The snowmachine shifts and drops, its rear half now submerged in the dark water, tilting backward like a sinking ship, pushing the rider under.

Richard's not going to make it in time.

In five seconds, the snowmachine will disappear.

In thirty seconds, the driver will be unconscious.

In a minute or two, they'll be dead.

He forces these thoughts from his mind and removes his helmet, backpack, and gloves, chucking them behind him as he sprints. Around the snowmachine, the ice is jagged and white, like shattered porcelain. The water is more black than blue.

Just moments after the lake swallows the machine, Richard breathes in sharply and leaps into a dive. Arching through the air, he's back at summer camp, where every morning he'd wake up before dawn to join the Polar Bear Club and swim in the glacial runoff.

He braces for the punch. No matter how many times you swim in icy water, it always smacks like a sledgehammer.

He hits the water and his capillaries tighten, his lungs shrink. The water is metallic, unforgiving. The headache is immediate. Bubbles rebound across his face, momentarily blocking his vision. He claws downward, past the disturbance of the splash. The water is ethereal cobalt, darkening the deeper he goes. The hole in the ice is a skylight—a shaft of gray light cutting into the eerie darkness. He sees the half-illuminated snowmachine, surrounded by a mushroom cloud of silt disturbed by the impact.

Practiced, purposeful kicks and strokes. Steady now. Just like the Polar Bear Club. No different. It's all a mind game.

By the time he reaches the machine, the pressure in his ears is like bottled thunder. The driver has ceased moving, their body drifts like seaweed in a fish tank. Richard grabs at the driver's shoulders—they're petite beneath the deceptive, bulky winter coat, and he realizes then that she's a woman—and attempts to drag her to the surface. But there's resistance, like a ball and chain around her right foot.

Ears throbbing, skin and muscles on fire, he gropes down the leg of her snow pants to the source. A cloud of blood reddens the dark water. The ice wasn't the only thing to fracture—the body of the snowmachine shattered upon impact, and it seems the uneven plastic has cut her leg. In any case, the fabric of her pants is snagged on the snowmobile's smashed hood.

His lungs are on the verge of bursting, but it's now or never.

If Richard swims to the surface for another breath, by the time he returns it may be too late.

He removes his knife from his pants pocket, unclasps it with his teeth, and saws away at the pant leg until her body breaks free. He tugs her up toward the surface, but his snow pants, heavy jacket, and wet winter boots have turned to concrete. He can barely kick. He drags her limp body in one hand, clutches his open knife in the other. Stars and comets orbit across his vision. His body screams in protest. He aims at the light like a marathon runner sprinting toward a blurry finish line.

He hits the surface and gasps, filling his lungs with oxygen—never has he had a sweeter breath. He ditches the knife, then dives back down. With one hand on her rear and the other gripping the edge of the hole, he shoves her up and out of the water like a human shot put.

Ignoring the temperature and the windchill, he clambers out of the water and focuses solely on the woman. He unstraps her helmet. Her eyes are closed, her face pale and bluish. He unzips her jacket, sweeps the pendant that rests on her ribcage over her shoulder, and begins to perform CPR.

Fifteen compressions. Two breaths. Listen.

Nothing.

Fifteen compressions. Two breaths. Listen.

Nothing.

Halfway through the next sequence, she coughs up water and sputters.

"Marty?!"

She's clearly concussed. He brushes his hands across her scalp, searching for a contusion.

"Do you know your name?"

"Where am I? Who the fuck are you?"

"You crashed your snowmachine into Crow Lake," he says, doing his best to stay calm. "And I'm Richard."

Like clockwork, her eyes roll back. She's out cold this time.

He finds a swollen bump the size of a gumball on the side of her head.

"Stay with me, now!" yells Richard, remembering that football coaches don't let players sleep after a concussion these days.

A trickle of blood from her calf paints the snow bright red.

He fetches the knife and makes a small incision across her pant leg, only to find that a shard of plastic from the snowmachine is lodged in her calf.

Breathing heavily, he runs back to his snowmachine, picking up his backpack and gloves along the way. He yanks open the seat compartment and grabs the med kit and his Nalgene water bottle. With fumbling fingers, he unties the compressed bug-out bag that's lashed onto the rack alongside the extra fuel. He huffs it back to the site of the crash—from far away, the hole in the ice looks like a black smear of graphite on an enormous piece of sketch paper.

As he runs through the snow, he ticks through the bug-out bag's contents: sleeping bag, emergency tarp, three days' worth of rations, rope, a few odds and ends for snowmachine repair, duct tape, a headlamp, flint and steel, waterproof matches, a lighter, Vaseline-soaked cotton balls, a small titanium cook pot, another knife and a dry set of long underwear. In his backpack, he has a shovel for digging out the sled, a sandwich, a few energy bars, his own Thermos still full of hot tea, and a spare puffy jacket. He hopes the satellite phone is still working—he didn't have time to remove it from his jacket before he jumped into the lake.

Now completely out of breath, he reaches his charge. The woman fades in and out of consciousness as he unscrews his Nalgene and drips water onto the wound, rinsing away the blood. The gash is broad, the plastic lodged in deep—it'll require stitches. He has a needle and surgical-grade nylon thread in the med kit. But if he pulls the plastic out too early, before he's ready to stitch her up, blood loss might be significant. One thing is for sure. He can't operate out here, he can barely see anything. The storm flicks back on as if by a switch—the snow is dumping now. Besides, his cold, wet fingers aren't exactly prepared for surgery.

No, better to stem the bleeding first and get her warm.

He takes a quick sip out of the Nalgene then stashes it in the bug-out bag. He removes his jacket, then his long underwear top, and ties the latter carefully around her leg in a tight tourniquet—not exactly hygienic, but he'll clean it as soon as he can. She grunts with pain as he cinches the shirt down. He puts the jacket back on. It's soaking wet, well on its way to frozen, but it's better than nothing.

Quickly but carefully, well aware that lives have been lost to rushing, Richard lifts the woman. She's smaller than his daughter. Ringlets of brown are frozen into rock-hard coils along her brow. He sidesteps the hole and carries her, floundering in the snow for what feels like fifteen minutes, until they hit the trees on the shore of the lake.

The forest is a welcome respite; the barricade of trees dampens the harsh wind. He puts the woman down in a small clearing, arms aching. He unfurls the tarp and lays it on the ground, then positions the sleeping bag on top of the tarp.

"You're not going to like this," he says, "but you have to trust me."

She groans again, out of pain or an attempt to respond, he can't tell. He takes a deep breath and begins to pull off her wet clothes. There's nothing remotely sexual about the act, but he's embarrassed nonetheless. He works as quickly as he can, trying his best not to look at her. This backfires, though, as she suddenly flails and Richard catches what feels like a right hook to the face. Immediately, blood spurts from his smarting nose. Swearing heavily, he pulls a wad of waterlogged toilet paper from his pants pocket and shoves it up his nostrils, then gets back to work, careful to avoid another haymaker.

He dries her shivering body with the fresh long underwear, shimmies her into the dry sleeping bag, and wraps the tarp over her to keep the snow off. Only then does she start to calm down. And only then does he realize that he's quaking like a Parkinson's patient.

The adrenaline is wearing off. His teeth chatter, his fingers are stiff, his toes are numb, and his flesh is textured with goose bumps beneath his sopping clothes. The ride back, he realizes, will likely kill them both. At top speeds, in these conditions, it will take at least two hours to return to the parking lot, and she's hardly conscious, let alone prepared to hold on and help weight and steer the sled while he drives full-tilt through this storm. She'll have to sit in front of him, like a child. It might take twice as long to get out, maybe more, depending on the visibility. Between the wet clothes and the windchill, hypothermia is all but guaranteed.

"Hey!" he snaps as she begins to doze off again. "No sleeping. Stay awake."

He checks his watch. They have a few hours till sunset.

"We've got to stay put," he says, to himself more than anything. "We've got to get warm, dry our clothes. Then tomorrow morning, we can head back. But tonight, we have to spend the night."

Chapter 7

James' knee was right. The storm is a prodigious one.

He fixes a caribou stew for dinner, as he always does the afternoon of a big storm. The rich, dark concoction simmers on the stove for hours, filling the small cabin with the scent of garlic, onion and game, and he enjoys a bowl for lunch and another for dinner. He feeds the dogs inside, then lets them out to take care of their business. There's no playing or messing around today—the storm is brutally cold, and James doesn't hear so much as a bark. He chuckles as they scurry back inside one by one, shaking snow from their white, brown and black coats. His dogs would gladly charge through the storm if he asked them to—harness the team to a sled and they'll run forever. But when they're so close to the iron-bellied stove and the warmth of the cabin, even his toughest pups soften up into little wimps.

"C'mon, you mutts," he calls cheerfully into the storm for the stragglers. "Last call for alcohol!"

Once the dogs are accounted for, he pours a glass of well-deserved whiskey and reads by the crackling fire. The dogs snooze in piles by the hearth, and the wind rocks the little cabin as if it were made of cardboard instead of solid timber.

He loves these nights. There are no choices to make beyond

what book to read. He stays inside and tends to the fire, because that's what survival demands. He can't hunt, or set traps, or do much of anything at all, really. He and the dogs can only stay warm and wait. Life during a blizzard, James thinks as he swirls his whiskey, is beautifully simple.

Chapter 8

Richard rips off his coat, wincing at the instant sting. The jacket, at least, is no longer dripping wet, as the droplets have frozen solid. He lays the stiff coat across the tarp, thinking it might at least offer some additional insulation. Out of the backpack he pulls his spare insulated jacket and puts it on, his poor fingers struggling with the zipper. The emergency layer is lighter than he needs, but at least it's dry. He puts his gloves back on, too, flexing his fingers, and the relief is immediate.

He assembles his shovel and finds a spot to his liking—a gentle five-degree slope on the far side of the clearing—and begins to dig. He scoops snow into a mound, occasionally patting down the pile with the flat of the shovel and chopping chunks with the blade. He keeps an eye on the woman, and barks at her every so often not to fall asleep, but there's only so much he can do. His pants are rigid, iced over, but the exertion thaws his core, and warmth slowly works its way back to his frigid extremities, aside from his toes, which he can no longer feel inside the wet socks and boots. He digs hard enough to defrost his body but not hard enough to sweat. After an hour or two, the mound of snow is a foot or two taller than he is at its peak, and eight or nine feet across.

The last time Richard built a quinzee was with the kids, last winter in the backyard. He remembers explaining the difference between a quinzee and an igloo as they bundled up in winter coats and gathered shovels from the garage. A quinzee, he told them, is a snow cave hollowed out of a large pile of compressed snow, much simpler and warmer than an igloo, especially when the snow is fresh and deep.

Sean got such a kick out of building the thing, even claiming that he wanted to be an architect as well as a professional skier. Sarah hated shoveling, and Caleb got claustrophobic scraping out the inside of the cavern, but the whole family enjoyed the finished product. The quinzee stood for weeks, and the five of them sat beneath the curved walls of snow and ice, candles flickering, swathed in sleeping bags, telling ghost stories, drinking hot chocolate.

Richard's not sure if he should focus on the happy memories while he works or banish them from his mind.

He collects an armful of branches from the surrounding pine trees, stripping them of needles and breaking them into sticks that are approximately a foot and a half long. These sticks will measure the thickness of the walls, and he carefully inserts them into the pile of snow until only six inches of each stick is exposed. When he's done, the quinzee looks like some abominable, spiny urchin. Satisfied, he removes the handle of the shovel and, using only the blade, starts excavating an entry tunnel.

It's long, hard, cold work to shovel out a quinzee, even when a second person hauls out the shoveled snow on a sled. Ideally, the second person spots the digger, too, in case of a collapse. But Richard is alone. On his back, he burrows into the quinzee. He makes sluggish headway, one shovel load at a time, cursing when snow falls on his face or down the back of his neck. Eventually, he has enough room to get onto his knees, then crouch. He scrapes the inner walls of the cave until they're semi-smooth, careful to stop whenever his blade uncovers one of the sticks so as not to weaken the structure. He digs out the floor, leaving a raised platform big enough for the two of them to lie on, as well as an even deeper entry tunnel all the way down to the dirt below, so that cold air won't collect where they sleep. He pokes out a fist-sized hole in the wall opposite the entryway for airflow. Finally, he starts a tiny fire in the middle of the quinzee, using a Vaseline-lathered cotton ball, flint and steel from the bug-out bag, and a few sticks he managed to find under the trees. This fire is not for warmth, but instead to cause condensation, which drips down the domed walls of the snow cave and coats them in an icy glaze. The quinzee isn't pretty, but at least it will keep out the wind and insulate them from the frigid temperatures.

He emerges from the shelter and trembles straightaway. He's pleased to notice how much colder it is outside in the storm—maybe twenty degrees difference, not accounting for the wind. Two inches of snow coat the motionless tarp. He gathers up the bug-out bag and, with a gloved hand, dusts off the light flakes. Grunting, he squats, scooping up the tarp-wrapped woman and carries her to the quinzee. He sets her down near the door, crawls in, and drags her in after him.

The quinzee is dimly lit, at least for now: Faint light passes through the entry tunnel, plus a few holes in the walls where Richard removed the sticks. He's not sure how much juice remains in his headlamp batteries, and he wants to save them as much as he can.

The cave will heat up with two bodies inside, but Richard begins trembling again, this time uncontrollably. Now that the woman is safe and he's stopped digging, it's as though his brain has given his body permission to break down.

He kicks off his boots, peels the wet socks off with fumbling fingers, and strips out of his wet pants and long underwear. He dries off his body with the spare long underwear and slides into the sleeping bag next to this stranger. Well, slide is perhaps too graceful a word. Despite his clumsiness, she hardly moves. Luckily, the sleeping bag is an extra-large zero-degree bag with premium eight-hundred-fifty-fill goose down, which costs more than six hundred and fifty dollars at the mountaineering shop. It's plush and roomy—the latter of which is a necessity for an outdoorsman of Richard's size. However, with the two of them cocooned in the bag, it bulges like a python's gut after eating a goat.

It will be a miserable way to spend a night, but they'll survive.

Pressed together, he shivers, soaking in the warmth emanating from her skin.

"Are—are you awake? Ma'am?" he asks, flustered, uncertain of what to say. He's uncomfortable being so intimate with a naked woman who isn't his wife—but the alternative, he reminds himself, involves her lifeless body at the bottom of a lake. He hopes he will eventually be forgiven—by both his wife and the naked stranger when she wakes. For now, though, she's unresponsive. She smells of sweat, perfume and, faintly, booze. She doesn't exactly seem like the snowmachining type. Her helmet was a rental, he could tell by the barcode on the back. What the hell was she doing out here all alone?

"Sym-sym-symbiosis," he stutters uncontrollably. The phrase had just come up in Sarah's science homework last week. "I saved you, now you save me, and you don't even know it."

If theirs is a symbiotic relationship, he thinks, the snow is parasitic. Beneath the sleeping bag and the tarp he can feel it, eternally hungry, leeching on their lifeforce.

Whoever she is, wherever she's from, Richard is, at the moment, grateful for her warmth. After a while, his body stops shaking and, exhausted by the day's events, he dozes off, too.

Richard wakes with a start. He checks his glowing watch: It's 5:32—p.m., he assumes, although he isn't sure. Either way, it's dark out, and the snow cave is pitch black. He should be getting home just now, right on time for dinner. But his family, and that warm home by the river, are a world away.

Now that he and the woman are both relatively safe, Richard's priority ought to be letting his family know where the fuck they are.

He turns on the headlamp. The beam reveals that their clothes and boots are frozen solid.

"Fuck," he says. "Fuck."

He should've expected that. He reaches for his frozen jacket, trying not to disturb the woman. He unzips the chest pocket, the zipper splintering through a thin layer of ice like the prow of a ship through arctic ice floe. He prays that the satellite phone still works, that they can call in a helicopter or a rescue team of sledders to bring them fresh gear and warm clothes, to bring them home. Coming clean to Jim is the least of his worries now—what he wouldn't give to hear Jim cursing at him over the phone.

But the prayer dies on his tongue when he pulls out the satellite phone. It's caked in ice, entombed in it, like a fly in amber. With the butt of his jackknife, he gently chisels away at the keypad. Once cleared, he takes another deep breath, prays again, and presses the power button firmly. The screen turns on and he whoops loudly, chastising himself instantly, but the woman doesn't move a muscle. Three black lines flash on the screen, followed by the image of a spinning globe.

Thank God, he thinks. Thank God.

But instead of transitioning to the home screen, the phone simply turns dark. He curses, then tries the process again. The second time, the screen illuminates, but there are no lines, no spinning globe, and the phone goes dark for good. He keeps pressing the button and pressing the button, calmly, as if patience is all the phone needs, like a car that won't start till the fifth or sixth turn of the key. Reality sets in when he flips over the phone and reads, in small, embossed letters on the black plastic: "water-resistant."

Not waterproof. Resistant. After being submerged to twelve or fifteen feet or however deep that cursed lake was, the phone is dead.

The phone is dead, Richard thinks, and we might be dead, too.

There's no time to dwell on the loss of the phone, however heartbreaking, and he forces his attention elsewhere. He has to maintain the shelter, dry their clothes or they're fucked. But first, he must tend to the woman's wound—he should've done it hours ago. He hadn't meant to sleep at all.

Mustering all his resolve, he exits the warmth of the sleeping bag. The long underwear is useless, but he puts on the stiff boxers and snow pants, cringing at the cold. He fell asleep wearing the spare jacket, which is a little damp from digging the quinzee but still relatively toasty. He slips his sockless feet into icy boots again, cognizant that he still can't feel his toes. Quickly, to get the blood flowing, he puts on his gloves and does a set of pushups, as many as he can. Then he flexes his fingers until full range of motion returns—he'll need all the dexterity he can get.

He unzips the sleeping bag, gingerly pulls her injured leg out.

He gathers a syringe, rubbing alcohol wipes, tweezers, scissors, and needle and thread from the med kit, lines them up carefully on top of the bug-out bag. Careful that water doesn't drip onto the sleeping bag, he inserts the syringe into the Nalgene, fills it with water, and flushes the wound, repeating this process several times. Under the bright beam of his headlamp, Richard can better assess the shard of plastic. It's not as bad as he thought but yanking it out is not going to feel good.

With the lighter, he burns and disinfects the needle and tweezers. There aren't any antibiotics out here; an infection could be catastrophic if they can't make it home tomorrow. He tries not to focus on that possibility and, gripping her thigh tightly with one hand—just in case she lashes out again—he tweezes the plastic out of her calf. It comes and comes and keeps coming, the tip of the shard buried nearly an inch and a half deep in her flesh, probably down to the bone, or close to it. Her eyes fly open. Like a wild animal, she kicks and cries and thrashes. This time, though, he dodges the blows. Blood geysers from the wound and he slows the flow, clamping down firmly with his now-blood-soaked long underwear top.

"I'm stitching you up," he says. "It's gonna hurt, but it's for your own good."

Her eyes roll back, and she passes out.

The gash looks like a backward "L." She'll have the scar for a lifetime, however long that might be. He flushes the wound a few more times, hunting for smaller pieces of plastic, but finds none. He swabs the wound with the alcohol wipes. When the sting registers in her sluggish brain, she kicks and punches and cries again.

He removes his gloves, picks up the needle and threads it.

He plunges the fire-blackened point into the stranger's calf.

She screams, and once again he dodges kicks and punches.

He pushes the needle through, ties the knot, pulls it tight, cuts the ends of the thread with scissors.

By the third stitch, he's found a rhythm.

By the sixth stitch, his fingers don't shake.

By the tenth stitch, the stranger doesn't cry or kick.

But twenty-three stitches later, he still doesn't know her name.

After playing doctor, Richard crawls out of the entry tunnel only to find that a snowdrift a foot and a half high threatens to seal up the entryway. He punches through the partition of windblown powder, out into the night and the worst blizzard he's ever seen.

Richard stands, or at least tries to. Bent by the force of the storm, he squints, his arm shielding his face to keep stinging snow from his exposed flesh. Flakes the size of locusts pelt him with biblical fury. Disoriented, he curses again. If only he had his helmet and goggles, but they're still on the lake with the snowmobile. The many boot tracks are covered now; the only evidence that anyone's stepped in the clearing before are slight furrows in the snow. He looks back at the quinzee—the sticks that protruded from the dome are indiscernible now. Entry tunnel aside, the quinzee doesn't look like a man-made shelter anymore, just a bump on the landscape, a hillock draped in white. Using the shovel, he scrapes the fresh snow from the roof, trying to gauge the accumulation. It's about eight inches, in some places as many as twelve or eighteen due to wind loading. The shelter is quite strong, and can handle the load, but he doesn't want the snow to test its structural integrity. He works his way around the quinzee, scraping snow as he goes. As he does, he carves a knee-deep path, a moat of sorts, between the castle of the quinzee and the snowbank beyond. The air hole, he notices, is completely choked with fresh snow, and he clears it with the shovel handle.

"I'm going to have to do this constantly," he says aloud, his words ripped from chapped lips by the wind. Defeated, he retreats inside the quinzee.

He had hoped to dry their clothes above a fire, but he had a better chance of fixing the phone than starting a fire in that blizzard. And an indoor fire in the quinzee—one big enough to dry clothes—would be a fool's errand, if not outright suicidal. The quinzee might collapse, leaving them buried and without a shelter; or the fire might silently suck up the oxygen, killing them in their sleep, especially if that air hole keeps getting clogged.

No, drying clothes by fire will have to wait. Instead, he gathers the pile of icy clothes and boots and knocks off what snow he can.

After another max set of pushups, he slides into the sleeping bag, wearing the damp boxers this time, if only for the sake of modesty, and the woman recoils at their touch. At this, he can't help but laugh.

"You're not going to like what comes next this time either," he says. "I'm sorry in advance."

He crams their long underwear, plus the socks and gloves, into the bottom of the sleeping bag, hoping that their body heat will dry them overnight. He does the same with both pairs of boot liners. The snow pants and jacket will have to wait for tomorrow—he doesn't want to soak the sleeping bag more than he has to, and space is limited as it is.

One of the liners drips slush onto her bare back, and she squirms and yells angrily, "What the fuck!"

"Relax," he says, as calmly as he can. "Relax."

"Get off of me!" she yells. "Who the fuck are you? Get off!"

She panics, flailing hard, elbowing him in the stomach, the ribs. He lets her go at it—he has no way of knowing what she remembers, if she knows who she is or where she is. He can't fathom her terror, waking up naked in a sleeping bag, in a pitch-black cavern, an enormous, shirtless stranger behind her. He considers exiting the sleeping bag but worries the movement will scare her further. Instead, he lets her scream and flail, shushing her quietly. "Shh. It's okay. It's okay. You're safe. My name is Richard. You crashed and fell in the lake. I saved you. You're safe," like it was Caleb after one of his nightmares.

She struggles unrelentingly and yells until her throat is hoarse. After more and more blows, he can feel her thrashing stretch the fabric of the sleeping bag, and he begins to worry that she'll tear the bag or break the zipper. Such an outcome could prove tragic. So he reaches his arms around her, pinning her arms to her sides in a firm but gentle bear hug, and repeats quietly, "It's okay. It's okay."

After a while, she drifts out of consciousness again—her breathing steadies, and her body goes limp—but he continues saying those words, if not for her sake, then for his.

The night is never-ending, and Richard is awake for what feels like every minute of it. He's ravenous, but his hunger is overshadowed by stress. He's worried about the woman's head injury, the storm, the shelter collapsing, making their way home, frostbite. All night long he tries to massage feeling back into his toes, which have begun to tingle and burn, but it's tricky to do while sharing the sleeping bag with the woman. He settles for pressing one foot, then the other, against his calves.

She panics a couple of times during the night, but mostly doesn't seem to be bothered by his movements. Richard has given up asking her to stay awake. Hopefully, she'll come to her senses soon.

At one point, he does fall asleep, only to wake to the unconscious woman relieving herself in the sleeping bag. Cussing, he cleans up the piss as best he can with his bloody long underwear top. He dons the brittle snow pants and semi-thawed, damp boots, then breaks through the snowdrift that's formed at the mouth of the entry tunnel again. The world that greets him looks the same as he'd seen it last—a vortex of snow and bitter wind and darkness.

Diligently, he wades around the quinzee, scooping another foot or more of loose, light, freshly fallen powder off the hard-packed dome. Once he's done shoveling, the snowbank surrounding the quinzee is up to his thighs.

He goes through this dreadful ritual three times before dawn—shoveling snow off the roof, clearing the air hole, and carving out a path between the quinzee and the snowbank. When the gray light comes at a quarter past nine—a blessed sight—the moat is waist deep, and the storm shows no sign of slowing down.

"We made it," he says, exhausted, speaking to the raging sky. "We made it!"

Delirious, he unzips his fly and takes a piss in the snowbank—his first in hours. The smell is unpleasant, the hue an unnatural, dark yellow, almost brown, reminders that he's hardly had so much as a sip of water since the crash. He tells himself that there's a Thermos of tea in his backpack, and he should drink some.

"Shit," he says. "Shit. Fuck. Dammit to hell."

He crawls frantically into the quinzee, hip-checking and partially collapsing the entry tunnel. Sweeping the cave with the headlamp, he searches beneath the tarp, the sleeping bag and the bug-out bag. His fears are quickly confirmed. The backpack is nowhere to be found. He can't remember exactly where he last had it. Not far, somewhere in the woods, probably close to where the woman lay on the tarp while he was building the quinzee. But the backpack is under some three feet of snow now, and he hasn't the energy to dig up the entire clearing for it.

He tries to calm down. What was in his backpack?

The Thermos of tea and a sandwich—the thought of which brings tears to his eyes and saliva to his tongue.

His cell phone—likely as useless as the satellite phone.

Three energy bars—potentially lifesaving.

He has his shovel, thankfully, and the Nalgene, which is

almost empty now.

He shakes his head. He needs to focus. Their survival depends on it. Jim had said the storm was only going to get worse. Even without the backpack, he has three full days' worth of emergency freeze-dried meals. Strictly rationed between the two of them, the food will hopefully still last four or five days in a pinch. But the meals are freeze-dried packets that require hot water, and the only way he can make hot water is by melting snow, and the only way he can melt snow is with a fire. A fire in this storm without dry fuel is a fool's errand, and making a fire in the quinzee goes against his better judgment.

He smacks his shovel down on the snow, frustrated, and the blade clangs loudly. The sound sparks an idea: It's possible, he thinks, to use the blade of the shovel as a rudimentary fireplace— similar to the "kudliks," the old seal-blubber lamps that the Natives used in igloos. The Native trick was to prop the tray-like wood or bone lamps up on sticks, so the burning seal blubber wouldn't melt the snow and cause the tray to sink. Conceivably, this could allow him to make an extremely small, controlled fire in the quinzee. He could poke a hole in the ceiling to ensure proper ventilation.

"A kudlik and a chimney hole," he says to himself. "That could work."

He's about to MacGyver a kudlik, but instead he starts laughing. "A hole—we don't need a chimney hole. We already have a water hole."

He gathers his Nalgene, cooking pot, and shovel and pushes through the waist-deep snow toward the lake. The fire wasn't necessary, although it was a good idea for cooking. There's as much water as they could possibly need, it's just underneath the ice. Luckily, the woman had done them a favor and cracked the lake open already.

But at the edge of the woods, his eagerness turns to horror. The lake is a nondescript expanse of white. He can't see far, but he sees enough to know that finding the crash site, as well as his snowmachine, will be like looking for a needle in a haystack.

Chapter 9

Jim lies awake early Sunday morning with no one to distract him. He stares up at the slow-spinning ceiling fan. It's hypnotic in the blue glow of his alarm clock. Sometimes, watching it rotate is enough to send him back to sleep. Not this morning. When his alarm goes off at 5 a.m., he's relieved. He throws off the covers and slips out of bed. He turns on the deck lights and gauges the night's snowfall. It's not yet dawn—the sun won't rise for hours—and two feet, maybe more, has stacked up on the deck. Thick flakes continue to drift down from the black sky. The skiing at Alyeska Resort will be excellent thanks to this storm, just as he'd hoped. Humming now at the prospect, he makes his bed, then changes out of his pajamas into a pair of loose sweats and a tank top.

Barefoot, he pads down the cool concrete stairs of his postmodern Glacier Point home. He ought to sell the place—it's too big for a bachelor—but he loves the wood-slat dock that juts into the pond, the grill and firepit for those late, sun-streaked summer nights, the hot tub for those cold winter ones, the quaking paper birch that frames Denali just so. He loves the house, despite the memories.

The kitchen is quiet and dark. He turns on the lights, puts on the kettle, and spoons two rounded tablespoons of a fair-trade Guatemalan medium-roast coffee into a stainless steel and glass French press. The press is his favorite gizmo in the kitchen - simple and elegant, it matches the aesthetic of the house—one thing that Jess couldn't take with her.

He pours hot water over the fragrant coffee grounds. While the java brews, he combines a cup of almond milk, a handful of spinach, a bunch of beet tops, a banana, an apple, a dash of turmeric, two massive scoops of almond butter and a nub of ginger into a blender. The aroma of Guatemalan coffee steams into the air. He punches the "chop" button on the mixer. He cools the smoothie in the fridge, pushes the French press, and pours the coffee into an insulated mug. Then he relocates to what he's deemed the Post-Divorce Gym, or PDG.

To a realtor, the Post-Divorce Gym would be known as a "living room without furniture." The very same day that Jess first ransacked the house—bitter Viking bitch, navigating a U-Haul instead of a longship—Jim realized that his empty living room made for a perfect gym. Sans furniture, it was suddenly spacious, well lit, and ventilated. Plus, there was surround sound for pump-up jams and a flat-screen on the wall for ESPN. He let her take the furniture, the artwork, the china—it just wasn't worth the fight. But he put his foot down when it came to the TV. He had no say if Mick the lawyer fucked his wife, but he'd be damned if a Yankees fan would watch his sixty-inch flat-screen.

"Keep it," she said. "See if I care. Mick will get one for me."

She wasn't lying. The lawyer wasn't stupid—he'd buy her whatever she asked for. Jess possessed not only a Machiavellian brain but also two functioning legs, and she wouldn't hesitate to use them to walk away.

Every morning in the Post-Divorce Gym, Jim puts his own legs to work. He stretches through ten sun salutations and then some prone twists for his lower back.

Not without a trace of irony, his yoga mat lies where the couch once squatted.

He breathes deeply into a downward dog pose.

He doesn't miss her. He doesn't miss the Crate & Barrel

sectional sofa, either. It was an ugly, beige, rectangular thing, as uncomfortable as it was expensive. Jess picked it out and Jim paid for it. In the frenzy of the divorce, Jess declared that she wanted the couch and Jim suppressed a smile—he wanted that thing out of there even more than she did. Like the statue of an evil dictator, it had to be toppled for a new administration to flourish.

He breathes in, feels the rubber mat underneath his fingertips. The shoulders of his tank top droop past his ears. His nose is inches away from the fossilized indents left behind in the carpet by the couch's legs. Oddly enough, he finds himself feeling sorry for Mick. A strange development, seeing as how that lawyer is a slimy, smarmy, cuckolding son of a bitch.

He exhales and drops his belly to the mat.

He wonders if Mick knows that he's betting the farm on a modern Circe.

Like the couch, the large, square coffee table that once held large, square coffee table books is now gone. Jess didn't get her hands on that one. He'd banged his shins on that hideous wooden table so many times that, when he got news of Jess's infidelity, he and Richard bashed it with sledgehammers in the backyard and inserted the fragments into a woodchipper while polishing off a bottle of Johnnie Walker Black. Splintering antiques, industrial machinery, and Scotch—a satisfying recipe for vindication.

In the coffee table's place is a set of kettlebells. Jim works through a sequence of swings, presses, and squats. Sweat drips on the carpet. Jess would've hated that, but Jim doesn't mind. If he decides to stay in the place long-term, he'll rip the carpet out anyway. And if he sells, well, it won't be his problem anymore.

Since revamping his diet and adopting this morning routine, Jim's lost twenty pounds and gained more than muscle tone. The physical improvements pale in significance to the mental ones. He sleeps better now, though he's still something of an insomniac. And he's quit drinking, save for a tumbler of whiskey or two on poker night.

The shelves are empty of books, the walls devoid of picture frames, though nails still protrude from the light blue paint like tiny islands on a map. Jim had purchased a couple of zodiac posters from a Nepali store in Anchorage. He's never been to Nepal, though he and Richard have talked about mountaineering in the Himalayas since they were in college. The authentic textured parchment looks good on the bare walls—ascetic, even—and the posters make him feel slightly monk-like, even though he'd never say so aloud.

He pinned the posters on either side of a large window that opens up to the backyard. On a sunny day he can see Denali in the distance, just over the tops of the birch trees. Jess had her desk here, in the corner, not that she ever used it; it was a section of the living room that Jim had all but ignored, preferring the time warp of the couch and the television. In the absence of both ex-wife and furniture, that little corner has become one of his favorites.

He's positioned a purple meditation cushion facing the posters and the window. Following his kettlebell workout, he lies down on the yoga mat for a few minutes, calms his breathing, and then sits cross-legged on the cushion and meditates. At first, when meditation was a scary, off-putting word, he started with guided meditations, soft voices recorded over singing bowls and harps. Now, he prefers silence.

As he's learned to do, he tries to let the thoughts in, watch them enter his consciousness, and then allow them to pass on by, like an autumn wind rustling through yellow leaves. But in the wake of Jess's visit the previous night, his mind is especially jumbled, and the thoughts come storming in.

Jess barging in with her key.

Mick awkwardly following like a puppy on a leash.

His former partner, treating her new man like a mover, directing him with a familiar coldness. A coldness he never knew when they first fell in love. Did that develop over time? Or was it always there, underneath the surface, and he just never saw it?

Mick carrying cardboard boxes, unable to make eye contact.

Richard deciding to continue onward.

The purr of a snowmachine.

Two years of separations and spats.

The suspicions, the doubts.

Opening emails. Screening text messages.

His own vengeful benders, his own digressions.

His mind wanders to the week he spent at Richard's remote cabin last summer, just to get away from it all. The evening he'd fly-fished until dark. Only then did he let long-overdue tears fall, let them wash away with the rapids. He decided that it was over, that he couldn't do it anymore.

That it was time to move on.

He breathes deep, and tries to find his center.

To let the thoughts come in, and the thoughts go out, like wind through yellow leaves.

Jim finishes meditating, then takes a shower. With his previously prepared smoothie and coffee in tow, he retreats to his office, the only room in the entire house that's remained unchanged by Jess's exit. A snapshot from the Iron Dog finish line sits on his desk next to his laptop. A painting of Denali hangs on the wall. A bulletin board is covered with Post-its, a calendar splattered with ink. File cabinets line the wall. Everything's the same, but he's changed dramatically. He flips open the laptop. It's now 7:15 a.m. A few months ago, he'd either still be passed out or tossing and turning, hungover as hell.

Jim sips his coffee, and immediately turns off his Wi-Fi before emails and messages load and derail his Sunday. He wants to get a head start on his work week while the blizzard rages, so that he has the flexibility to hit the ski resort midweek when the storm eases. Rumor has it the chairlifts will be shut down for a day or two. It sounds like a doozy of a storm. When the resort does open, the skiing will be all-time, and Jim doesn't want to miss it.

Disconnecting has, funnily enough, become a part of his post-divorce self-improvement kick. Any day he's serious about working,

Jim doesn't check his email or look at his phone until lunch. This allows him to work from home, be productive, and get shit done. Whenever he goes to the office to manage his team, he always jokes, he has nothing to show for it.

Usually, his disconnecting habit is harmless. Usually, by lunch, he has a missed call or two, a few texts, and ten or so significant emails (plus the expected slew of spam). But by 9:30 a.m., on a Sunday no less, his phone has ten missed calls and twelve messages—all from Anne. He's oblivious to this fact, though, and is crushing a marketing proposal for the Glacier Point Tourism Board, quite pleased with himself for completing his early morning routine and working on the weekend, when the doorbell rings.

Anne's at the door, and she looks furious.

"Hey," says Jim, confused. "What's going on?"

"Why the fuck haven't you answered your phone?"

Jim's never heard her curse before.

"I'm sorry, I don't usually check it before noon."

"He didn't come home last night."

"What?"

His heart sinks.

Trembling, she repeats herself.

Snow's whipping around behind her. The driveway has been recently plowed, but the banks on the side are two and a half, maybe three feet deep.

It could be three times that in the mountains, maybe more.

"Shit. Come in."

She walks into the hallway but doesn't bother to take off her snowy jacket or boots. She just stands there, dripping.

"What happened, Jim?"

"Nothing. We, well, I came back early, Richard wanted to keep going."

"What?!"

It's Jim's turn to repeat himself.

"You separated?"

"He insisted."

She slaps him across the cheek. Her tiny palm packs a surprising amount of force.

"You should have called last night! To check if he got back at least."

"I know, I'm sorry, I was dealing with my ex-wife. She came with that lawyer to get some boxes…" he breaks off. "I don't mean to make excuses. You're right, you're right."

Anne's silent, steaming, sorry for lashing out but unwilling to apologize.

Richard should be back by now. Why wasn't he? Did he get lost? The visibility was terrible by the time Jim got back to the parking lot, but Richard wasn't an idiot—that shouldn't have thrown him off. He had GPS and a sat phone. But there were a million things that could have happened, that's why they always operated on the buddy system—he could've crashed, gotten lost, fallen into a lake—they weren't all fully frozen yet. But again, Richard would've known that.

"Did you call his sat phone?"

"Of course."

"Have you called 911?"

"No, not yet. I wanted to talk to you first."

"We've got to move fast."

He jogs through the house, heart thumping, and grabs his cell phone from the kitchen counter. He ignores the messages and the notifications and dials 911.

"Jim?" says Anne.

"Yeah?"

"Is it going to be okay?"

"Yes," he says, with a confidence he doesn't feel.

"Nine-one-one, what's your emergency?"

Jim takes a deep breath. "I'd like to report a missing person."

After getting off the phone with the cops and dialing Search and Rescue separately, Jim drives Anne back to her house. Her hands are shaking. She's in no state to drive, not in this storm.

He makes her a cup of tea—an ancient remedy for bad times. Anne sits in an armchair, steam rising out of her teacup, and gazes forlornly out the window. She looks exhausted. Jim bets she hasn't slept. He can't imagine what she's thinking. He feels as helpless as she looks.

The doorbell rings. It's Allen Bogle, former fire chief, current Glacier Point Search and Rescue director. He also lives nearby and is a frequent member of their Thursday night poker games—he knows Richard as well as anyone.

"Hey, Al, thanks for coming."

"No problem." Al removes his wool beanie and runs a burned right hand through thin gray hair. He speaks solemnly as he hangs his coat on the hook and knocks snow from his boots. "It's coming down out there. It'll be something else in the mountains."

Jim nods. "Coffee?"

"Wouldn't say no."

They walk through the living room to the kitchen. Anne smiles weakly at Al.

"Hello, Anne," he says delicately, with the bedside manner of a seasoned surgeon. "We're going to do our best to find your husband."

"Thanks, Al. I know you will. I—I can't thank you enough."

"We're going to talk over the details over some coffee," says Jim, extending an invitation.

"I'll—I'll just sit here, thanks. I trust you both."

In the kitchen, Jim fiddles with the K-cup machine. "Sorry, all Richard has is damn Dunkin' Donuts coffee in these godforsaken containers."

"I'm not surprised," Al laughs. "That'll be fine with me." His voice grows serious again. "I have confirmation from folks out there that his truck is still in the parking lot. The vehicle was damn near completely buried."

The words are devastating.

He's still out in the storm.

Jim only nods.

"Now, why don't you tell me what happened," says Al.

Jim goes over the details. He tells Al what Richard was wearing, how much food he had, what emergency gear was in his sled. Embarrassed, Jim admits that they'd separated. He spreads out a map, draws a line of their projected route, and marks specifically where he left Richard.

"He was going to the base of the pass, then turning around, south along the Hope."

"That's good, Jim. That's exactly what we need to find him," says Al, who carefully snaps a photo of the map and emails it to the relevant government bodies and Search and Rescue personnel.

"Park Service, rangers, they're already aware of the situation. Search and Rescue teams from Fairbanks, Anchorage and Glacier Point are ready to go."

"Great. When can we move?"

Al furrows his bristly eyebrows. "Well, we can't mobilize until the storm stops. You know that."

Logically, Jim does know that. But there's nothing logical about this situation, so why should it merit a logical response?

Al continues. "Given his equipment and skill set, if he's alive, which there's a good chance he is, he's built himself a shelter and hunkered down for the storm. If we were to go out there now, why, we could be standing ten yards from him and never know."

Al gets up to leave. "Stay strong now, Jim. Try not to blame yourself. I'll keep you updated as I work on this."

Jim nods as Al claps a hand on his shoulder.

He listens to the door slam, then pours two half-empty coffees into the kitchen sink.

Anne is on her third cup of tea. Jim paces the living room. Since Al left, he's been on edge.

"Al says he can't send out teams until the storm breaks," he says, as much to himself as to Anne. "I checked the weather. That might not be until three, maybe five days from now. Maybe more. And the long-term forecast doesn't look promising, either."

"He's got food, shelter, and a sleeping bag, right?"

"Right. But three days, that's a mighty long time."

"You're supposed to be assuring me that everything's going to be okay," she says flatly. "Not the other way around."

He stops pacing to look at Anne, who sits in the armchair like a queen on a throne, her original shakiness replaced by stone-faced strength.

"You're right."

Jim sits down on the couch. Tears start to flow. He hasn't cried since he decided that it was over with Jess. But here they fall, splashing onto a worn, well-loved couch covered in dog hair.

"That's my brother," he says through the sobs. "That's my brother."

He can't see her, but he feels Anne's presence near him, her thin arms around his shoulders.

"Hush, Jimmy. It's going to be okay. We're going to find him."

"That's my brother!" Anguish racks his body.

"I know, I know."

He wipes tears from his eyes.

"I'll go today. I'll drive out. I'll go by myself if I have to."

Anne smiles sadly at his foolishness. "And you'll find him yourself?"

"Yes."

At least if he dies out there, Jim thought, he won't have to live with the guilt.

Anne reads his mind. "You can't punish yourself for this, Jimmy."

"But it's my fault."

"It's no one's fault, no one's but Rich's," Anne speaks softly and rubs his back. "I don't blame you. And if you blame yourself, you're going to be more hindrance than help in this search. I need you to pick yourself up. I need you to be a man right now. You're the godfather to my children, remember?"

"Yes."

"Well, it's time you start acting like it." Her voice betrays no malice.

"What can I do?"

"That's better. Can you please pick up the twins this afternoon? They're at a sleepover at the Darcys. And don't say a word about Richard, mind you. I want to tell them and Sarah both at dinner."

"You got it, Anne." He hugs her tightly, then gets up to go.

"Oh, and Jim?"

He turns.

"Pick up some of your things. I'll make up the guest room. I—" her voice falters. "I'd like for you to stay here until this is all over."

He nods, wipes at his eyes, and heads home.

Duffel bag over his shoulder, Jim locks up his house. He wonders when he'll return, and under what circumstances that will be. He hitches the snowmachine trailer to the back of his truck. Just in case.

He picks up the twins from their sleepover in time for dinner, which, unsurprisingly, doesn't go well.

Anne breaks down the situation as best she can.

Sarah bursts into tears and flees to her room.

Sean shatters his plate on the floor then sprints out of the house, barefoot and in a T-shirt.

Jim runs after him, grabbing a jacket and what look to be Sean's boots from the foyer. He follows footsteps through the snow to the treehouse that Jim and Richard built when the twins were in kindergarten. He clambers up the snowy ladder into the cramped little room and holds Sean tight as he shivers and cries.

Only Caleb remains at the table. He looks at his mom.

"Are you okay?" he asks, concerned and compassionate beyond his twelve years.

"Yes, honey, I'm fine," says Anne, almost taken aback. "And your dad's going to be fine, too."

At this, Caleb jabs at his asparagus and growls. "Don't say that if it isn't true."

Chapter 10

She doesn't remember where she is or how she got there. She doesn't even remember who she is. All she knows is that a headache pounds at her temples and her leg throbs.

As her eyes adjust to the gloom, a curved ceiling comes into focus. She tries to get up but fails. The pain is severe and she's inexplicably weak. With concerted effort, she cranes her neck and takes in her surroundings. She's wrapped in a sleeping bag and a cold tarp. She reaches her hand out, ignoring the pain, and brushes the low ceiling above her head. It's cold to the touch. The walls, the floor—all seem to be made of snow.

She lies back, physically spent, and stares at the ceiling. She probes the foggy recesses of her mind and her memory starts to come back bit by bit. Her name is Mel Drummond. She's thirty-five years old. Her parents never married. These are major memories, the core of her identity. But Mel reaches back further, for details only she would know. She loves Chinese food but can't stand chopsticks, hates cats but empathizes with their standoffishness, has one small tattoo of a daisy on her left ankle that she regrets deeply. Her passwords are all related to actor Johnny Depp (CaptainJack89, DeppDiva999, ?!Blow!?, etc.), and she subscribes to two fitness magazines that she never reads.

At least she knows who she is.

But her short-term memory, it seems, has gone to shit. Where is she? How did she get here? And why does she feel like she just got hit by a truck?

The small room, or cave, or whatever it is, is virtually empty as far as she can see. She runs her hands up and down her body and concludes that she's naked. Panic sets in. The pain, the headache, the lack of memory; she's been drugged and brought upstate to the lair of some sicko and… She doesn't even want to think about what's happened to her, or how long she's been unconscious. She just needs to escape.

She's preparing to throw herself out of the sleeping bag when her hand hits a small fabric box by her side, spilling a few small items onto the snowy floor. She picks them up and identifies them one by one: alcohol wipes, a syringe, a roll of bandages, scissors and needle and thread. She picks up the box last. It's a red first aid kit.

Involuntarily, she shudders, remembering how the disinfectant burned when it touched her flesh. Another memory materializes; a man leaning over her, saying, "I'm stitching you up."

Inhaling sharply at the pain, she reaches down and feels a bandage on her calf, under which she assumes are stitches.

Who was this fucked-up sadist? What did he want with her? What happened to her calf and head? Had she tried to resist? Was she tortured?

She tries to picture his face, wondering if she'd ever met him before—they say kidnappings are often committed by acquaintances of the victim—when a faint light flashes across the sleeping bag. She can hear something, presumably the man from her memory, crawling toward her on the snow, and the light grows brighter and brighter, filling her with fear. She grabs the medical scissors and hides them inside the sleeping bag. She tests the point against a thumb. The scissors are small but sharp, and through an eye or jugular they could inflict gruesome, potentially fatal, damage. Just before the source of light pokes into the room, she shuts her eyes.

The beam rests on her face, and she doesn't dare move a

muscle. Her act must be convincing, because soon the light turns away from her. She cracks an eye open, and watches as a large man busies himself on the far side of the cave, scraping the bark off a small branch with a pocketknife. His knife makes her scissors look like a toothpick. And knife or no knife, the hefty man is more than a match for her, especially in her compromised state.

Still, she's debating whether to attack while his back is turned, imagining jabbing the scissors into the side of his beefy neck, when she hears the click of a lighter and sees a small orange glow. He's building a fire, she thinks.

Sure enough, the stranger blows on what appears to be a ball of moss and a flaming cotton ball. Carefully, he places the sphere on top of a bed of more moss, wood shavings and small sticks, all stacked in a metal tray that looks as if it might be the blade of a shovel. The tray sits several inches above the snow, perched on stilt-like sticks.

When the moss finally catches, the man claps and cheers joyfully, and then looks in Mel's direction quickly, as if concerned that he might wake her. Unable to close her eyes in time, she grimaces and turns away from the brilliant beam, which twists the screws of her headache deeper and deeper into her temples.

"You're awake," he says, seeming relieved. "How are you feeling?"

She considers staying quiet, but it's obvious now that she's awake, and she needs to learn more about her captor. It's not a good idea to anger this man, whoever he is.

"My head hurts. And my leg."

"To be expected on both accounts, I'm afraid," says the man, prodding the small fire. "You've had quite the adventure." Mel watches serpentine smoke spiral up and out through a hole in the snowy ceiling. The man adds on more sticks until the flames are bright enough to cast orange light on the curved walls, and then turns off the headlamp.

"What have you done to me?" she asks, doing her best to sound brave. Enough beating around the bush. She wants a straight answer.

There's a pause, and then the man laughs so loudly that she worries the cavern might collapse.

"What have I done to you?" the man chuckles.

Mel fails to see the humor.

"My head. My leg. I'm naked, with no idea where I am. Forgive me if I don't find this as hilarious as you do," she says stiffly.

The man stops laughing immediately. "Ah. Yes. I understand it might not be a funny question from your perspective. The only thing I've done to you is saved your life."

Mel says nothing.

"You don't remember, do you? You hit your head when your snowmachine crashed, before you went underwater."

Underwater. Mel remembers that—sinking like a stone in that icy, black and blue water, the light fading into darkness.

The levees break, and the memories all come flooding back.

Traveling to Alaska on vacation. Booking the snowmachine tour. Getting lost in the snowstorm. Digging out the sled. Turning around and eventually finding a set of tracks. Wrenching the handlebars, losing traction on the ice, spinning out of control on the frozen lake.

"I remember some of it," she says slowly. "But not all of it."

"You're probably concussed—very concussed, I imagine—but I'm no doctor." He pokes another slightly bigger stick into the fire, and stoops over the bed. "That being said, I did a fine job on your leg. I'll show you if you like."

Mel nods, and he unzips the sleeping bag from the bottom so that he can pull out her leg without exposing the rest of her body to the cold.

While he's bent over her, Mel thinks: This would be her time to strike. Except the scissors no longer seem necessary. She believes him.

His hands are immense, cold to the touch but gentle. He turns on the headlamp and unwraps the bandage. Mel does her best not to cry out and leans forward so she can see the train track of stitches curving up her calf. The wound is red and fresh, but clean.

"When you crashed, the body of the snowmachine cracked on the ice," says the man as he wraps up the wound again. He reaches for something near the fire, then hands her a jagged piece of plastic an inch and a half long. "That little bastard," he says, "speared through your pants. It went pretty much to the bone. Twenty-three stitches. But don't worry. You'll be fine."

Mel remembers it vividly now, and replays those moments in her mind. Spiderwebbing cracks. Fracture lines spreading outward across the lake. And then blue, deep blue, fading to black. She remembers falling through the ice. She remembers the terror. What she doesn't remember is her salvation.

"But the water. I was underwater," she says. "I don't understand."

"I saw the crash and dove in after you."

He makes it sound so simple.

"And you pulled me out?"

"Yes. I pulled you out. Dug us this shelter. Luckily, I had a survival kit in my snowmachine with this sleeping bag in there. I took off all of our wet clothes. Um, well, we laid next to each other in the bag for warmth."

"We slept together in a sleeping bag? Naked?" Mel asks, surprised to feel that nakedness seems rather trivial.

Embarrassed, he looks down.

"Yes."

For such a large man, he seems remarkably small when unnerved.

"Oh."

There's no space in her clouded brain for a witty retort.

"And then I've been trying to maintain the shelter, dry our clothes, and melt snow for water," he says, as if trying to change the subject. "It was a miracle that I was snowmachining nearby. A little farther away and I wouldn't have been able to see you."

"A miracle," she repeats. Who is she to argue? This might as well be the work of God. Never has she been so close to death.

"How long have I been asleep?"

He pauses. "On and off for forty-eight hours."

"Forty-eight hours!"

"Approximately—my watch just froze up and stopped working. I thought about bringing you back right away, but I was scared you were going to be hypothermic," the man says, putting the back of his hand to her forehead. "Better now, though, you've warmed up quite a bit." He looks out the entryway. "And it hasn't stopped snowing. It snowed over four feet in the first twenty-four hours or so. Incredible. I've never seen anything like it. Then it slowed down to an inch an hour, which is still no joke. The damn snowbank outside is over six feet tall at this point. Almost taller than this cave of ours. But enough negativity." He claps his hands again. "You must be hungry."

She hasn't noticed until he says it, but she's suddenly famished.

"Yes. And thirsty, too."

"Would you like some soup? We have chicken noodle. I'm just heating up some water now."

"I'm a vegetarian."

He turns toward her and stares blankly. And then he starts laughing again—deep, uncontrollable rolls of laughter. He doubles over. Tears form at the corners of his eyes.

Mel doesn't laugh. She doesn't understand why he finds it so funny.

"It's a personal choice."

He wipes away the tears. "What's your name? I feel like after saving your life I've earned at least that."

"Melissa Drummond. Call me Mel."

"Richard Maynard."

With a tenderness unexpected from a man of his stature, he shakes her hand.

"Nice to meet you, Richard."

"You too, Mel." The formality seems belated, given the intimacy they've already shared; not only the nakedness in the sleeping bag, which Mel doesn't remember, but also the fact that this stranger risked his own life to save hers.

"Right. Soup," he says, getting down to business. "Vegetarianism out here is synonymous with starvation. We have three days of hydrated meals, but I'm trying to make them last as long as possible. I've been making tea from pine needles—it's kind of bitter, but it's an old Native trick and helps take the edge off. I also have a few energy bars and a sandwich in my backpack, I just need to dig it up."

"Dig it up?"

Richard pauses. "It's somewhere in the clearing outside, buried under the snow, I'm just not sure exactly where. It was a mistake. But in my defense, I did have my hands full."

Mel nods, but something isn't computing. This all seems unnecessary. She props herself up on her elbows. Woozy and wobbling from the head rush, she nearly collapses sideways before Richard catches her.

"Easy now, easy now."

"Richard," she says. "I don't understand. Why do we need three days of food to last as long as possible? Let's eat, get our strength back, then get the hell out of here. I'm awake."

"I wish it were that easy."

"Let's get on the snowmachine and go. I'm fine. I feel better."

"Your machine is at the bottom of the lake."

"And yours?"

Richard's smile disappears. The fire hisses. Richard cracks his knuckles.

"Did you poke your head out of the cave yet?"

"No," Mel says.

"It's dumping snow. It's been dumping snow. For two days straight."

"So, we wait for it to get sunny?"

"My snowmachine is out there, somewhere on or around that lake. The storm was so intense, I couldn't see shit. And in the chaos of saving you, I left the snowmachine there overnight. I knew I'd have to dig it out, but it's buried out there and, quite honestly, it could be anywhere within a square mile, under six feet of snow and counting. It's impossible to figure out where you fell in right now. Any footsteps are long since buried. It may take a few days—weeks, even—to find the snowmachine."

Reality sinks in, like a sled through the ice.

For now, they're stuck here.

Failing to maintain a vegetarian diet seems like the least of her concerns.

"I guess I'll have some soup then," she says.

Chapter 11

Richard cuts open an empty packet of dehydrated chicken pot pie with his pocketknife, unwilling to let so much as a pea go to waste. The math is simple. They started with nine packets. At a rate of one packet per day, they'll get through nine days. By then, Richard figures, the storm will break, and Search and Rescue will come calling. Until help arrives, though, he's as disciplined as a drill sergeant when it comes to rationing their food. Every morning they split half a meal packet for breakfast and then finish it for dinner.

If Search and Rescue doesn't come, well, that's a different story.

Mel, wrapped in the sleeping bag as always, says, "I am the worst vegetarian in the world. What I wouldn't give for a cheeseburger right now."

He snorts in agreement. "Our bodies are craving meat. I'd settle for another packet of dehydrated chicken pot pie."

This is, for the most part, the extent of their conversations. Not because they don't have anything in common—which they don't, it seems, aside from hunger and missing home—but because they don't have energy to spare. If they aren't starving, they're damn close, closer than either has ever been in their lives, and expending brainpower on pleasantries feels like a waste of calories. It's been four painfully slow days and even slower nights since the crash—an endless cycle of scraping snow off the quinzee, melting snow for water, and trying to stay warm huddled together in the damp sleeping bag. What little food they do eat is delectable, easily the best part of the day. But it's never enough.

In the end Richard's investigating pays off. He finds a chunk of carrot, which he sucks on like a throat lozenge, and a corn kernel, which he hands to Mel, who accepts it as if there were no finer gift.

After dinner and a shared pot of pine needle tea—their saving grace—Richard attends to the usual quinzee maintenance and then joins Mel in the now-putrid-smelling sleeping bag—he hadn't the heart to tell her she'd pissed in it, but it isn't exactly a secret, given the smell. Accidents notwithstanding, they've managed to dry their underwear and long johns with their body heat, and he's relieved that sleeping naked is no longer necessary. He imagines what his wife and children are going through, as he always does before he falls into fitful slumber; but before sleep can offer him respite, Mel's body begins to shudder, as she's overcome by intense sobs. He's pressed so tightly against the poor woman that he can't even pat her back. He just puts his arms around her and doesn't say a thing. This, too, becomes part of their routine.

Later that night, he gets up to go pee. Groggily, he searches for the headlamp, which should be in the bug-out bag next to the sleeping bag. After a few seconds of fruitless scrabbling, he realizes that the sleeping bag is glowing from the inside out. It takes him a moment to realize that Mel, snoring lightly, is holding the lit headlamp in her hand.

"Mel," he says, shaking her roughly. "Mel!"

She wakes with a start, clearly frightened, but Richard has no capacity for empathy right now.

"The headlamp! Turn off the motherfucking headlamp," he says angrily. "That battery's going to die and we're going to be living in darkness."

"I'm sorry," she says, frantically fumbling for the off

button. "I must've fallen asleep."

"No shit," he says curtly, then extricates himself from the sleeping bag and heads out into the storm to piss.

Sure enough, while shoveling snow before dawn the following morning, the headlamp flickers and dies.

"Motherfucker," Richard swears into the dark.

Back in the quinzee, he pours hot water into a packet of dehydrated chicken teriyaki for breakfast and relays the news brusquely.

"Headlamp just died," he says.

"I'm sorry, Richard," Mel says sincerely, and tears begin to stream down her stricken face.

Content to let her shoulder the burden of her blunder, he doesn't say anything else. His stomach growls, and his thoughts are dark ones. He wishes he hadn't jumped in after her, that he'd just let her die.

Breakfast, though, is hot and hearty and it helps. The quarter serving is not nearly enough to fill him up, but he regains his senses enough to apologize.

"I'm sorry I got so mean. I'm just hungry," he says. He crouches down by her side and wipes her tears away with a gloved finger. "And don't worry about the headlamp. We all make mistakes. If I knew where the backpack was, we'd have an extra day of food. If I'd pulled the snowmachine into the woods, we'd be home by now."

She snivels, and he hands her the packet of chicken teriyaki.

"Have some breakfast. It'll make you feel better."

Chapter 12

Mel can't sleep. Rich drug addicts and alcoholics go to rehab in the woods. They escape into nature and get away from the distractions of the city to face their problems. It's just them and their addiction—plus the well-paid staff, luxe amenities and three square meals a day. But they don't do it like this—starving, wrapped in a piss-stained sleeping bag for twenty-three hours a day, the only way to avoid frostbite getting spooned by some gruff, snoring Alaskan giant.

Her calf isn't infected, thankfully, at least according to Richard; but the concussion is impossible to diagnose, and a splitting headache comes and goes. Whether she has a traumatic brain injury or not, her brain chemistry is off-kilter. It's been five days since the crash. Granted, she's only been conscious for three of them, but that's five days without taking her anxiety medication. Five days without drinking. She didn't exactly think to pop her prescription and a pint or two into her snow pants pockets. No, she's doing it cold turkey. No "titration of the dose," no "tapering," none of that medical bullshit that Dr. Meyer sprayed in their sessions. She's moody as hell, and her stomach hurts, like she's got the flu—it's possible these symptoms are just manifestations of her hunger, but she'd bet a thirty-day prescription of Zoloft and a bottle of Tito's they're side effects of withdrawal.

Her mind doesn't feel like home anymore. It's a foreign land in there. It's like she's back in high school again, lost, low, constantly on edge. Her normally sharp wit has dulled. She's no stock market whiz, no financial guru, not successful in the slightest, just a useless lump, completely dependent on a stranger. The days are all the same, each a horrible clone of the last, and she wants them to end. It's not the first time she's wanted out, but she's never wanted it more. She fantasizes about Richard's pocketknife, the vertical slit she'd make across her wrist. She thinks about black lake water filling her lungs, how welcome it would be to greet nothingness. She'd been there already, hadn't she? If Richard hadn't jumped into that lake and saved her life, she'd be gone, nothing but a name on a gravestone, no body to be found. The crash wasn't painful, at least not compared to the aftermath.

Richard, ironically, is the reason she doesn't give up. She can't. He risked his life for her sake. And if she takes her life, it'd be like taking his, too—he needs her body heat when he comes back in from shoveling snow. To abandon him now would be beyond cowardly. So she fights as hard as she can.

Inspired to make an effort, she slips out of the sleeping bag, puts on her stiff snow pants, jacket, boots and Richard's dryish gloves, then retrieves the shovel. Today she'll wage the war against winter—the man has earned a break. She crawls out of the entry tunnel, happy to register a feeling of motivation instead of her usual melancholy. Immediately upon her exit, she's forced into a squint by the sun.

"The sun," she says, skeptically, as if questioning its existence. "The sun!"

How different it is, Mel thinks, to have no idea what the weather holds. No iPhone app to check, no weatherman to watch on a hotel flat-screen. You just wake up and see for yourself. She thinks about shaking Richard awake, but decides she'll shovel first and surprise him.

She starts to dig, humming as she scrapes a foot of snow off the roof and chucks shovelfuls over the tall walls of snow—the imposing banks are now ten feet tall, significantly taller than the quinzee. In her elation, she works quickly, ignoring the pain in her temples and calf, and she's soon out of breath and lightheaded. As she stops for a quick rest, in the distance she hears a sound, a roaring sound, like a waterfall—but it keeps getting closer, as if there's a DJ with his fingers on a mixer, slowly bringing up the volume.

It's the drone of a helicopter.

"Richard," she yells into the quinzee. "Get up! There's a helicopter! Get up!"

The walls of snow are daunting—she can't shovel a path to the lake, that would take hours. She leaps at the bank, jabs the shovel blade into the top of the wall, and kicks her boot toes into the hard-packed snow toward the bottom. Huffing, she climbs the snowbank and scrabbles up into the untouched powder.

She wallows up to her waist, panting and soaking wet. Powder creeps into her boots. She hasn't had her medication, or a drink, or a proper meal, in days. Her body is running on fumes. But none of this stops her. She's on a mission. Get to the lake. Wave her arms like a lunatic. Get picked up, go home, forget this ever happened.

The quinzee is only fifty yards from the lake, but it's slow going, like swimming through gumbo, and the roar is getting steadily louder.

The helicopter is deafening. Then she sees it, the chopper, careening across the lake.

They've come at last.

She pushes out of the forest, yelling hoarsely, waving the shovel.

The helicopter is so close she can feel the blast of the rotor wash as it surges by.

But it doesn't stop.

She keeps pushing, out into the lake, chasing the helicopter west, hoping they have a rearview mirror.

But it continues onward, fading into the sky like a pebble dropped into a bottomless blue pond. On and on, disappearing into the horizon.

The roar of the rotors fades to silence, and with it, Mel's hope sputters and dies. A lump the size of a pinecone forms in her throat. Her arms fall to her side. How could they not have seen her?

She can't believe it. All she can do is laugh. Hollow and pained, the laugh threatens to crack her in two. She collapses onto her knees, suddenly aware of the dizziness, the icy snow, the wetness of her sweat, the tears freezing against her cheeks, the sheer exhaustion. It's too much. Shivers run down her skin like avalanches down steep mountainsides.

They came. Search and Rescue came. And they won't come again. They'll check this section and scratch it off their maps.

She's never been so hopeless.

Head buried in her hands, she hears Richard crashing through the trees.

He doesn't say a word. She's grateful that he doesn't.

She hears him breathing hard beside her, feels him crouch down. He pulls her close to him. She doesn't look up. The tears fall silently and steadily now, rivulets dripping into the snow.

Mel stands, her breath ragged, ready to return to the quinzee, ready for the wave of depression to sweep her up again, but it doesn't come. Instead, she stares with wonder at the long, flat expanse of the lake, the snow sparkling like trillions of minuscule diamonds in the sunshine. On the far shore of the lake there's more stretching forest, behind which are mountains unlike anything she's ever seen, enormous spires of rock and snow, scraping skies like New York high-rises never could.

"It's beautiful," she says.

Richard nods.

"I'm happy to be alive," she says, brought to the verge of tears again by the beauty and the power of her realization.

At this, Richard laughs, and looks at her sideways. "I should fucking hope so."

She laughs, too, hard and long, until it hurts. This time, the laughter feels good.

"Hopefully they'll come back," says Richard, starting to walk back. "Let's go make breakfast. You've earned it after that sprint. We can come look at the mountains again afterward."

Mel's about to follow suit when the sun flashes off something, metal or maybe glass, on a spit of land on the far shore of the lake.

"Richard," she calls. "You didn't park your snowmachine on the far shore did you?"

He stops and turns. "No. Why?"

Chapter 13

Richard insists they have breakfast before they investigate. "It's too far," he says. "We need the energy."

They break camp, bringing everything with them. It's not much, just repacking the sleeping bag in the bug-out bag and collecting their food, but doing so fills them both with hope. It's hard to tell what she saw—it's a half-mile or so across the lake—but Richard agrees that it's worth exploring.

They forge a path across the lake. The going is slow, and Mel is exhausted from her earlier effort, but Richard breaks trail.

"I think you're onto something," he says excitedly when they're halfway across.

Mel turns and looks back—their old camp is invisible in the trees. To the left, the valley opens up even more broadly. She points down the valley. "Is that where you came from?"

"Yes, ma'am. That's the Hope River Valley. I looped around those peaks, came from the north, and my car and trailer are that way, south." He plods on hurriedly, then whoops, "Mel! You're a genius! An eagle-eyed genius!"

By the time Mel catches up to Richard, he's dancing an odd jig in front of an old, abandoned cabin. It's buried to the eaves, and a steeply angled, rusted metal roof, complete with a thin black chimney, protrudes out of the snow like a volcanic island in a sea of white.

"Say goodbye to the quinzee," howls Richard. "We're sleeping good tonight!"

Mel laughs and claps her hands. She throws her arms around Richard, and he spins her until she's dizzy. They celebrate like the ball just dropped on New Year's Eve, minus the drunken kiss.

Digging out the cabin is a Homeric quest—the snow is dense and heavy, and Richard is weak with hunger. While Mel shivers in the sleeping bag, Richard digs out a narrow staircase of snow down to the deck, clearing a path to the door just as the sky turns from pink to deep violet.

He grabs the rusty doorknob. The door's unlocked. He grins at Mel. "Home sweet home."

In the dim light, they examine their new abode. Compared to the quinzee, it's palatial.

"Likely a trapper's cabin, from the looks of it," says Richard. "A decade out of use, at least."

He can't believe it. Shelter. True shelter. A godsend. A miracle. What are the chances?

There's a musty smell, the beams are rotten, it's drafty as hell, and the place is full of cobwebs, but that's to be expected.

"What's this?" asks Mel, pointing to the back wall, sounding creeped out.

Handmade wooden cages with rusted metal grates for doors are built into the rounded-log wall. There are ten cages total—two rows, five columns wide. Above each cage is a name clumsily burned into a wood panel. It's tough to see in the darkness, but Richard reads a few as best he can: Marie. Waldo. Augustine. Louis. An assortment of ropes and harnesses hang from hooks.

"A backwoods torture chamber, of course," answers Richard, then bursts out laughing at the look of horror on Mel's face. He points to the cages. "Just kidding. These are dog kennels, not for people. Sled teams are a great way to get around out here."

Mel rolls her eyes, and they keep taking inventory of the cabin. Four grime-covered windows flank a roughly hewn timber doorframe. There's a potbelly woodstove and a basic kitchenette with a cutting board, a broken mirror, a few shelves, and a pot and pan. There's not much in terms of furniture, just a basic table with two chairs and a narrow bed draped in a musk ox hide.

Richard laughs. "I've never been so happy to see a cot."

There's a stack of dry logs next to the stove.

"Aged to perfection," says Richard as he gets a fire going, shaking his head at their luck. He leaves the grate open so they can watch the dancing flames, and the cabin warms up quickly. It's the first time they'll be dry—properly dry, not damp—in days.

He melts snow on the stove, and Mel wraps herself up in the musk ox hide, which is thick and warm.

"What's this? A bear fur?" she asks.

"A musk ox," says Richard. "Big, furry Alaskan bastards."

"Just like you," she jokes. Richard snorts, and she cracks another one. "You can have the sleeping bag to yourself tonight—that thing smells like piss."

Chapter 14

Their day in the sun, it seems, was a fluke. The bad weather returns with a vengeance overnight. Still, at dawn, Richard ventures into the storm to dig out the deck so they might actually look out the windows. "It's a waste of energy, and I know it," he says. "But I was going crazy in that dingy cave. Days are short enough as it is."

"Looking out for your mental health isn't a waste of energy," says Mel, and Richard guffaws before seeing Mel's perturbed expression and realizing she wasn't being facetious.

As he shovels away, slowly, so as not to overexert himself, Mel explores the small cabin more thoroughly. She assumes the owner was a man, and a tidy and simple one at that—even under the layers of dust, the few belongings are just so. With a rag from a hook over the sink, she dusts the place and scrubs grime from the windowpanes. Gagging, she wipes up small mountains of petrified rodent droppings and the shredded evidence of their numerous nests.

"Let me know if you find any live ones," says Richard as he hauls in snow to melt into water. "We sure could use the protein."

With a hatchet he found hanging by the stove, he chops the small stack of dry logs into stove-friendly sizes, then traipses in and out, restocking their stores with wet logs from a rotting woodpile under the deck. When he opens the door, snow creeps in,

144

a reminder of the cold they came from. The fire—a lovely, roaring fire—gives Mel life.

She finds a few treasures, most in a small storage closet that's tucked unobtrusively behind the dog kennels: a small box of tools, including a whetstone, which pleases Richard to no end—the hatchet is dull—a shotgun and two and a half boxes of shells, a fishing rod, more dog harnesses, leashes and collars. Beneath the cot, she finds an extra blanket and a stack of old books.

"Look at this! Books! Most of them are in French," she says. "Except for *Robinson Crusoe*."

"Useless," says Richard as he fiddles with the broken shotgun, irritated that it's so far proved immune to his tinkering.

"*Tu te trompes!*"

"You speak French?"

"*Oui.* I was born in France."

"I thought you said you were from New York?"

Mel goes quiet. There's a story there, and Richard can tell she doesn't want to tell it.

As dusk falls Richard sits down by the fire and removes his boots, wincing in pain.

"What's wrong?" Mel asks, realizing it's the first time she's seen the man take a load off.

"Oh, it's nothing," says Richard quickly.

In the firelight, though, Mel can tell that something's not right. Brushing off his half-hearted dismissals, she kneels and peels off his fetid socks. The tips of his mottled, pruned toes are crowned in grayish blisters.

"Jesus, Richard," she says.

Frowning, he flexes his toes. "They look a little worse than I thought," he reasons.

"Are they frostbit?"

"I don't know," he admits. "Maybe. But they could just be frost-nipped."

"What's the difference?"

"One of 'em I get to keep my toes."

"No more going outside for a bit," Mel says, with more authority than she feels. "You've got to warm up those fucked-up feet of yours."

For dinner, they pour extra hot water into their dehydrated beef Stroganoff, turning it into a watery soup. Mel is still hungry, but the hot broth heats her from the inside out. And if Richard, who's nearly twice her size and has been chopping firewood all day with frostbitten or frost-nipped toes, doesn't complain, then she won't either.

She's looking for something to clean their utensils—it's amazing how much she's missed something as simple as a spoon. There's a tall stack of old newspapers under the kitchenette, only some of which have been shredded by mice, and she figures she can dip a few pages in boiling water and turn that into a questionably sanitized semblance of a sponge. But when she grabs the top stack of newspapers, her knuckles wrap on metal.

She moves the papers, and yells loudly at her find.

"What is it?" asks Richard, concerned. "Did you cut yourself?"

She points to the prize: a twelve-pack of baked bean cans.

Richard howls with joy, hugs her close, and kisses her on the cheek.

"Twelve cans!" he says. "Twelve cans!"

"Wait a second," says Mel, not wanting them to get ahead of themselves. "Won't this make us sick? It's got to be at least five years past the expiration date."

Richard pulls out a can and angles it toward the firelight. "Nine years," he says cheerfully. "It won't taste great, perhaps, but it won't kill us."

"Are you sure?"

"Nope," he says. "But the alternative will."

Richard cracks a can with his pocketknife to celebrate. The beans don't smell sour, although they've ceased to identify as beans and have instead turned into a gelatinous maple glop.

"It's the best bean soup I've ever had," says Richard, testing a spoonful and passing it her way.

"Let's make the whole can," says Mel after taking a bite. "Let's get full—properly full."

Richard looks at her sternly. "Did you realize we only had two meal packets left? We were about to starve. I know it isn't much, but with this score we can last another two weeks maybe, ten days easy."

Stomach growling, Mel watches him pour half of the can into the pot, then carefully place the half-empty can in the freezer box, an uninsulated box that's cut through the logs and keeps food just slightly warmer than the outside temperature.

She doesn't fuss when Richard insists she take the bed. "You earned it, bean queen," he says.

"Don't ever call me that again," she says. Exhausted but pleased, she gets into the sleeping bag. He lays the musk ox hide on the floor by the fireplace, sprawls out, and is snoring within minutes.

Mel lies on the stiff, dank, narrow mattress, wide awake, listening to Richard's snoring, her stomach gurgling with bean goop, and the roaring blizzard.

The beans ease the pressure of starvation, but only briefly. The snow continues to stack up, and the stormy skies, according to Richard, will keep helicopters from flying.

"How do you know?" asks Mel one afternoon, frustrated by his self-assuredness, hating the fact that he's been right about rationing.

"I know the man who runs Search and Rescue. We play poker together. Or, at least, we used to."

Time is measured not in days but in feet of snow, pages of books, cans of beans. The cabin is almost completely buried, Mel has read three books in French, and they have a single meal packet and five cans of beans remaining when the weather breaks and the sun shows its face again.

"Finally," says Richard, relieved, looking up at a blue sky only partially shrouded by clouds. "We'll start trapping, hunting, and fishing today. And we'll find the snowmachine and get the hell out of here."

Using snowshoes they found stashed in one of the kennels, the two unlikely roommates walk out onto the lake.

Richard carries his shovel, as well as an ice auger to drill into the lake and the fishing pole procured from the storage closet. He also brings along a broom handle that he whittled into a point during the storm.

"Is that a spear?" Mel asks skeptically.

"A probe," he says. "To find the snowmachine."

The task is a daunting one. Flat, pristine and expansive, the snowfield over the lake seems preternaturally perfect. Mountains cloaked in white rise on the horizon. There's no sign of another human. There are no helicopters, no rescue planes. For all she knows, no one is even looking for them anymore. Richard pokes his wooden stick down into the snow to measure the depth of the snowpack, and it disappears.

"Falling in is no longer a concern," he says half-jokingly as he pulls up the makeshift probe. "It's more than six feet to the lake, maybe eight, I'll have to dig down to see," he grunts, poking the stick again into the snow. "The snowpack is firm as hell halfway down, probably from that last break in the storm—the sun baked it into an icy crust, then we have this heavy layer on top of that, perfect recipe for avalanches. I expect we'll see some serious shedding on the peaks."

"I don't speak Alaskan," says Mel. "What does that mean?"

"It means this blizzard was one of the craziest in history. It means that finding the snowmachine is going to be next to impossible right now. I can't dig and probe all this. It would take weeks. Months." He stretches a hand out at the endless white.

"But you'll try?"

"Of course I'll try."

"And until we find the snowmachine?"

"We survive. Until they come and get us, or the snow settles and melts once we get some more sun and we can find the sled. But before we can start probing, we need food. I can't waste my energy on that goose chase right now."

Richard jabs the probe into the snow and starts digging a hole.

Mel tramps away from Richard in a determined line, hoping to help. She's tired and hungry, deflated by Richard's assessment. Half an hour later, she rejoins Richard, who dangles a fishing line through a hole in the ice. He nods gravely at her.

"Good idea," he says.

"Thank you," says Mel, looking back at her handiwork: a giant "S.O.S." spelled out in her footprints, each letter as big as a house.

Chapter 15

Richard skirts the lake on snowshoes, the mended shotgun slung over his shoulder, daydreaming about a rare ribeye steak rubbed with thyme, rosemary, and garlic salt. It took him hours to disassemble the gun and discover the problem—a pockmarked, rusty, and bent firing pin—and then an entire evening to wiggle the bolt free, scrape the rust off, and get the shotgun functioning again. If there's one thing he has in spades out here, it's time. The shotgun works fine, he's shot it twice to test it, but Richard's yet to shoot so much as a field mouse, as both Mel and his grumbling stomach always remind him.

They've presumed the original owner of the cabin dead. Mel found a worn leather-bound journal gathering dust behind the stack of books, the name "Jean Pierre" inscribed inside the front cover. Unfortunately, the diary didn't provide any insight into the mystery of what happened to the man. After nearly daily records for five years straight, the entries—stoic prose, according to Mel, mainly about his dogs, hunting and trapping—stopped short fourteen years ago with no explanation.

"Maybe the diary just fell under the bed and he forgot about it," she guessed.

"I don't think he'd forget about that. He lived alone with a pack of sled dogs—that diary was his one attachment to humanity." Richard shook his head. "And it seems like he was a meticulous man.

I don't think he would've just left this place unattended. Whatever happened, he wasn't expecting it."

Jean Pierre, dead or alive, was their savior. Once the storm broke, Richard discovered a ramshackle outhouse and a dilapidated shed behind the cabin stocked with scrap metal, tools, more shotgun shells, snowshoes and other miscellaneous implements and building materials. In addition to providing the necessary ingredients to return the shotgun to working order, Richard found a few rusted steel traps that, with a bit of elbow grease and some tinkering, snapped shut when triggered. He waded through the snow to the junction of Crow Lake and the Hope River, then positioned the traps in a short trapline—one every half mile or so upriver—picking sites that were protected from the wind. He baited each trap with a foul and fragrant pile of trout guts, which he hoped would be a toothsome, irresistible treat. However, the critters were either unconvinced or few and far between, as the first two trips to check the traps had proved fruitless. With any luck, this time around the traps will be full. He and Mel have been living off inconsistently caught trout from the lake, and the thought of rich, fatty meat is enough to make him drool.

He shimmies his pants up, reties his makeshift belt. Even at its tightest, his old belt is useless—his snow pants are now secured by a length of cord he dug out of the shed. Earlier that morning, as he stoked the fire and made pine needle tea, he caught a glimpse of his half-naked body in the mirror: His belly has all but disappeared. He needs to shoot something, to trap something. Not just to quell the hunger, but to restore his confidence.

Since childhood, Richard has ravenously consumed survival stories, and he's always assumed that, if put into a survival situation, he'd come out on top. He'd return to civilization triumphant, a changed man. A piece of him even envied the bastards who got mauled by grizzlies or crawled out of canyons with broken femurs and lived to tell the tale. Iron is forged only in fire. But as he checks the trapline, he feels no self-assurance. He'd rather be anywhere else in the world. The cabin is a dream compared to the quinzee, but still, it's a nightmare all the same. There's no glory in this hell.

Outwardly, he still projects confidence to Mel, assuring her that today's the day the helicopters will come, the day the traps will be full, the day he'll bring home dinner. She's not an outdoorswoman, but she's not an idiot, either. Quite the opposite, in fact. He does his best to convince her that everything's going to be all right. The problem is, he's starting to have trouble convincing himself. Doubt creeps into his psyche, and not simply because a Search and Rescue team hasn't dropped out of the sky. For all the years he's adventured in the Alaskan wild, he's never been so entirely at its mercy. And for all those hunting trips and winter expeditions—what he considered training for precisely a moment like this—he keeps coming up empty-handed.

The shotgun digs into his back, as if it can read his mind. He adjusts the strap and scans the forest ahead of him. Only now, slogging through these cursed woods in his snowshoes, hunger like a tapeworm tunneling away in his gut, does Richard realize the difference between the recreationist, which he's always been, and the survivalist he's always admired. The recreationist purposefully ventures into wildlands to derive pleasure from the experience. The survivalist's sole purpose, on the other hand, is to do just that - to survive, to escape, to end the ordeal as soon as possible. The former chases life, the latter evades death. The line between them, Richard's learned, is thin.

He snorts and shakes his head. He'll blow his shot at dinner unless he's focused. Thoughts don't get a man fed, after all. Actions do.

He concentrates on putting one foot in front of the other. Yesterday's slushy snow has frozen into a solid crust overnight—his snowshoes don't sink so much as a millimeter, the rusted cleats bite into the ice like the claws of a jungle cat into hard earth. Richard moves quickly along the lake, hugging the trees to avoid squinting into the bright morning sun. His retinas have been seared like tuna steaks already. His sunglasses are unhelpfully buried in the seat compartment of his snowmachine. Even the low-light yellow lenses of his goggles would do wonders right now, but they're long gone, too, attached to the helmet he threw off in his urgency to get to Mel. His snowmachine is entombed beneath well over 100 inches of snow, Mel's is at the bottom of the lake, the pair of them like pharaohs mocking him from frozen tombs. Their ticket home is so close, yet so impossibly far.

If only he'd returned to pull his snowmachine to the trees. It would've taken twenty, thirty minutes. He'd be home right now, not desperately walking through the forest, crossing his fingers that he'll find a frozen animal carcass to bring back for dinner.

He snorts again. Thoughts don't get a man home, either.

The first trap is untouched. Richard replenishes the bait with a pinch of fresh entrails then continues onward. The second trap has been all but annihilated, its steel jaws smashed to bits, crumpled like tinfoil. When he gets closer to the mutilated metal, he sees the paw prints and curses. He swings the shotgun round and grips it tightly—not that buckshot from this antique would so much as slow the party responsible. It might as well be a BB gun. From the look of the dinner-plate-size paw prints that surround the crime scene, the grizzly was full grown.

Not the kind of neighbor you'd invite over for a cup of pine needle tea.

After spending several decades in Alaska, Richard knows that hibernation is mostly a misconception. These magnificent, terrifying bears don't simply pass out in November and wake up in April—though they're slower, lethargic and stay in their dens for extensive periods in the winter. They're still a threat, however, even when groggy. That's why he always has a gun with him in the bush, no matter the season. His .44 revolver—a much better weapon to take down a bear, but still far from perfect—is buried in the ice as well. He thinks of the kennels in Jean Pierre's cabin; he wouldn't mind having a pack of sled dogs right about now to keep him company.

Hairs stiff on the back of his neck, he gathers up the mangled trap, unsure if he'll be able to piece it back together, straps it to a loop on his haversack, and keeps moving.

At the third and final stop, marten tracks—tiny, compared to the bear paws—lead up to the trap. The trap is set, the bait is gone. There's nothing in the steel jaws, not even a scrap of fur, a bit of blood.

Empty-handed yet again. He replenishes the fish guts, then carries on. His stomach howls on the long walk home. He prays for a weasel to run into the end of his gun.

On his way back to the cabin, he walks past Mel's S.O.S. letters. Like his own trails and tracks, the marks from her snowshoes are frozen into the crust of the lake. They're clear as day, might as well be written in Sharpie. No need to touch them up. He wonders how visible they are from the sky. More importantly, he wonders how frequently someone flies overhead.

Not frequently enough.

Scowling, he eyes the fishing hole. Before this little adventure, Mel had never cooked a piece of fish in her life that wasn't already breaded, fried and flash-frozen. She burnt his last catch, a gorgeous thirteen-inch rainbow, past recognition. Some creole seasoning would go a long way. Some cornmeal, too. And some oil? Salt and pepper? Butter? Dare he be so bold—tartar sauce? Tabasco?

He wrenches his mind away from such fantasies. That's a slippery slope. He must ignore things that are out of reach—family, friends, real food. If he focuses too intensely on them, he'll never survive. It's not until all of his chores are done and the sun has gone down that Richard grants himself the painful luxury of thinking of home. He tells himself over and over again that if he lets his mind wander back home, he'll never see home again.

He turns from the river onto the lake, following the trail back to the cabin.

When he steps through the door, she doesn't ask him how it went. She knows how it went. Same as always. She hardly looks up from her reading to scan his empty hands.

"One of the traps was set, but no luck," he says.

She continues reading.

"Another one was destroyed," he says, knowing this will get her attention. "By a bear. Full-grown grizzly."

At this, she raises an eyebrow. "Aren't they supposed to be asleep?"

"That's somewhat of a myth, they can wake up from time to time."

She shrugs. "I didn't catch anything at the fishing hole. I probed for the sled, too. I didn't catch anything there, either."

Richard nods. He doesn't have energy to laugh at her joke.

"How long did you fish?" he asks, unable to hide his disappointment.

"Long enough to realize they weren't biting," she says defensively, crossing her arms.

He thinks about grabbing the fishing rod or the broomstick handle and trying his luck, but it's almost dusk. The nights are growing longer now. They're just days away from the winter solstice, when the sun will be in the sky for less than four hours. Which means, he thinks with a heavy sadness, Christmas is just around the corner.

"Tomorrow," he says, removing his boots. He softens his voice and does his best to sound sure. "Tomorrow, we'll catch something."

"Tomorrow," she echoes. "Tomorrow, tomorrow."

He can't tell if she's making fun of him. If it's a jibe, it's well-deserved, and he ignores it. He looks at the kitchen shelves. There's half a packet of dehydrated Stroganoff and two cans of baked beans.

They'll go hungry tonight. Tomorrow, too.

They make pine needle tea and split half a can of beans, then read to distract themselves from their empty stomachs. Jean Pierre was a gifted writer, and Mel enjoys navigating through his journal. She reads slowly, and usually exclaims at one thing or another, commenting on the behavior of one of the dogs, enviously recounting the moment that his traps caught a beaver, affirming the existence of grizzlies based on the Frenchman's observance of tracks in the mud and a pile of mauled salmon carcasses by the river, only their eyes and organs missing. Tonight, though, she's quiet.

Richard sticks to *Robinson Crusoe*. He reads slowly, too. He wants to savor it. Once the book is over, he's afraid his mind will come undone.

He eyes his roommate over his book. She's smart, clearly, but she needs to do her share. She should be out there fishing from the moment he leaves until he comes back. He shouldn't have to remind her that they're starving. And she takes the bed every night, too. What's with that? Richard took to the floor rather easily, but it would be kind of her to offer the bed up, at least for a night or two. He had, after all, saved her life, and he's twice her size. She makes him worry about what dealing with Sarah will be like in a year or two. Assuming he ever makes it home.

Marking days by books and beans makes for inefficient record-keeping, so every morning Richard notches a stick with his pocketknife to keep track. It's been twenty days, give or take, since he's seen his family. Twenty days without a proper meal. How many nights they spent in the quinzee was up for debate—it was a long, torturous blur, one he hopes to forget.

While water boils for tea, he carefully cuts a notch into the bark, then places the stick back on the windowsill. One of these days, he might just throw it into the stove. How easy it would be to lose track of time. At least a prisoner has some idea of what he's counting down to. Richard is just counting, that's all. With no end in sight.

"Richard," Mel whispers, furtively. She's standing at the door, which is cracked open slightly. "Get your gun. And come here. Quietly."

From the way she's whispering, he imagines it's the neighborhood grizzly that mauled his trap, a towering specimen of fur and flesh, groggy and peeved, and he almost snaps at her to shut the door. The shotgun won't so much as sting that apex predator. Their only hope is that it won't choose to smash the door off its rusty hinges. But he springs to his feet and does as she asks.

He looks over her shoulder, out the door, into the small clearing. He sees nothing in the subdued light of dawn.

"What is it?"

"There," she points, and he follows her outstretched finger beyond the door, down the steps, to a patch of snow that seems nebulous and fuzzy. Then white contrasts against dark brown: a snow-white ptarmigan, camouflaged in its winter colors, given away by the trunk of a pine tree.

They're impossible to spot, these little, round birds, and they often scare the shit out of Richard when he's checking the trapline, squawking only when his snowshoes come too close, flying away in a frenzy of feathers. It's tough to get a shot off quickly then, as he's usually wearing his mittens. And the stealthy fowl take off surprisingly fast for being the size and shape of a cantaloupe with wings.

Never has he spotted a bird on the ground. Those white feathers make for impressive camouflage.

It's twenty feet away. Within striking distance. But Richard has only one shot; as soon as the blast rings out, if the ptarmigan is unharmed, it will take off and squawk into the woods.

"Back up," he says quietly. "I need a little space here."

Mel does as she's told. He can feel her desperation, the hunger. He raises the barrel of the gun, aiming it through the cracked door. The ptarmigan shuffles back and forth between the white background of the snow and the brown of the pines. Richard breathes in and out like a sniper, trying not to think about the young woman looking over his shoulder or the potential of a fat little bird sizzling in the cast-iron pan over the fire.

When the bird hops in front of a pine tree, he tightens his finger on the trigger.

Inside the cabin, the blast is deafening. His ears ring. Mel yelps at the shock.

Outside the cabin, the ptarmigan squawks and jumps into the air.

"Shit!" says Richard, fearing all hope is lost. He won't be able to get a second shot off in time. He's pumping the shotgun when he hears Mel screech.

"Look!"

The ptarmigan can't fly straight. The buckshot put a hole through its right wing; it looks like a chopper with a damaged rotor, spiraling down toward the snow.

Blood speckles paint the snow red. Feathers drift downward like snowflakes. The ptarmigan squawks and lands in a clump. It starts to hobble away, hopping into the forest. Richard's about to raise the gun and take a shot and finish the job when he feels Mel push past him.

"Mel!" he yells, lowering the gun.

She pays him no mind. Barefoot, she runs down the steps and into the clearing. She bounds through the snow like an Olympic sprinter and snatches up the injured ptarmigan, which clucks and writhes in her grip. Instead of snapping its neck, as any ethical hunter would do, she acts on instinct, grabbing the bird by the legs and smashing it into the trunk of the nearest pine tree—once, twice, three times.

The ptarmigan dangles limp and bloody in her hands as she walks back to the cabin.

She hands him the bird. "Nice shot," she says, grinning breathlessly, a shimmer in her eyes. Richard is shocked. It's like he's never even met this woman before. "Maybe you should cook this," she pants. "After my blackened fish."

Surprise is plastered across Richard's face. All he can say is, "Your feet must be cold."

She looks down at her bare feet, glistening with snow,

then grins up at him mischievously.

"I suppose they are."

Chapter 16

Before the ptarmigan, Mel had never killed anything in her entire life, aside from the occasional cockroach. She'd caught a few fish, but Richard was the one who bashed them over the head with a stick, and she'd looked away as he did it. Yet, despite her past dietary preferences and convictions, she doesn't feel an ounce of remorse when she smashes the ptarmigan against the pine tree. Her breath ragged, warm blood and feathers on her hands, she feels only the flush of the kill, the anticipation of a good meal. She took a life, but only to save her own.

That evening, Richard teaches Mel how to pluck and prepare the bird. They pick fatty flesh from bones by the light of the fire, filling their bellies properly for the first time in weeks.

"Holy shit. I've been to some ridiculously priced restaurants in New York," she says. "And this is by far the best thing I've ever tasted in my entire life."

Richard chuckles. "To think, a couple of weeks ago you were a vegetarian."

"A decade of delusion," she says.

Mel's on the verge of tossing a picked-clean drumstick bone into the fire, but he throws a hand out to stop her. "No, no, don't toss that."

He grabs the bone, snaps it, and gives her half, then demonstrates how to slurp out the marrow.

"We've got to be like the Inuit. Zero food waste. Only way to survive out here." Richard says. "Even after you suck out the marrow, don't throw it into the fire. Tomorrow, I'll show you how to make a broth out of the bones and carcass."

"That sounds good."

"It beats pine needle tea."

Something about the kill—maybe the full bellies, maybe the fact that they took the bird down together—cuts at a tension that's been present since the crash. She has been, at times, difficult to live with, and she knows it. Stuffed for the first time in weeks, happy for the first time in months, Mel stares at the orange flames in the stove more intently than she ever watched television.

"This is going to sound funny, but this is the happiest I've been in a while," she said.

"Me too," smiles Richard. "It's been a tough couple of weeks."

"I don't mean weeks," she says, surprising herself with her forthrightness. "I mean, months. Years, even."

"Stockbroking sounds like a taxing gig," says Richard kindly.

"It's complicated," says Mel, unsure of how much of herself she's willing to share with Richard. Despite their closeness in the quinzee, he's still very much a stranger. Dr. Meyer, she knows, would encourage her to open up. "The money's good, but I feel at times like a hamster on a wheel, just anxiously pursuing a check, my whole life passing me by, without any true purpose."

Richard nods. "I get it. I've been so focused on building my company—and, more recently, selling it—that I haven't been able to enjoy the things I truly love."

"Like what?"

"Like spending time with my family. Being out here, in the wilderness, although obviously not under these conditions."

"What's your wife's name?" Mel asks.

"Anne," he says, twisting his wedding band around his greasy pointer finger. He's too skinny now, if he tries to wear the band on his ring finger, it slips right off. "She's my world. Tiny little lady, but the biggest heart you've ever seen. A real firecracker. If I don't die out here, she may kill me herself."

Mel laughs. "She can't blame you for this. You saw me crash, you saved my life."

Richard gazes into the flames. "She can blame me, and she should blame me. I shouldn't have been there. I should've gone back with Jim."

"Who's Jim?"

"My snowmachine partner. My best friend. The godfather to my children. He and I were riding together, and he wanted to turn around. He did turn around, and I kept going, even though he wanted me to head back with him. I lied to him, told him I'd turn around at the pass, but I kept going, because I wanted more time out here to clear my head. That's the only reason why I was out here."

"It's also the only reason I'm alive."

"True. Maybe I was supposed to be there to save you," says Richard, considering the repercussions of his actions. "Ironically, the lie that saved you is the only reason why Search and Rescue hasn't saved us. They have no idea we're this far north."

They watch the dancing flames for a while, listening to the hypnotic hiss and crackle. Richard didn't have to jump in after her, but he did anyway, and the debt, she realizes, has made her uncomfortable. Like a couple of shots of tequila and the right pharmaceutical cocktail, a belly full of ptarmigan seems to loosen her tongue.

"Thank you," she says. "I never thanked you. For saving my life." The levees break, and tears run down her cheeks.

Richard turns to her, clearly surprised. "You're welcome. I'm just glad I was right there when it happened."

Mel feels like a weight has been lifted. She wipes the tears from her cheeks and laughs again, baffled by the range of sentiments she can feel in a matter of minutes, especially now that the Zoloft has run it's course. "Fuck me. What a roller coaster. My emotions are all over the place."

Richard nods. "This has been stressful."

"No, you don't get it. I've been going through shit since I was a teenager, shit I never talk about, and on a hefty dose of antidepressants for the entirety of my adult life. If I've been bitchy, it's because I've been going cold turkey—didn't think I needed to bring any pills on a two-hour snowmobile tour. And—damn, saying sorry is harder than thank you—I'm sorry. I know I haven't been carrying my weight."

Richard lets her words sink in, then replies carefully. "Thank you for sharing that with me. I had no idea. I don't have much experience with antidepressants—I was taught indirectly by my dad to bottle that shit up, and when I was young I just directed all of my anger into hitting people on the football field. I might not be the most empathetic, but I imagine that what you're going through hasn't been easy. So there's no need to apologize. And you more than carried your weight today—you spotted the ptarmigan, and then when I missed the shot you tore after it like Tarzan and smashed it against that tree."

Mel sniffs and smiles. "Enough about me or I'm going to throw up. How many kids do you have? I can't believe I haven't asked you this already."

"Three. Sarah is a teenager, and Caleb and Sean are twins, in middle school."

"You must miss them."

Richard laughs, if only so he doesn't join her in tears. "More than anything."

She places a hand on his shoulder, patting him awkwardly, unsure how to console such a man.

"What about you?" asks Richard, wiping away the start of a tear surreptitiously with the sleeve of his long johns. "Who do you miss the most? Boyfriend?"

Mel retracts her hand. Her instinct is to shut down, close off, tell him anything but the truth, but she resists the compulsion. She's already shared more with him than anyone aside from Shawna and Dr. Meyer. "No boyfriend. My mom. My dad. My half-sister."

"They're divorced?"

It's Mel's turn to snort. "They never married. As far as I know, the last time they slept together, they had me."

Richard whistles.

"We're not as close as we once were. My own fault, I got caught up in work. But I'm sure they miss me. I'm sure they're worried sick."

"They'll see you sooner rather than later. If Anne and Jim have any say in it, search parties will be here any day now."

"Tomorrow," she sighs melodramatically, and the two of them burst out laughing.

Chapter 17

As always, the whines and whimpers from the kennels are a reliable alarm. James sits up in the creaky cot and yawns, stretching until his fingertips graze the angled log ceiling of the loft. He climbs down the ladder in total darkness, operating strictly out of feeling. He locates a box of matches and lights the kerosene lamp. In the dim glow, he stokes the fire and puts the kettle on. Once the coffee's ready, as first light tinges the surrounding mountains' deep indigo, he lets the dogs out for their morning constitutionals. Shirtless and shivering, wearing nothing but his long underwear bottoms, he watches them alternate between playing and relieving themselves. Later, he'll go out and shovel shit so his snowy yard doesn't resemble a tub of chocolate chip ice cream. Once they've finished their business, he lets out a whistle.

A whistle means breakfast, and the dogs come running.

Feeding a sled team is a task exceedingly more laborious than your average pet owner's morning ritual. The demands of James' muscled Chinooks and huskies are startling. Each of the ten members of his team chow through four thousand five hundred calories daily. That's more than twice the suggested caloric intake of a full-grown human male, and that number doubles if the dogs are out on the trail. James would never be able to haul a winter's worth of kibble on his two annual trips to town—he'd need a semi-truck, not a dogsled. So he doesn't bother. Instead, he buys a few bags of dog food for an emergency stash, in case he breaks an ankle and can't hunt for a couple weeks, but for the most part he feeds the dogs off the land.

His bare feet on the splintery deck, a curved breaking knife in his hand, he slices off hamburger-size hunks of moose meat and tosses them to the dogs. They scarf breakfast even more quickly than usual, thrilled to gnaw fresh steaks as opposed to the smoked, dried standard.

It's a simple relationship, thinks James, as the dogs chow down with gusto. He provides sustenance, the dogs supply transportation. Their lives are intertwined, their survival interdependent. And to ensure their shared existence, they spend the majority of their days chasing calories. James hunts, traps and fishes relentlessly. Predation swallows most of his waking hours, but his chores begin in earnest upon his return to the cabin.

After dressing his kills in the field, he butchers them carefully at home and then determines which cuts to freeze and which to cure in the smoking shed behind the cabin. If the shed and freezer box are ever less than half full, he feels panicked, uneasy. He's had enough close calls to know that hardship is heralded by empty shelves. And yet, even when the larders are full, his work is far from over. He pursues the ancient, Sisyphean task of chopping and stacking wood. He makes home improvements, trains the dogs, mends equipment, boils snow for drinking water. And he shovels shit. Lots of shit. Forty-five thousand calories' worth of shit daily to be precise.

He doesn't mind shoveling shit—at least in winter, when the frozen turds don't stink. He doesn't mind being busy, either. He enjoys it. Busy is fulfilling, busy is satisfying—infinitely more so than when he walked work-shy and listless through the streets of New York, fluctuating between loathing and lethargy, uncertain of place or purpose, contemplating knocking off this liquor store or that bodega. In the bush, his life is hard but simple. His mission is clear: survive. His place is with the pack. The lack of human contact, the loneliness, it doesn't get to him, at least not most of the time. He's too damn busy staying alive.

"Boredom and solitude exist on separate planes," he wrote in his journal once. "That the former follows the latter is a perception of those too weak to live alone."

This particular morning, however, James' chores go quickly. The dogs are fed, snow melted, wood chopped, meat butchered, shit shoveled. The smoker and the freezer box—James had ponied up for solar panels and an electric freezer box a few years prior—are both stuffed to the brim with moose meat. And so, come early afternoon on a beautiful, cloudless day, James finds himself with time on his hands.

Only once in a blue moon does he get to sit and read his book before dark mid-winter. A lit tobacco pipe in his hand, a mason jar of whiskey on the arm of the old deck chair, snowball bobbing in the glass like an icecap in an amber sea—it's a pleasant way to spend an afternoon. Such an occurrence means that he's so ahead of schedule, so on top of his chores that he has daylight to spare. Come summer, when Apollo is a tireless, whip-wielding insomniac who drives in circles across the Alaskan sky, James often falls asleep while the chariot's still tipping across the heavens. But in winter, when the sun slinks south, when the moon becomes an inescapable comrade, when James has to check the traps by headlamp, when the darkness falls like icy velvet around his cabin and the glow of the fire becomes fundamental to not only his physical warmth but his mental well-being, daylight is more precious than gold.

For the first time in weeks, James reclines on the deck chair, a sleepy dog blinking lazily at his feet, and savors the lull. He plans to take a leaf out of the pooch's book and do absolutely nothing for the rest of the afternoon, save for sip his whiskey and watch the packed snowball twist and melt, receding slowly like a miniature calving iceberg.

Thirty-six hours prior, James was checking his trapline. The trapline has expanded over the years, and in many ways, it's his life's work. Ten traps form a serpentine route, a trap every two miles for twenty miles total. It starts winding south from the cabin, down valley, then crosses a snow bridge and returns on the other side of the river. The loop closes via another snow bridge just north of the cabin. He generally takes a team of six dogs, eight if the snow is deep. He can complete the trek in a day if he leaves at dawn and the mission is uneventful. This last trip was anything but.

Halfway through his loop, after trapping a beaver and two rabbits, he spotted a mother moose and her calf, likely two years old based on the size—maybe six hundred fifty to seven hundred pounds, nine to ten feet from nose to tail—clomping across the snow bridge. The mother smelled the dogs on the wind. Spooked, she panicked, plowed forward across the bridge, aiming for the woods, but sprinted inadvertently into a deep wind drift. Tall and strong, she swam through the snow at top speed, vapor spewing from her nostrils like the twin chimneys of a steamship. The calf, slower and less surefooted, attempted to follow his mother's path but wallowed in the deep snow.

"Yah! Go!" The dogs knew to give chase. He didn't need to guide them across the snow bridge; they chased the calf of their own accord while he calmed his breathing and readied his rifle. The mother disappeared into the trees just as they pulled up alongside the calf.

It almost wasn't fair, to skate above the snow on his sled, the floundering calf looking sideways at him with one panicked milky-brown eye.

But there was no remorse in James, only the ruthless motto he'd followed since his childhood in Queens: If it's you or me that's got to go, it's always gonna be you.

From ten yards away, James pulled the trigger. The bullet ripped into the young moose's neck. The calf tripped, bellowed, stumbled forward. James brought the hammer back, shot again, then prepped the weapon once more, just in case the mother came back seeking vengeance. The hooves of an irate mother moose scared true Alaskans just as much as the paws of a grizzly.

The dogs howled. The calf dripped a pool of red, momentarily melting the snow into a bloody, steaming slush.

A grim grin on his lips, his heart thumping through his patched fur jacket, James held the rifle in one hand, the hunting knife in the other. He waded into the red and gutted the calf, its warmth leaking out through its belly, steam rising up out of the snow, its brown eyes open and glazed. James tossed the organs to his team, praising them one by one in order of the hierarchy, letting the team leader eat first and feeding him the heart.

"Good boy, JP," he said, and watched his leader snatch up his prize.

Kidneys. "Good girl, Donner."

Liver. "Good boy, Samuel."

Tongue. "Good girl, Lanka."

The kill was a noteworthy one. The calf would feed him and the dogs for weeks. It was a rare gift, rich meat that was a welcome change from the oily beavers and martens he so often pulled out of the trapline. By the time he'd finished field-dressing the calf, the sun was setting, and he decided it was better to make camp for the night and head home at first light. That night he didn't sleep. He sat huddled in his sleeping bag, his flashlight off but close at hand, his gun across his lap, watching the shadows in case wolves came for his kill.

There's nothing James loves more than coming home with a bounty after a successful hunt.

To hear that howling symphony of appreciation from his pack, his tribe.

That moose calf now fills the freezer box, the smoking shed, and the bellies of man and beast.

James pours himself another celebratory whiskey, noting a red spot on the back of his hand that he'd missed as he washed the blood from his hands that morning. He returns to his chair, tamps his pipe, and flips open a book.

He breathes deeply and tries to relax. It's a strange feeling, slowing to stillness from constant motion.

JP, clearly oblivious to his master's opinions on relaxation, snores contentedly at his feet.

The Frenchman introduced the brothers to sled dogs, and then, well…

They did what had to be done.

Naming the tawny Chinook pup Jean Pierre all those years ago—it was a token of thanks. Respect. James wouldn't have been able to survive without that pioneer's help.

Involuntary as it was.

James wasn't remorseful. He was grateful. There was a difference.

He slipped into that man's life like he was trying on a coat.

If it's you or me that's got to go, it's always gonna be you.

James is packing a snowball for his fourth whiskey, tipsy and relaxed, thinking about how lucky he is to have shot that calf, how lucky he is to have a moment of peace, when he hears an unmistakable sound.

The paranoia-inducing whir of a helicopter.

Might as well be sirens.

He abandons his drink, accidentally knocking over the mason jar. Valuable whiskey seeps into the snow as he hustles inside. He hurls his book onto the table and grabs his rifle.

When he comes back outside, suddenly sober as a nun, the chopper is blowing snow off the tops of the trees.

He knew this day would come.

If they come out guns blazing, James will do the same.

He doesn't intend to see another cell.

They can't have more than five or six men in that chopper. He'll hole up and withstand the siege, pick them off one by one from the loft window like a sniper from one of the war movies he used to watch as a kid. At the very least, he'll go out shooting.

The chopper lands on the bank of the river. The rotors slow, the trees stand up straight again. When the engine shuts down, he can hear the frantic barking of his dogs.

"JP! C'mere, boy," he calls. "The rest of you, back inside."

He shuts the door on the baying dogs, shaken. The tensed Chinook at his side can sense it and growls low.

A pair of men disembark from the chopper and wave. They've got no guns, as far as he can tell—at least nothing automatic.

Calm down, he says to himself. Maybe this isn't your day of reckoning.

At twenty yards, he waves back and calls: "What can I do for you fellas?"

There are three of them in total. The pilot stays in the chopper. The first man is gray-haired, lanky, and tall. He walks a half step in front, clearly in charge. His lackey is shorter, muscular, clean-cut, with a once-broken nose—a military type. Both are wearing black wool beanies and red GORE-TEX jackets adorned with Search and Rescue of Glacier Point patches.

The slim man extends a gloved hand. "Al Bogle, Search and Rescue. This here's Cliff."

"Stephen. Nice to meet you. This is JP."

Bogle eyes the rifle on James' shoulder. "Ain't this Bishop's old place?"

James raises an eyebrow. He tries not to let tremors creep into his voice. "It sure was. Did you know him?"

"Yessir," says Bogle, taking off his cap and sweeping a heavy hand through thin gray hair. "Tragedy, what happened to him."

"The wreck's still down yonder, beneath that waterfall, if you want to pay your respects," says James, shaking his head gravely. "That's what you get for flying a relic, I suppose."

"Bush planes," says Bogle, and they all nod, as if that explained it.

"I didn't know anybody was living out here," says Bogle, after a brief silence. "To be honest, that's why we stopped. Figured this place would be abandoned now. Saw the tracks and wondered who was home."

"I'm surprised you know of the cabin in the first place," says James, forcing a laugh. "He didn't tell many folks."

"We played pool together whenever I was in Anchorage, bowled a bunch, too," says Bogle, shrugging. "And he brought me fishing here once, long time ago."

Suddenly, James remembers Rusty, barging in from the bar, drunk off moonshine, raving about some kooky stranger he'd met. He hears the clinking of cue balls, feels the texture of chalk wiped on his blue jeans. The first time James met Bishop, they played pool at that dive bar in Anchorage.

The intricacies of fate baffle him. It could've very well been that this Bogle man was in the bar that night. Bishop might've introduced them, Rusty might've leaned over Al to grab a beer at the counter. He might've talked shit as Al lined up a shot at the eight ball.

"Loved pool, the degenerate," says James, veiling the unexpected memory in counterfeit sadness. "I'm actually his nephew. I moved out here shortly after his crash."

"My condolences to your family," says Bogle.

"Not much family left, but thanks all the same," says James. "Now, with all due respect, Mr. Bogle, I assume you didn't come out here to mourn my uncle fifteen years after his passing. What can I do for you?"

"We're out here looking for a couple of lost snowmachiners. Two separate instances, both occurred at the beginning of these crazy storms. They've been missing a few weeks now," says Bogle. "One woman—damn New Yorker if you can believe that—got lost from a tour group coming from Anchorage. The other is a longtime Glacier Point resident, was out riding by himself and never came home."

Bogle pulls a pair of folded photographs from his jacket pocket and hands them to James, who scans the photos. The woman is pretty and put together, seems like a big city type. It's the man, though, a handsome bald fellow, that makes James stop listening altogether. Bogle's lips keep moving, but the sound is muffled, as if

James is suddenly underwater.

How could this possibly be? What are the chances? Talk about the intricacies of fate.

His knee twinges.

The wide-open expanse of the river valley fades into a bustling New York street.

Rusty's at the wheel of a stolen Seville coupe, toothpick in the corner of his mouth, waiting for the light to turn green. His gloved thumbs tap at the steering wheel like a courtroom reporter on a stenotype machine, on beat with the Metallica CD in the deck.

James sits in the passenger seat, trying to keep his cool. The combo of dex and adrenaline has his heart jumping out of his chest like a stripper out of a birthday cake.

"Turn left."

"I know, I know."

The wheel spins through his brother's black leather gloves. James told him the gloves were overkill.

To which Rusty had responded, "What's the point of being a bad guy if you don't get to dress the part?"

Fair enough.

They pull into the alley behind Lionhead Jewelry.

They weren't trained heist men with electrical skills. They couldn't cut the power at night and rappel in through the vent and dodge the laser beams like some stealthy thieves in a blockbuster flick. But what they lacked in skill, they made up for in balls.

James pulls his wolf mask on, hefts the sawed-off shotgun in one hand, an eight-pound sledge in the other, and slides out of the car. Right on time, the counter girl comes out for her morning smoke. Before the door closes, James has his foot in the crack and thwacks the back of her skull with the butt of the shotgun. The poor gal crumples and sprawls out like a starfish next to her pack of cigarettes.

"Go time, baby," says James. He hits his stopwatch and charges in. Rusty puts the Seville in gear and peels out.

They'd timed this part. It would take Rusty forty-five to fifty seconds to pull the car around front without speeding. Enough time for James to run through the jewelry store, hit the cash register, blast the shotgun at the diamond display case, smash it with the sledge, fill up his backpack, and run out the front door.

A frightened clerk, hands shaking, fills up the backpack with cash. James levels two shots at the diamond display and quickly reloads. The blasts rattle the store. Screaming customers drop to their knees. The shatterproof glass fractures but doesn't break. An alarm sounds. Red lights flash.

Five frenzied smacks from the hammer and the door doesn't break, but it does pop open at the hinge. Enough to shove a hand in. James rakes his fingers across the display, knocking over velvet necks and hands, ripping rings from disembodied digits, tossing them into the bag.

His watch beeps. It's been fifty seconds. He zips up the backpack and sprints out the front door.

Everything according to plan.

That is, until he runs out into the throng of frightened people on the crowded sidewalk. As he scours the street to find Rusty, he's blindsided by a punch so hard his mask almost flies off the back of his head.

He hits the pavement, probably concussed, though he manages to keep his hand on his shotgun.

He looks up at a big man in a flannel shirt who seems, even in the frenzied chaos of that moment, decidedly out of place in New York.

The man backs up as he stares down the barrel of James' shotgun.

"That's right," James hears himself saying. The man stands in front of a screaming woman so small James almost doesn't see her. "Don't be a hero. You want your wife to see you die?"

"I don't want any trouble," says the man.

James laughs and spits blood out of his mouth onto the

sidewalk. Later, he'll deem this an idiotic move. DNA handed to the cops on a silver platter.

"It's too late for that," he says, and cocks back the shotty.

"Watch out!"

Rusty's rounding the corner, screaming out the Seville's window, pointing down the street behind James. James hears the approaching sirens—he doesn't need to look.

James scrambles to his feet. He's running around the car when he hears the unmistakable pop of a handgun, feels a bullet bite into his leg. His knees buckle—the pain is unfathomable. Crouching, he blasts back at the cops. Rusty leaves the motor running, jumps out, and throws James into the backseat.

Rusty burns rubber as bullets shatter the rear window. James yowls in the backseat, trying to stem the bleeding with his bare hands. Cursing, Rusty whips through the city, pulling away from the police by a full block before skidding through a narrow alley. According to plan, he turns into a rundown parking garage where they'd stashed a second stolen car, a Honda Accord with lightly tinted windows. As the sirens fade, Rusty finds a roll of duct tape in the trunk of the car and tapes a rag around James' leg. He helps his injured brother into the clean car and then drenches the bullet-riddled Seville in gasoline. Rusty strikes a match, torches the Cadillac, and they slip out of the city.

"Stephen?"

It was a miraculous escape. But if Rusty had been on time, and that big motherfucker hadn't laid him out on the sidewalk, they wouldn't have had to turn the streets of New York into a scene straight out of one of Rusty's Grand Theft Auto videogames. And James wouldn't still have slivers of a cop's bullet buried in his knee.

"Stephen?"

The memory crumbles but remains intact, like

shatterproof glass after two shells and five blows from a sledgehammer. New York disappears. And yet, there he is, the bald man who'd knocked him to the sidewalk, staring at him from a piece of paper. Older, sure, but that's a face James has never forgotten.

James shakes it off. "I'm sorry, not used to having visitors, haven't spoken to anyone in months."

"No problem," says Bogle, but he looks concerned.

"You were saying?"

"That we'd like for you to keep an eye out for these folks. Although in both cases, they probably didn't make it this far. We saw your tracks down south. Trapline?"

"Yes, sir."

"At the southernmost tip of your trapline, maybe twenty or thirty miles farther down the valley past that snow bridge, that's the last place the tour group saw the girl."

"And the man?"

"He's likely nowhere near here. Even farther south than the girl. This is as far north as we're checking, and it's only because we saw your tracks."

Cliff unfolds a map and shows James the highlighted route the man purportedly took.

"Richard," says James. He knows the name. He'd read the paper the day after the robbery, seen the interviews on TV while sweating it out with a bottle of bourbon in a rundown motel.

"Sorry?" says Bogle. "You know him?"

They hadn't said the man's name. Scrambling, James catches a glimpse of a note on the map and points. "Richard's Track."

"I wouldn't have been surprised if you knew him," says Bogle. "Half of Glacier Point knows him. Hell, half of Glacier Point is out looking for him. At least they were. Many have given up hope by now. Can't say I blame 'em at this point."

"It's a small world," says James. "Maybe you'll find 'em. Or maybe I will."

The two men shake James' hand and say their goodbyes. The chopper lifts up and away, blowing snow like smoke. James stands on the porch with JP, wondering if God has sent him a gift or is up there in the clouds, laughing.

Chapter 18

Mel holds a tattered, yellow book in one hand, a fishing rod in the other. Whenever she turns the page, she jerks the rod up and down, hoping to entice the otherwise uninterested fish below.

The ptarmigan is a distant memory now. Sunny windows and storms have come and gone, and still no sign of rescue. Three days ago, Richard trapped a lean rabbit. The stringy meat was a revelation, and they boiled the carcass into a rich soup. But yesterday, as always, the broth thinned to water, and hunger knocks at their resolve once more.

And yet, the hunger doesn't feel as oppressive as it once did, perhaps because Mel isn't the same woman she was before. She's still hungry, but she's not helpless anymore. Going cold turkey in this wilderness wasn't at all what the doctor ordered—although Dr. Meyer did say she needed a vacation—but it seems to have worked better than anything else she's tried. She feels different—even-keeled, capable, strong, a huntress and an angler. With the same resolute determination that got her into Columbia and onto Wall Street, she decided that if she's going to be stuck in this godforsaken cabin, she might as well make the most of it. And besides, as much as she's toyed with the idea of her own death, now that it's a real possibility, she deeply prefers the alternative.

A changed woman, Mel has taken on her fair share of cabin chores: cleaning, stoking the fire, chopping wood, hauling and melting snow. While Richard hunts and prowls the trapline, she fishes most afternoons—even the stormy ones—though without much success. They even switch off who takes the cot each night.

Richard notices her efforts. He nods appreciatively when she hauls snow, thanks her when she boils tea in the morning. The silences between them are fewer and farther between, although they try not to talk too much about life back home. It's too painful. But no longer are they two victims of circumstance forced to live under the same roof—they're partners, teammates, friends, even.

While organizing the shed earlier that morning, Mel found the book she reads now. It's a slim, faded survival text written in French, annotated in JP's tidy hand. Her French is better than ever from all this practice—maybe she'll take her mom on a girl's trip to France when all this is over, or bring her dad to see the French Open. Mel once would've scoffed at such an idea, instead aggressively saving money for her retirement; but money seems alien, almost trivial, now. She misses her family—she doesn't miss grubbing for pennies shoulder to shoulder with colleagues who felt more like competitors.

That world is a lifetime away, though, and instead of scrutinizing spreadsheets and crunching numbers Mel reads about making tea from pine needles, which Richard had already taught her to do. The text mentions that it's an excellent way to ward off what she guesses is scurvy, as the needles are packed with vitamin C. Below, in JP's handwriting, there's a scribbled note: "Inner layer of pine bark. Shred it, fry it. Bon appétit!"

She chuckles to herself, wondering what Richard might say if she comes back with tree bark for dinner. As she's contemplating how awful pine bark must surely taste, her rod jerks. There's a tug at her line—bigger than any she's felt so far. The rod tip arches toward the hole in the ice, bending so far she's worried it might break. Her pulse quickens. The water roils and then calms as the fish retreats and the reel unspools. She lets the fish take the line, maintaining light tension to keep the hook set and tire it out, like Richard taught her. After five minutes of cat and mouse, she reels the tuckered-out fish in, closer and closer to the hole. There! A flash of pink, a thrashing tail. It's bigger than any fish she's seen so far. Her arms strain. She jabs the rod butt into the snow and reaches down, her frigid fingers following the taut string into the water below.

The fish is so large it won't fit out of the hole sideways. This hasn't been an issue for any of the rainbow trout they've caught so far. Giddy, she angles the fish's nose toward the hole. She plunges both hands into the icy water, grasps the fish firmly around the belly, and flings it onto the snow.

Before the angry, flapping behemoth can shimmy back through the hole, she smacks it soundly with the broomstick handle until blood trickles from its gills into the snow.

It isn't a trout, at least not a rainbow trout. A pink stripe marks the fish's underbelly. Its back is gray, its jaw hooked. She's never seen a fish like it. Maybe a salmon? Richard will know.

It's a big catch, nearly twice the size of Richard's biggest trout, as big as the rolled-up yoga mat she used to take to overpriced, heated classes in Manhattan. It will feed them for days.

As with the ptarmigan, she feels no remorse. Only pride.

She closes the book, gathers up her rod and her catch, and hikes back to the cabin. On her way, she has an idea.

After she guts and cleans the fish—saving the entrails to bait the traps—she packs it in ice on the porch. With a hatchet and a hunting knife, she goes to the tree from which they gather the pine needles for their morning tea. Skeptically, she chops into the bark, scraping back the cold, hard outer layer to find a softer, lighter layer underneath. A laugh plays at her lips. If only her family could see her now. The laughter fades, however, when she thinks about the anguish her parents must be going through.

She wants to go home. How is it that they haven't been rescued? Was Richard's lie to Jim enough to throw them off his tracks? How far could she possibly have veered off the tour's route—forty miles? Fifty?

A sharp pain shoots through her fingers. She's dragged the hatchet across two knuckles on her left hand; twin gashes trickle red into the snow. She curses her inattention and heads back to the cabin to bandage her fingers, bringing with her a small bundle of thoroughly unappealing bark.

After cleaning and bandaging her wound, she gets to work on cooking the bark. She checks JP's instructions: "Shred it, fry it." They're certainly not detailed, though she forgives him. He didn't imagine anyone would be reading his recipes.

She stokes the stove for her experiment, then cuts the bark into carrot-size strips. Richard collected grease from the rabbit in a baked bean tin, and she dollops a glob of oily brown fat into the cast-iron pan on the stovetop.

The smell of sizzling fat alone is enough to make her stomach growl.

The first batch of shredded bark is chewy and tastes much like one would expect tree bark to taste like. She shreds the bark into thinner strips until it looks like a julienned potato. In the hot oil these smaller strips burn until black, and she chucks them. She never was much of a cook in New York, always opting to eat out or order in.

She hurries to the tree, scrapes off more bark. The third time, as they say, is the charm. She pokes at the thin strips with a wooden spoon until they're crispy and brown, and, frankly, appetizing. They look like the crispy onion rings that tower atop hamburgers.

Tentatively she tastes one. Soaked in grease and fried to a crisp, the pine fries aren't half bad. She hoots and gobbles a second, then a third. Hungry and deprived of vegetables for the last month, the tangy pine fries are a treat to be savored. She eats a few more to stave off the hunger—though it almost makes it worse—and peers out the window. The sun is down, it's dusk now, and Richard should be home. She won't let herself worry that he won't make it back, she won't think about the grizzlies and wolves and all those other fatal possibilities—a broken leg, a wrong turn. "God," she says to herself, laughing. "Here I am, wilder than ever, and I'm suddenly domestic as fuck, worrying like a damn housewife."

To distract herself, she goes to work on the fish. She's careful not to overcook it this time.

As the fish crackles in the pan, she hears boots on the steps outside. Her heart flutters, and she tells herself it's because she wouldn't want to stay in the cabin all alone.

The door swings open.

"Smells delicious!" says Richard, weary yet beaming, a small animal swinging from his hand. He holds it up. "I caught a weasel."

"We can save that for tomorrow," she says, grabbing the critter without cringing and putting it in the freezer box. "Dinner's almost ready. Let me help you with that." She takes his shotgun and sets it in the corner. She shakes out his snow-dusted coat and hangs it on a hook.

"It's starting to snow a bit," he says. "Nothing thick yet. What's cooking?"

She smiles and says, "I caught a fish."

"Really?" he says, pleased.

"Really. A big one, too!"

Richard pats her on the shoulder, kicks off his boots, and goes to the counter where the thick fillets are steaming. "Holy cow, you weren't kidding!"

"There's a bunch more in the freezer box, too, I brought in some ice from the porch."

"Excellent! What kind of fish was it?"

"I was hoping you might tell me that," says Mel, turning away from him so he won't see her smile. She retrieves the fish head from the porch and shows it to Richard. He takes it in his hand, grinning.

"Well, I'll be damned. An arctic char."

"A what?"

"It tastes like a cross between salmon and trout. It'll be delicious. And," he looks back at the fish sizzling in the pan, prodding it approvingly with a finger until the flaky flesh separates, "you didn't burn it at all!"

"Not this time," she laughs. "Take off your boots, sit down. I'll serve you a plate. How are your toes?"

"Not falling off yet." Gratitude is etched on his tired face. His boots steam by the fire, their musky stink strangely comforting. He sits down at the kitchen table and accepts a cup of pine needle tea.

She gets a couple plates, and from a warm bean can shakes out her surprise: the pine fries. On top, she scoops up generous fillets of char. On a whim, she minces several fresh pine needles into tiny green flakes and then tops the fish with a sprinkling flourish.

Richard claps when she brings the plates over. He grins and shovels the fish into his mouth. For a few moments, she doesn't even bother eating her own food, she's satisfied merely watching Richard's contentment. He pokes at a crispy pine fry, looks up at her with bewilderment and tosses it into his mouth. A look of curiosity comes over him. He shovels home another bite of fish. He's halfway done with his plate before Mel, grinning, starts in on her own.

Richard asks, "What are these things?"

"Guess," she says.

Richard tugs at his beard, tips back on his chair's two back legs, delighted by the change in their diet. "I have no idea. Some sort of wild potato?"

"Nope," she says proudly. "Pine bark."

"Pine bark!" he guffaws, and the front legs of his chair come slamming onto the wood floor. He slaps the table with open palms and laughs heartily. "Good fiber, I guess. How'd you figure that one out?"

"JP," she says. "I was reading the survival book, and he made a note about it in the margins."

"I'll be damned," says Richard. "I leave you alone for one day and you catch the biggest fish we've had yet and find a completely new and entirely endless food source, not to mention make me the best dinner I've had in decades. And all I did today was trap a lousy weasel!"

She feels a flush coming over.

Richard raises his tea. She does the same.

"To JP," she says, "for the recipe."

"And to you," says Richard, "an Alaskan in the making."

She sits in the rocking chair and reads while Richard hums and scrapes dishes. She watches over her book as he chisels burnt fish grease from the cast iron pan with the wooden spoon.

"They say the charred skin causes cancer," he says, holding up a strip of blackened scales, then crunches it between his teeth, "Delicious. Worth the risk!"

After he finishes up the dishes, Richard lowers himself to the musk ox hide and reads. They sit quietly, turning pages, listening to the crackling logs, and sipping tea. For a surreal moment, life seems like the vacation Dr. Meyer recommended, as if they'd rented this little cabin in the woods just to get away from it all.

When the logs are low and her eyes droop, Mel announces that it's time for bed.

Richard says nothing. His book is spread open on his chest like an upside-down clamshell. His eyes are closed. A snore escapes his lips.

Usually, she'd let him lie there, but it's his turn for the bed. Mel rises from her creaky chair and bends down to wake him.

"Richard," she says, gently touching his shoulder. "Richard, you fell asleep on the floor. It's your turn for the bed."

He doesn't wake. She kneels down next to him on the thick musk ox hide. She's tempted to just lay her head on his chest.

He mumbles something. She leans closer. "What was that?"

He mumbles again. The whisper brings reality back into sharp focus.

She stands up and drapes a blanket rather unceremoniously on his prone body. He harrumphs and turns on his side, still snoring.

Lying in bed, she knows she has no right to be angry. Still, she can't help but repeat the word he whispered over and over in her head.

"Anne."

Chapter 19

A funeral with an empty casket is one thing Anne will not allow.

The frenzy that began when Richard disappeared has died down, so to speak. The Search and Rescue teams have been called off on newer assignments. Daily front-page stories have turned into weekly updates below the fold. The flow of lasagnas and casseroles has ebbed to a trickle, although this Anne doesn't mind.

But a funeral? That's a finality she won't allow. That's giving up. She won't accept it. She doesn't even consider it until Al Bogle sits in her living room, a half-drunk cup of coffee in one hand, his hat in the other.

"I'm sorry, Anne. We've had weather window after weather window. We couldn't find him. I can't have my team out there. The trail is ice cold. We've got other fresh cases now."

"I understand," Anne nods. Al's team was the last to keep looking. "Thanks for your help."

"I wish we could've done more," says Al, looking between Anne and Jim, his eyes glazed, professional demeanor momentarily abandoned.

"Well, what can we do?" asks Anne. "How much would it cost to keep a team in operation? To hire a helicopter?"

Al wipes his eyes with his scrunched up woolen hat.

"It would be a lot of money. A helicopter, especially. We're talking multiple thousands of dollars a day."

"Anne," says Jim. "What are you going to do? Spend all of the kids' college savings on this?"

"I'll do what I have to do!"

"Think about Richard," says Jim.

"How dare you? I'm always thinking about Richard!"

"No, think about what he'd say if you spent all your money looking for him. He'd want you and the kids to be taken care of."

Anne shakes with anger and grief. Her options are fading, the same as the headlines, the rescue teams, the damn lasagnas.

"Anne," says Al. "It's been over three months. It may be time to accept that he's gone."

"You can believe that. I don't."

"I know you don't want to hear this," he says wearily. "But I'd put some of that money to a funeral, rather than a rescue party."

"What are you saying?" she yells. "That my husband is dead? That I should bury an empty fucking casket under a headstone that has a date we don't even know?"

"It might be good for the kids," says Jim, trying to hold it together. "To have some closure."

"We have to live without closure," says Anne, fire in her eyes. "He might still be out there."

Jim moves out of the guest room and back to his own lonely bachelor pad. He can barely stomach it, living alone, unable to call Richard for a snowmachine ride, just to chat, to grab a bite after work. There are reminders everywhere. His snowmachine. The photos in his office. The spot in the empty living room where the ugly coffee table used to be.

He wakes up late, then wallows in bed for hours. He doesn't open the shades. He doesn't go skiing, doesn't date. He doesn't eat well, falling back into fast food and frozen TV dinners. He gains weight. He stops going into the office and tells his assistant to make up excuses. He buys a leather couch and spends most of his time watching sports with the sound off and music blaring, drinking heavily. A line of empty bottles grows along the baseboards in the living room.

He takes long showers, letting his tears mix in with the stream of warm water. He constantly thinks about dying, about killing himself. Just drive his snowmobile into the middle of the woods and put a gun to his head. Whip into a light post at a hundred mph on the freeway. Hang himself in the garage. He wouldn't be the first Alaskan to take the easy way out—suicide and winter go hand in hand at this latitude. He probably would, too, if it weren't for Anne and the kids. Whenever he's near the edge, he pulls himself back for them. He does it for them.

These thoughts run through his mind on an endless loop, especially when he traces that out-and-back route on his snowmachine—he's ridden it fifteen or twenty times now, searching for a sign of his friend, always coming up empty-handed and brokenhearted.

Two weeks after Jim moves back to his own place, he gets a call from Anne. These calls aren't rare. Every day she calls him, as much to make sure he's doing okay as to ask for his help. To pick up the kids, to grab takeout, to handle some life insurance paperwork. Just because Anne doesn't believe that Richard is gone doesn't mean the insurance company thinks similarly.

He picks up the phone, sees the caller ID, and shakes his head, trying to brush off the fog of scotch.

"Hey, Anne, what's up?"

She's silent.

"Anne?"

Maybe she can tell he's drunk.

"The doctor called," she says slowly. "It's bad."

Jim hears only a few words that follow: malignant tumors, biopsy, chemo, nine months to go.

It'd be too easy just to find Richard and have everything go back to normal. It'd be too easy for Richard to disappear and for Anne to keep on as a single mother. That's the evil of cancer. It's indiscriminate in its timing, in its victim selection, in its violence.

He drops the bottle of Scotch.

Amber liquid mixes with the old sweat stains on the living room carpet.

"Jim," says Anne. "Jim. Say something."

Jim gulps. "I'll pack my things and move back in."

"As soon as you sober up."

"As soon as I sober up."

"Thank you," she says.

Jim and Anne decide not to tell the kids for a bit. Winter's been hard enough.

Sarah hasn't withdrawn as Jim expected she might. Instead, the event of Richard's disappearance has seemed to age her, to cause her to shoot right past the moody teenage years. Almost overnight, she's an adult, no longer worried about what movie she's seeing or what the boys think of her at school. She becomes indispensable to her mother, making lunches, keeping the boys organized.

Caleb and Sean, however, have drastically different reactions. Caleb pulls inside his shell like a hermit crab, rarely using full sentences and staying silent most of the time. On the complete opposite end of the spectrum, Sean acts out. As the headlines about his father cease to pour in, a stream of carefully worded complaints from Sean's teachers replace them.

"He's obviously terribly saddened by his father's death," wrote one. "But he's become a menace in the classroom."

One afternoon, while Anne's at a doctor's appointment, there's a call to the house. Jim answers. Sean's in the principal's office. The secretary refuses to give a reason for the call and only mentions that a parent or guardian must pick him up.

"I'm not his father," says Jim, peeved. "You do know who his father is?"

"Yes, sir," she says. "Are you related in any way?"

"I'm his godfather."

"That will do."

Sean is one of four boys sitting in a row of chairs outside the principal's office. They look like criminals awaiting processing. The other boys seem primarily unscathed, save for a black eye on one and another missing a shoe. Sean, however, is clearly the worse for wear. His lip is bleeding, his shirt is torn. Through the ripped fabric, Jim sees a gash of blood and a bruise on his ribs. Jim waves at Sean, who nods and says nothing, then fixes his gaze back on his shoes.

The principal, a tall and imposing man with an upturned nose who looks like a British nobleman, bids Jim to enter. The office is large and stuffy, with sunlight pouring through the windows, illuminating flecks of floating dust disturbed by the swinging door.

Jim shakes the man's hand.

"Jim."

"Principal Ford."

"Nice to meet you. What happened?"

The principal gestures to a small, uncomfortable chair and sits behind the large carved wooden desk. "Please, sit."

Jim sits. "What happened to Sean?"

"It seems he got into a fight against those three eighth-graders. He won't tell us why."

"He's going through a hard time."

"Will you be pressing charges? It was three against one, and those boys are all a year older."

Jim looks out of the office's floor-to-ceiling glass windows at Sean, who's gritting his teeth and staring down at the carpet.

"I don't see why. If his father were here..." Jim falters. "If his father were here, he'd probably be quite pleased that he stood up to three bullies and wouldn't rat them out to you. No offense," he adds.

Ford stands up slowly and strolls to the window. "I understand that his circumstances are... tragic. And were this the only incident, we wouldn't be having this conversation. However, it seems that every day I have more on my plate from this boy. You're his godfather?"

Jim nods.

"Then have a talk with him."

"What do you want me to say? Straighten up and fly right, your father is dead?" There's more than a hint of anger in Jim's voice. Who does this man think he is? He has no idea what Sean's been through. And the poor boy still has no clue about his mother's illness.

The principal sighs. "I can only imagine what it's like to lose a father so young. But Sean is at a key moment in his life. If he doesn't pull himself together, he'll be going into high school with a rebellious attitude and a reputation for trouble. The decisions he makes now will define his future. Despite what you may think, I'm here because I care about these kids, not because I like to swing a ruler around."

On the car ride home, Sean takes on his brother's silence as he looks out the window. In the reflection, Jim sees his swollen lips, the anger in his eyes.

"Sean," Jim says. "What happened?"

Sean's quiet.

"C'mon. Talk to me."

"They were talking shit."

"You can't just jump into a fight when kids are talking shit," says Jim. "If I got into a fight every time someone insulted me, I'd always be walking around with a bloody lip and a torn shirt."

"They were talking shit about Caleb," says Sean, tears falling down his cheeks, mixing in with the blood on his shirt. "They were pushing him around, and one of them said that dad went and got lost because it was better than having a pussy like Caleb for a son."

"Oh," says Jim. He pulls over and parks. He doesn't know what to say. He'd probably have beat their asses, too, the little snots. He imagines Caleb, wrapped up in his journal, quiet and keeping to himself when the three eighth-graders started to, as Sean so aptly put it, talk shit.

"You know, Sean, your dad—"

"What about my fucking dad? You're not my dad."

"You're right. I'm not. Your dad was the best man I've ever met. And," Jim sighs, "I don't think your dad would be the least bit mad at you right now."

This deflates Sean. He looks up at Jim, tears in his eyes, a miniature, angry, confused version of his father.

"He wouldn't?"

"No," says Jim. "He'd want you to protect your brother. Do you know why?"

"Why?"

"Because it's family first," says Jim, finally knowing what to say. "It was always family first with your dad. And that means it's got to stay family first. Now more than ever, more than when he was around. Have you noticed how your sister's been stepping up to the plate? How she's taking care of you and your brother? How she's helping out your mom? And did you notice how your mom's orchestrated everything? The search teams, the rescue operations? She's been involved in all of that. She reached out to every snowmachiner she could. She put the hounds out, and we've combed that route every which way. And you know what? Me, too. Do you see where I am right now? I'm here, taking care of you, making sure everything's okay. Because it's family first. And that's what your dad would've wanted."

The anger's gone now. Sean's chest convulses with sharp sobs. His head hangs low.

"Look at me. Chin up," says Jim, firmly but compassionately. "Never stop taking care of your brother. If people talk shit and your words don't work and you need to use your fists, I understand. Family first. There's no better reason to fight. But you need to step up and be the man your dad raised you to be, and I don't just mean with bullies at school. I mean at home, too. And by that, I mean that you need to make things easier on your mother. She has enough on her plate without worrying about getting a call about you from a juvenile detention center."

Sean nods. Jim puts his arm across the armrest, grabs Sean's neck gently, and kisses the top of his head.

"I love you, Sean. I'm not going anywhere."

"Are you going to tell my mom I got sent home?" Sean asks once his breathing slows.

"No. I think she has enough to deal with," says Jim. "Don't you?"

Sean nods.

"Good kid." Jim turns the key, and the truck roars to life.

"We're not going back to school, are we?" says Sean.

"No," Jim laughs. "I thought we could both use a trip to Donna's."

After the fight, Sean and Jim become close, and the flow of complaints and calls from the school tapers off like the headlines and the casseroles. Caleb is tougher to read, namely because he's always reading. Jim can't help but think that he's the polar opposite of his father.

To bring the boys closer together, Jim decides to take them out snowmachining. It's the first time he's used his sled for anything other than joining the search parties.

Over dinner, he asks them where they want to go.

Caleb, with unexpected boldness, says, "I want to go where dad went."

Sean looks up at his twin, shocked, and then agrees. "Yeah, where dad went."

Anne shakes her head. "No, absolutely not. It's too far."

"Please, Mom," says Sean.

Caleb puts his fork down next to his journal, which he carries everywhere now, and looks directly at his mother. "Mom," he says calmly. "We have to. Don't you get it?"

They go to Donna's in the morning and order three of Richard's Usuals. Susan drops off hot chocolates for the boys, on the house. Photos of Richard now decorate the walls.

On the drive Jim has to stop three times: twice to pee and once because Sean and Caleb are squabbling. He even makes the classic parental threat of stopping the car and turning around.

They get to the trailhead around 11 a.m. The snow is slushy down low, but the snowline is yet to reveal itself. Jim unloads the snowmachines, and Caleb and Sean tape duct tape to their cheeks, though the skies are sunny and the temperatures much milder than when he and Richard last unloaded their sleds together.

He triple-checks to make sure they each have a working radio.

"What channel?" he asks.

"Channel seven," they reply in unison.

"What's the rule?"

"Stick together."

There's a tattered "Missing" poster stapled to the trailhead, and Richard's torn face smiles out at them. Caleb goes back into the truck, pulls out a new poster and staples it to the sign. He doesn't throw away the old one, but instead folds it carefully and puts it into his pocket.

Finally, they take off. Caleb and Sean each drive their own machine. Jim remembers when one of them would be on the front of his sled, the other on their father's. They ride for an hour. The sky is blue and bright. Jim watches the boys ahead of him, a lump in his throat.

He pulls in front of the boys and slows down, and gestures for them to do the same.

They stop and turn off their sleds. The twins are flushed, excited.

"Have you seen a sign of him?" asks Sean.

"No," Jim says sadly. "This," he points at the surrounding mountains, the river valley, the snowmachine track, "this is where I last saw your dad."

Sean's smile disappears. They sit on their sleds in silence for a while. Jim pulls out a Thermos of Dunkin' Donuts coffee and takes a sip.

"Have you boys ever tried coffee before?"

They shake their heads.

"This was your dad's favorite. It doesn't taste great to me, but he loved it."

He hands the Thermos to Sean, who takes a sip and gives it to Caleb.

Caleb stands there holding the steaming Thermos, and for a second, Jim's sure he's about to cry.

Instead, Caleb reaches into his jacket pocket and brings out his journal. He flips to a page, clambers up to stand on the seat of his snowmachine, and begins to read.

"*Past tense.*
They speak of my dad in a tense of the past,
They speak of my dad like his legacy won't last.
When they speak of my dad they always tread lightly,
They speak of my dad sweetly, politely.
They say my dad wasn't just sweet, he was strong.
They say he wasn't just polite, he knew when to carry on.
They say a lot of things, all of them false, all of them true.
True not just because of what he was, but what he is, too.
False because he lives on in me, and he lives on in you.
Such a spirit can never be dead.
He exists in our hearts, he exists in our heads.
He exists on this Earth, even more than in heaven.
So when you speak of my dad, do so in the present."

Caleb's lines are spoken softly, but they reverberate as if amplified, bouncing off the mountains, filling the valley with meaning. They knock the wind out of Jim, who has himself used the past tense when talking about Richard. They bring tears to Sean's eyes, so clearly full of admiration for his odd brother. Caleb sips the coffee, makes a gagging sound, but swallows the piping hot brew. He then pours a small stream into the snow. Brown coffee sizzles into crystalline white.

They mount their snowmachines in silence, turn around, and head back to the trailhead.

The night before Anne starts her chemotherapy, she tells the kids about her illness. Before dessert, she gathers her strength with a long, yogic inhale.

She feared the conversation would go as poorly as the one when she announced that Richard was missing. She told Jim as much.

"I don't think so, Anne," he said. "They've changed. All of them."

And sure enough, he was right.

Upon hearing the news, Sarah gasps and then reaches out to hold her mother's trembling hand. Caleb stands up, and then Sean, and they gather around her, hugging her.

"You'll get through it, Mom," says Sarah confidently. "You're the strongest woman I know. And I get my driver's license soon, so I can take you to appointments and the boys to school."

"Don't worry, Mom," says Sean. "I'll stay out of trouble."

"You've always taken care of us," says Caleb. "It's our turn now."

Jim sits on the opposite side of the table, a half-eaten fish taco in his hand, watching this through blurry eyes, thinking to himself that, for a man who cries once every ten years, he sure has been getting his fill over the past couple of months.

Chapter 20

Richard and Mel fall into a routine—most of which involves chasing calories. After deciphering some of Jean Pierre's scrawled notes in the margins of the survival text, Mel digs several new fishing holes, focusing on a far corner of the lake, where a wide, iced-over waterfall steps down to a creek that snakes into the Hope.

"The flow under the ice and the proximity to the bank make it a good spot, according to Jean Pierre," she says hopefully. "What do you think?"

Richard voices skepticism—his father always taught him to fish farther out toward the middle of a frozen lake. But Jean Pierre's tip proves invaluable: Whenever Mel drops a line in the new zone, she brings home supper.

While Mel plucks trout, char, and grayling from the lake, Richard patrols the trapline. Thanks to Mel's angling acumen, there's no shortage of bait. He refills the steel jaws of his traps generously with whole fresh fish carcasses instead of small pinches of guts. This new methodology is much more productive, and he often brings home marten, ermine, and similar small game. Sometimes, when they have ample fish frozen in the snow, Mel joins him and they hike together, tracing the now-familiar trapline, following his old tracks or breaking new ones, sometimes chatting, but often in contented silence.

Occasionally, he takes out the snowshoes and a backpack of

overnight survival essentials—sleeping bag, food, water, fire starters and the like—and goes hunting. The hunts are a less reliable method of gathering food than the trapline—and they're certainly less fruitful than Mel's new fishing hole—but they do sometimes supply larger and tastier game. Mel crafted him a fingerless mitten out of marten fur, which allows him to be much quicker on the draw, and as a result he brings home plump ptarmigans regularly. A couple weeks back, he even took down a young moose. The meat was a delicacy compared to the gristly game he pulls from the traps. The two ate their fill, froze some of the choice cuts—the backstrap steaks, the tenderloin, the rump—before smoking and storing what was left.

The hunts do wonders to calm Richard's nerves, center his thoughts and provide him with a sense of purpose. His initial feelings of embarrassment that he might not be cut out for this survival game are long gone, expelled with every shotgun shell, every fishhook, every steel trap that brings home sustenance.

Between Richard's hunts, the new fishing holes, and the addition of pine bark to their otherwise carnivorous diet, their stores are well stocked, especially when compared to their early days of rationing rancid baked beans. Much has changed since those miserable nights following the crash, nights spent hungry and waiting for a rescue. They're certainly not hungry anymore. And they're not banking on a rescue, either.

According to the notched sticks leaning against the windowsill—there are four of them now—it's been three and a half months since Richard dove in after Mel. Three and a half months without rescue.

Each day, the sun lingers longer in the sky. Spring is coming. And as much as Richard welcomes lengthier days and warmer afternoons, the changing of the seasons is a direct threat to their lives.

In addition to the endless chores of hunting and maintaining the homestead, Richard obsesses over two essential tasks. The first is finding his snowmachine. He's sure that, by now, all but his wife and Jim have stopped looking for him. Since that fateful flyby, they haven't seen or heard another helicopter. The snowmachine is their escape, their only way out, their only way home.

The winter has been a prodigious one, with weekly snowfall totals averaging multiple feet. Stacking up on top of the original blizzard, it's surely a record-breaking snowpack, at least based on Richard's rudimentary calculations. The cabin is constantly buried, despite regular shoveling, with corridor-like paths leading to the woodpile, the outhouse, the shed.

Richard retired the broomstick handle after he found an old, ten-foot-long tent pole in the shed, and every afternoon he uses it to probe through the snow in search of his snowmachine. It pokes through the drifts on top of the lake better than the broomstick, but he worries that the snowmachine is now encased in ice, that it will be impossible to strike with a probe, that his efforts are entirely in vain. And even if it isn't entombed in ice, if he doesn't strike the cushy seat, the metal and plastic of the snowmachine might feel just like ice. There's a possibility he could hit it, continue moving, and miss it altogether.

It's a daunting, frustrating task, one that proves fruitless day after day. He scours the lake, retracing his steps, poking the probe into the snow like a sandpiper jabbing its beak into the beach. After a day or two of searching, the footprint-covered lake looks like a game of connect the dots. And then the snow falls again and his efforts are erased. Despite his failures, despite the implausibility of his search, he continues at it anyway.

He can't think of a better use of his time.

It's both his greatest duty and his greatest desire to get home, to return to his family.

Richard's second obsession is a zealous study of the snowline. It's a perpetually shifting perimeter, the line where snow meets dirt, the point at which winter recedes and acquiesces to spring.

Most importantly, the snowline is the key to their survival. If the snow melts, snowmachines are as good as useless, and they'll be stuck. And with spring on its way, the snowline can rise quicker than a desert river in a flash flood.

The irony of the situation is that by the time the snow melts enough to locate the snowmachine, the machine may be worthless in the muddy, rocky terrain.

They have to move, and they have to move soon.

Remnants of dinner—moose rump roast—stick to the cast-iron pan on top of the stove. Mel's rereading the survival book, searching for any tips she might have missed. He watches her dark eyes scan the text, her lips mouth out difficult words as she searches for their meaning in a tattered French-to-English dictionary they found, like everything else of use, in Jean Pierre's shed.

The woman continually surprises him. Her transformation into a grizzly pioneer has been as unexpected as it's been welcome.

"I think we ought to climb the peak on the other side of the lake," he says.

She looks up from her book, taken aback, and then a small smile flits across her face. "You aren't getting enough exercise? I'd say you've lost some weight since we got into this mess."

Richard grins back. He's in better shape now than when he was a football player in college. An all-protein diet, zero pizza or beer, and hard labor have made him lean and muscular.

"No," he says. "But this sunny streak, it's got me worried about the snowline."

Her smile disappears. They've spoken at length about the snowline. How winter's their only way out.

"But there's still so much snow," she says simply.

"A couple weeks of sun like this and the whole landscape will change, especially down lower," says Richard. "We'll see the river rage and the lake melt out."

"If the lake melts, we should be able to find the snowmachine, right?"

"True," says Richard. "But…"

"It could fall into the lake?"

"I'm honestly not sure how that would work, assuming that it's now caked in snow and ice. It might even be on the bank rather than on the lake itself. But it's not exactly something I want to gamble on. If that snowmachine goes, we go too."

"If that snowmachine goes, we're going nowhere," Mel corrects him.

"Exactly. But the biggest concern is that by the time we pull it out of there, the snowline will be so high that we can't even use it."

They sit quietly for a bit, and then Mel asks, "And the mountain?"

"Summit's probably three and a half, four thousand feet above where we are. It would give us the ability to see if the snowline is starting to reveal itself down-valley. On a clear day, we might even be able to see some semblance of civilization with those binoculars you found in the shed. Maybe another cabin. Maybe a way out."

"Four thousand feet," says Mel. She whistles. "That's almost three Empire State Buildings."

"There's a ridge we can follow pretty much to the summit. That will keep us out of avalanche paths and deeper snow." Richard pauses. "If you don't want to…"

"Of course I'll come."

"Wonderful." Richard is relieved. He'd do it on his own, but it's always better to take on a mission like this with a partner. He's learned that lesson the hard way. Had he gone back with Jim in the first place, none of this would've happened. Although, in that scenario, Mel would be dead at the bottom of the lake.

"Then it's settled." Mel puts her book down and stands up. "I'll make us a big bag of jerky and pine fries for lunch. We'll need the energy."

The next morning is cloudy, and they postpone their plans out of fear of a storm. But the following night is clear, and before the sun rises, in the pale light of a full moon, they strap on snowshoes and make their way toward the mountain.

The snow is crusty and they cross the lake quickly. "It'll get warm, quick," says Richard. "When our snowshoes start to penetrate the surface and we feel slush around our boots, we should've been off the peak already. When the snow gets wet like that, it becomes weaker, and we could be dealing with wet avalanches."

They make their way through the trees: first the pines, then the willowy scrubs that dot the foothills. If only the snowline were as constant as the treeline, Richard thinks as they break into the alpine.

Richard's legs feel fresh, and he's pleased with their progress. The going is difficult, as the ridgeline is steeper than expected, but Mel stays on his tail and doesn't complain. By the time the sun rises, they're approximately halfway up the ridge, with sweat sticking to their backs. They break for a quick lunch of moose jerky. Mel offers him a Thermos of pine needle tea, which he gratefully accepts.

Refueled, Richard powers up the ridge. He stops again beneath a steep section, one of the final pushes to the summit. There's a mellow pitch beneath them to their left, and on the right, a rolling drop. Mel is behind him by fifty yards.

The sun is high now and their snowshoes sink more and more into the snow. He's not sure if they should keep going. He'd prefer to reach the summit, get a view of the entire range, but from this vantage point Richard has an excellent view of the valley. He can see the lake below, the glint of the cabin's roof. He takes out JP's binoculars and aims them south, down the valley, tracing the Hope River—their way out. The snowline is still nonexistent; the landscape is blanketed in white. They don't need to worry, at least not yet. He sees no trace of civilization, although he does see a speck that may very well be the roof of another trapper's cabin.

Richard looks up from the binoculars, ready to relay to Mel what he's seen, when he sees Mel nearing the steep roll, peering over the edge.

"Mel! No!"

He leans out and grabs her hand, flinging her back from the edge. She falls into the snow behind him.

"What the hell!" she yells.

The roll she was standing on is a cornice, a snow formation that looks like a wave, shaped by wind beating repeatedly over ridge tops and depositing snow on the leeward face of the slope. It's unsupportive, prone to break off and catalyze an avalanche. But before he can explain this to her, hairline fractures form underneath his snowshoes. Mel looks helplessly at him from behind the fracture line. With a whump, the ground beneath him drops out, and suddenly he's plummeting through a waterfall of moving snow. Chunks of cornice crash around him. It's like he's swimming through a collapsing tower of cars in a junkyard. He fights with all his might to stay above the surface of the avalanche.

If he's buried beneath the debris, she'll never find him in time.

It's all over in a few seconds. Snow clouds his vision. A sharp pain flashes across his forehead, likely where the binoculars smashed in the fall. They've probably been ripped from his neck at this point. He can't check, because he can't move his arms. The snow has solidified—it's like he's encased in concrete. More terrifying still, he can't see anything but darkness, can't hear anything, can't breathe.

Like his snowmachine thousands of feet below, he's entombed in snow.

His thoughts go to Mel—he wonders if she can survive without him. He thinks of Jim, of his children, of his wife. If only he could spin the clock backward, just go back to that fork in the road with Jim, make the right decision, live to ride another day.

Richard is in the process of coming to terms with his death when the darkness turns to blackness, and he passes out.

He hears hoarse screams and wonders if he's dreaming. His legs are numb, but he feels a rhythmic pounding on his chest. The pounding stops and chapped lips brush against his own. Air unnaturally fills his lungs. A drop of water falls on his cheek. The sun is uncomfortably bright. He squints into the brightness and makes out a tearful Mel. She's panting and panicked.

"Are you giving me CPR?" he asks.

"No, I was giving you a kiss, you idiot," she gasps.

"You might've," says Richard. "Second time I've saved your life."

"I think this one's a wash," says Mel, "you'd be buried if it weren't for me. Your glove was sticking out of the snow. Only way I found you."

Using the back heel of her snowshoe as a shovel, she digs him out. It's a slow process. The snowshoe's broken in two places now, and she uses it almost like brass knuckles to scrape the ice and snow from his legs. Once he's free of the snow, she sits down, breathing heavily.

"I've never climbed a mountain before," she says sheepishly. "I didn't know that was going to happen."

"Don't worry about it," says Richard, checking his body for injuries. Pain shoots through his back, his old football injury flaring up again, and his forehead throbs; but other than that he seems to have emerged remarkably unscathed. "I should've told you about cornices before you got up onto that ridge. Those rolls make you want to see the edge, but you never want to do that. They can break, and then…" His voice cracks, and he sweeps his arm out as if to say, "This shit happens."

He looks down the mountain. The debris of the avalanche stopped where the slope peters out. Luckily, there wasn't a cliff or a band of trees below. He's seen skiers go through trees before. He'd have been lucky to get out of that with a broken leg. And out here, a broken leg might just be a death sentence.

Up the mountain, he eyes the avalanche path. The cornice broke and ran for a couple hundred yards. The crown of the avalanche was up to six feet thick. Doing the math, it was a miracle he wasn't buried deeper.

"C'mon," he says to Mel. "We've got to get out of here."

They hike back up the ridge, skirting to the left of the avalanche path. It's slow going—Richard's snowshoes were ripped off his feet in the avalanche, and he sinks deeper and deeper into the snow with every step—but they need to retrieve their packs.

Once they've got their gear, Richard shows Mel how to glissade down the peak. Sitting on their heels, they slide down the ridgeline, making quick time back to the foothills.

Crossing the lake is the worst part of the journey home. Mel only has one working snowshoe, and Richard has none. They wallow through the deep, slushy snow, and by the time they make it to the cabin, the sun has set and both are soaking wet. Richard's back aches with sharp pain. Mel fixes dinner, and they eat in silence, exhausted.

She insists that he have the cot, even though it's her turn. Richard doesn't argue. He wonders if he'll dream of towers of junkyard cars collapsing around him, but he's asleep within minutes and dreams of nothing at all.

Richard wakes not to the brush of lips against his own, but to severe pain in his back. It's so excruciating that he can't even push himself into a seated position. He grits his teeth and barks involuntarily.

Mel's already up, fixing tea, and she puts down the kettle, concerned.

"What's wrong?"

Richard speaks through clenched teeth. "My back. I can't move."

With Mel's help, he props himself up on a stack of pillows.

She brings the steaming mug of tea to his lips, and he takes a sip.

"Fuck!" he exclaims, frustrated, bedridden, helpless.

"Is there anything I can do to help?" asks Mel, her eyes teary. He knows that she feels like this is all her fault, and at that moment, he wants nothing to do with assuaging her guilt.

"In the medical kit," he says, "there should be a small plastic bag with white pills in it."

She rummages in his kit, happy to have something to do, and brings him the pills.

"What are they?"

"Oxycodone," says Richard, counting twenty pills in his palm. He takes one, despite wanting to down the lot.

"Why didn't you give me one of those when I crashed?"

Richard winces. "Because you were likely severely concussed. And I'm no doctor, but I don't think you're supposed to take these after a head injury. I didn't want to risk it."

Once the painkiller kicks in, he's able to stagger outside to pee with Mel's help.

"I don't think I can make it to the tree," he says, referring to the pine they've designated as their pee tree. The point of the pee tree, as Richard explained to Mel when they first made the cabin home, was to avoid both overburdening JP's decrepit outhouse and tainting the snow just off the deck. "We collect and melt this for drinking water," he'd told her sternly, pointing at the virgin snow along the porch. "No peeing in the water supply."

Mel hasn't forgotten. "Just 'cause you're on painkillers doesn't mean you get a free pass to pee in the water supply," she groans, shouldering as much of his weight as she can.

Richard laughs, then grimaces at the subsequent shooting pain along his spine. "Hopefully we get some fresh snow soon, then." He grasps the rough wooden railing of the porch to stabilize himself.

"You got it?"

"I got it," he says, waving her back. He pisses off the deck, breaking his own rule and cursing his luck.

For days, Richard is useless. He's moody, constipated from the opioids, and in pain. His routines become hers. She handles all the cabin chores. She checks the trapline for the first time by herself, bringing home a pair of hares. She fishes and hunts and chops wood and stacks it and keeps the fire going. She collects untainted snow and melts it for drinking water. She probes for the snowmachine, though he tells her not to, that it's not worth it. In addition to these essential tasks, she plays the role of caretaker. She rations his painkillers and helps him to the bathroom. At night, by the fire, she has him lie on his stomach on the musk ox hide with his shirt off and, using a pinch of animal fat, massages his tweaked muscles, working out the kinks as the snow falls lightly outside the cabin.

Chapter 21

The wind rips down from the green, jungle-wrapped mountains and whips across the sand. Spray blows off the feathering tops of the turquoise waves.

The morning light is still pale and pink. Few surfers are in the water. It's Sunday, after all, meaning that most tourists who flock to the surf town are drunkenly asleep, not yet nursing hangovers with cups of Nicaraguan java.

More than a few of the hungover have Rusty to thank.

Rusty walks the beach, grateful for the droves of drinkers who allow him to make a living. He took only $25K from the stash when he left Alaska, but that was enough. Enough to make his way through Central America for a few months before falling in love with Nicaragua. Enough to start a bar. A proper Irish pub. Well, as proper an Irish pub as one can have when it's easier to import cocaine than Guinness and the patrons hardly ever wear shoes.

Back then, the tiny town of Santa Catalina was just a small hamlet, a little slice of heaven, with a few expats, a handful of surfers, and a bar or two. These days, hostels spring up all the time, there are sushi joints and pizza places, and the main drag is overrun with Australian surfers and Dutch yoga chicks. There's a steady vortex of vacationers, soaking up the sun and the attractive exchange rates, drinking and surfing their brains out, fucking each other silly, going home with smiles, stories, and sunburns—plus the occasional intestinal parasite or STD.

Rusty walks the beach for an hour every morning, sometimes starting well before first light. He does so more for his mind than his body—he gets plenty of exercise surfing, but he doesn't sleep well. He hasn't, not for a decade and a half now. Though these days, it's better than it was.

He got his first taste of surf in Mexico. While he was hitchhiking down through Baja California, he got picked up by a couple college graduates from Washington who were, in their own words, "squeezing in one last adventure before joining the real world," and they pushed him into a few waves. Since then, he's been hooked. On a great wave, all his troubles fade away.

Not a single soul from his old life knows his whereabouts. Those he once called friends think he and his brother fell off the face of the earth. And to be completely honest, Rusty nearly did. When he left Alaska, he was depressed, leaning heavily on drugs and drink, tumbling in free fall. If it hadn't been for surfing, he'd still be coked up in Mexico; or he'd have gotten shanked in a Honduran jail cell. But once he realized his passion for waves, he cleaned up and made a plan to surf his way from Mexico to Chile.

Love, however, has a funny way of changing plans.

He met Victoria his second week in Santa Catalina. She was compassionate and witty and sarcastic as hell, though that he discovered later. It was her beauty that ensnared him first. She had smooth skin, almond-shaped eyes that were pure espresso brown, and long, dark hair that curled well past her slender shoulders down to what he'd later come to call the "Eighth Wonder of the World." One look and Rusty was smitten. Like the national export, she was caffeinating.

Raúl, a local fisherman and Victoria's father, had high hopes for his daughter, and marrying a drunken, broke tourist wasn't among them. And despite his best efforts, Rusty couldn't ply Victoria with winks and whiskey. She was well and truly out of his league, and for the first time in his life, he put in the work. He walked with her around the town square and wrote her love letters and poetry in shit Spanish. She was the reason he started the bar in the first place. Victoria told him that if he owned a business, her father would be more likely to offer his blessing. After all, Rusty wasn't the only suitor for Victoria, though he was the one she wanted. Somehow, he won both her and her father over, despite the awful poems.

Raúl, once his mortal enemy, is now a regular at The Rusty Nail, which The Lonely Planet travel books describe as, "Irish pub meets tropical outpost; a must-stop post-surf watering hole for any visitor."

Rusty was born to tend bar. At least, tapping kegs and pouring beers suits him better than planning and executing heists. It's certainly less stressful. He's a gracious host, renowned for his bawdy jokes and good nature. His weekly happy hour specials draw locals and tourists alike. He drinks less these days, now that he's a family man, though he still has a pint or two every shift.

Rusty wrenches his gaze from the sea. Briskly, he walks back toward town on a dirt road. A hand-painted sign nailed onto a palm tree announces "Casa de Rusty," and he makes a left up his rutted, muddy driveway.

Victoria's up when he gets back, bustling in the kitchen of their three-bedroom bungalow, a tour de force even at dawn. The scent of coffee fills the open-air kitchen, a dented tin percolator bubbles on the stove. The wood is rough on his feet. The breeze is gentle and steady. Palm fronds sway outside. There's a monkey on a branch, nibbling on a mango rind.

It is, as the welcome mat reminds him every time he comes home, *paraíso.*

"Good morning, *mi amor,*" he says, then wraps his wife up in his arms. She smells of coconut and fresh linen.

"How was your walk, *guapo?*"

He gratefully accepts the café con leche she offers him and sits down on one of the wooden stools around the small kitchen table.

"Paradise, as always," he says, "Ah, *gracias, café con leche.*"

She smiles, as she does every time he says those three little words. His favorite coffee and his nickname for her, all in one.

"Why do you call me this?" she asked him once, after a six-month-long courtship when they lay together for the first time, in the attic bedroom above The Rusty Nail, not long after it first opened. "Is it just because of the color of my skin?"

Rusty laughed into her hair. It smelled like coconut then, too. He'll always remember that smell, as long as he lives. "No, my love. It's because you're the first thing I want in the morning."

She responded then that it was a cheesy thing to say; but later, many years later, she admitted that it was then that she decided they would be married, and he would be the father of her children.

Into the kitchen walks a product of these sentiments: his nine-year-old son.

Café con leche, with extra *leche*, Rusty always jokes.

"Good morning, Papa."

"Come here, *hijo*," says Rusty, setting aside his coffee. Jaime protests half-heartedly as Rusty pulls him onto his lap.

"Mami, can I have some toast?"

"Mami what?" says Rusty, tickling Jaime in the ribs.

"*Por favor*, Mami," says Jaime, squirming.

"Where is your sister? Still sleeping?" Victoria puts a plate of toast and jam down next to a bowl of fried plantains, a fresh banana, and a pitcher of mango smoothie.

"I think so."

Victoria sighs and goes to roust Juliana, who, at thirteen, never seems to wake up on her own.

Rusty watches his boy munch at the corner of the toast.

"Can we go surfing when I get home?" he asks.

"Only after you finish your homework."

Jaime picks up a piece of plantain with his fingers and nibbles it slowly, as if mimicking the monkey on the branch outside.

Juliana enters the kitchen, a young, light-skinned, blond version of her mother. Rusty loves her more than anything, and wonders, as lady-killers turned fathers often do, if her blossoming beauty is a curse for the years he spent in dive bars and brothels, chasing women with a recklessness he now regrets.

"Morning, Dad."

"Good morning, sweetheart."

Victoria reads the paper. Juliana finishes up last-minute math homework and eats a bowl of cereal. Jaime looks at the pictures in a surf magazine—Rusty's found it's the best way to teach him English. Rusty's Spanish is near perfect now, though his accent is still abysmal, and a constant source of jokes amongst their Nicaraguan friends.

His heart is full as he kisses Victoria and walks his kids to school, down the winding dirt road and back into town. Juliana tells him about the latest gossip. Jaime runs ahead, kicking rocks as if they were soccer balls.

After Rusty drops them off, he stops by the bar—he keeps a few of his surfboards in the storeroom. It's the right size for a bar - not so big that if only a few customers are inside, it feels cavernous and lonely, but it's not cramped, either. On a good night, he'll have a hundred people packed in here. On a massive party night, he'll fill up the backyard—a sandy stretch with horseshoe pits and a volleyball court and an additional outdoor bar—and he'll have three times that.

Photos framed in bamboo grace the corrugated tin walls. Legendary parties. Him building the first bamboo bar—they're now on the third rendition. Wave after wave after wave. Participants in The Rusty Nail's annual Beer Olympics. In one corner, there's a photo of Rusty, James, and Bishop, taken on a timer right in front of the bush plane before Bishop hauled their gear to the cabin.

He doesn't often see that picture; he'd put it in the corner for a reason. But Señora Mendoza, the cleaning lady, had left a mop leaning against it when she finished work early this morning. As he reaches for the mop, he sees Bishop's smiling face, his own grin and James' scowl.

Standing there in a pair of board shorts, in his perfect bar, in his perfect life, his thoughts turn north, and he feels what he always feels when he thinks of his brother: sadness, curiosity, lingering animosity. The thoughts cast shadows over his contentment. He wonders how James is doing, if he's still alive. They haven't communicated in fourteen years. There's no way to do it, no way to send a letter, let alone an email.

He picks a surfboard from the rack in the storeroom—a six-foot twin-fin fish, pale yellow with bright red rails. Well-suited for a mellow day of well-shaped waves.

He locks up and heads out back. A small dirt bike with a board rack is parked outside. With care he straps his board onto the rack like a baby into a car seat and drives fifteen minutes north, to a break that old Aussie expats nicknamed "Deviled Eggs" for its oval-shape waves and its propensity to be spicier than expected. Now, locals just call it "Huevos," because that's what it requires when the swell gets heavy. Huevos. Cojones. Balls.

The surf school has a group or two out, but they're hanging on the inside, catching the whitewash. On the outside wave, Rusty recognizes a couple local surfers and Rozzo, an Aussie pro who frequents Santa Catalina and is a constant customer of The Rusty Nail when he's in town. The waves are shoulder- to head-high, with the occasional set coming in a couple feet overhead.

He paddles out, smiling at the surf school pupils.

"The first one to stand up gets a free beer at The Rusty Nail tonight," he shouts in English, then switches to Spanish to say hello to the surf instructors. He keeps paddling out toward the breaking waves. Rozzo rips by him on a peeling right, his face contorted in focus, as though what he's doing is the opposite of fun. He zooms out of the tubing wave, crouched like a kung fu master.

"Yew!" calls Rusty, shaking his head. For all his dedication, he'll never surf like that. Rozzo's been surfing just as long as Rusty has, but he's twenty years younger. If you don't start surfing as a kid, you'll just never get to that level. That's why Rusty's so pleased to see Jaime taking to surfing at a young age. In a few years, if he wants, the kid will start competing and doing well at that.

Rozzo paddles past on his way back to the lineup, grinning at Rusty.

"Mornin', barkeep."

Rusty watches as Rozzo catches another textbook wave. The off-duty surf coaches both snag waves before Rusty turns and paddles into a right himself. He doesn't do it with the same grace as Rozzo, but he stalls and tucks into a small barrel, crouched as a fanning spiral of turquoise shimmers above him, below him, all around him.

The crew remains small, and they trade waves through the morning. Catching his breath for a moment, Rusty bobs by himself beyond the cluster of surfers waiting for waves. He's too far out to sea to catch anything, yet still close enough to shore to feel the rise and fall of the swell as it begins to form into waves, catching on the reef beneath the surface, curling into cresting peaks.

The day is perfect. And for some reason, the perfection gnaws at him; it makes him feel guilty. He gets to go back to his beautiful wife and have lunch with her on the deck. Maybe he'll make love to her before the kids get home. Assuming Jaime finishes his homework, they'll go for an evening surf, leaving his bar in the hands of his capable staff. He can't believe the life he leads now. It's like karma has forgotten all about his past.

He sits on his board and looks north, up the jungle-cloaked coastline, and thinks of James, thousands of miles away, countries away—a lifetime away. Up there, all alone, in that cabin. Rusty imagines him turning into some sort of monster, a shadow of a man, a hunter closer to his dogs than to any other human. And it haunts him for the rest of the session.

He catches a last wave, a sloppy right that crumbles in front of his board, and rides it back to shore. He dries off and secures the board back onto his bike, unable to shake the feeling that he ought to somehow send word to his brother.

As predicted, Rusty goes home and makes love to his wife on the veranda, though he's admittedly distracted. They have a lunch of gallo pinto and fried fish—courtesy of Raúl, who often sends his regards along with the catch of the day. The kids come home from school, and he helps them finish their homework, just in time for a sunset surf.

Rusty sleeps less than usual that night. He tosses and turns, listening to the wind rushing through the open window and the rhythm of his wife's gentle breathing. When the clock reads 4 a.m., he pads out barefoot onto the dirt road. He walks and walks, but instead of going to the beach as usual, he heads inland, following an old cattle path that winds up the mountains. He should have grabbed a flashlight, but at least the moon is bright.

The sun lights up the Pacific just as he gets to the top of the hill. He's drenched in sweat, his tongue dry. He didn't think to bring water. He didn't know where he was going. He just wanted to clear his head. He stares at the ocean and watches the sunrise.

By the time he returns to the house, showers and makes coffee, his mind is made up. Victoria, yawning, enters the kitchen.

"Good morning, love," she says. "You surf already?"

"No," he says, handing her a cup. "I just went for a walk and got sweaty, so I took a shower."

They sip coffee as the jungle around them purrs and the insects and birds and monkeys start to stir.

"Baby," he says. "I have to tell you something."

The last time he said that was right before he asked her to marry him. When he told her about James, about the robbery, about Alaska.

When he told her about everything.

Well, almost everything.

She puts down her coffee. He can tell she's thinking the same thing.

"What is it, *mi cariño*?"

He pauses, sucks in a big breath, and then says, "I need to go to America."

She says nothing.

"I need to see my brother."

Still, she says nothing. Her almond eyes are dark brown twin comets, and right now he's doing all he can to resist their orbital tug. He wishes it were easy to just stay put, to forget about James, as he has for fifteen years, to let him gather dust, become a memory, nothing more. But to have such a beautiful life and to share none of it with his older brother, who might still be all alone in those desolate woods—it fills Rusty with shame.

That is, if James is even alive. And if he isn't alive, Rusty has to know. He needs closure.

"Why now?" she asks.

"I'm not sure. It's just, everything I have here is so perfect. I need to make sure he's doing okay. It's my duty, as his brother."

"I don't understand. After everything he did to you?"

And she doesn't know the half of it.

"Even so. Perhaps especially because of everything he did to me."

A pause. Finally, Victoria speaks. "I don't like this."

"I don't either. But I have to go."

"When we married, I gave you my word," she says. "That I would always support you. I support you now. But I ask one thing."

"Anything."

"Promise me you'll come back."

"I'll come back."

"Promise me."

Rusty imagined she'd blow up, put on a fireworks display, admonish him for his stupidity, tell him to be grateful for his blessings. But this calm, this acceptance, it requires unnerving strength. It makes him love her even more. It makes him want to stay.

"*Te lo prometo.*" I promise.

"Good," she says. "Is it safe? With your passport? What about the police?"

"They didn't flag me at the Mexican border. My passport's

expired, but I should be okay. I'll go to the consulate in Managua first." He takes her hand. "I'll come back."

"I know that," she says. She raises her hands and gestures to the jungle around their little bungalow. "How could you leave this behind?"

The question stings. But Rusty answers. She deserves an answer.

"He's my family. My blood. He's all I've got. I've got to go."

She smiles sadly and strokes his neck. "*Cariño*. You have me, too. And the kids. I am your blood. They are your blood. Never forget that."

"Never."

James hums as he harnesses the dogs to the sled.

He's off to check his trapline. He'll keep an eye out for signs of Richard, though at this point, James figures, the man is dead.

Too bad. He wanted to find Richard. He wanted revenge. He wanted to brand him with a red-hot poker, to break his legs with the back of a hatchet, to tie him up and drag him behind the sled, to starve the dogs then let them tear the man to shreds. But James didn't find him, despite scouring the range for weeks based on the Search and Rescue official's tips.

What a tease, to have Richard come so close.

As he's mindlessly tightening the straps, he hears the rare and worrisome drone of a helicopter. It grows louder and louder.

Maybe it's Search and Rescue, coming back to check.

Sorry, boys, my luck was as poor as yours.

The helicopter kicks up snow in the fierce rotor wash. James shoulders his gun. This is starting to feel like a routine. He ought to write "No Solicitors" in big letters on one side of the roof of his cabin. "Beware of Dogs" on the other.

Excited by the interruption, the dogs bark like mad.

"Hush now," says James gruffly.

But it's not a government chopper. It's a private bird—an old war relic, by the looks of it, probably the cheapest charter flight you can find.

The passenger gets out, but the pilot doesn't. The rotors don't even stop spinning.

He's a tall man, well built, athletic. That much James can tell, even through his brand-new puffy coat.

"What can I do for ya?" he yells off the porch.

At the sound of his voice, the tall man slings a small duffel bag over his shoulder and waves to the pilot to take off.

The rotor wash picks up again, the chopper takes off and disappears, and the man ambles toward James and the cabin.

James is furious. Who the hell does this man think he is? And why is he telling the pilot to fly off? There might be two beds in the cabin, but one of 'em has remained unused since—

And then he sees the man's face. He's tanner now, with a scruffy beard.

"Hey, James," says the man, standing an arm's length away. "It's been a while."

James says nothing. He can't believe his eyes.

He reconnects the wiring between his mouth and his brain, and a single gritty word spills out of his lips.

"Rusty."

Chapter 22

The shotgun is loaded, and Mel isn't afraid to use it. Two weasels collected from the trapline are swinging by their tails from her belt.

Mel, who once shirked her duties, has become the sole provider for their odd, two-person tribe.

Mel, who once haughtily voiced her vegetarianism, is now a hunter. In fact, her diet is entirely carnivorous, save for pine needle tea and bark fries.

Mel, who once showered daily, paid for pedicures weekly, and got her hair done by Leo, her overpriced Manhattan hairstylist, twice monthly, has become content with the occasional "bath"—a bucket of hot water and a rag.

With a grimy, trout-gut-stained finger, she flips back a matted lock of her hair that would cause Leo to curse in Italian and drink a bucket of Barbicide.

She chuckles, imagining what the meticulously manicured Leo would say if he could see her now.

Her old life is ancient history. The New Yorker Richard pulled from the lake has disappeared. In her place, as though the icy water contained some slow-acting potion, is a woman reborn.

She misses her family, but she's a daughter of Alaska now. Adopted by circumstance, baptized by a blizzard.

She knocks the slush from her boots. She steps into the warmth of the cabin and, with a sardonic tone, yells, "Honey! I'm home."

Hunched like an arthritic senior citizen, Richard busies himself at the stove.

It's good to see him up and walking again.

"Hello, darling," he says, going along with her shtick, draping a beaver pelt around his waist like an apron. "How was work?"

"Meh," she says, plopping the weasels down on the counter and picking her teeth with the tip of one of JP's old hunting knives.

"We'll sup well tonight," says Richard, clapping his hands.

"What are you doing out of bed?"

At this, Richard drops the act. He grimaces. "I couldn't stay in there anymore."

"The painkillers are almost gone. You've got to slow down."

"Ah," he says, smiling. "On that note, I've got a surprise for you." Reaching into the cabinet, Richard pulls out a dusty bottle.

"What is that?"

"Bourbon."

"Where did you find it?"

"The back of the very top shelf," says Richard, his eyes twinkling. "I was looking for spices, thinking maybe there might be salt and pepper stashed in one of those cupboards that we just missed, and in the back I found this, just sitting there, caked in dust."

Mel hasn't had a drink in months. Now she recalls the taste of Champagne. She remembers the Bloody Mary she had that morning before the snowmachine tour. And though she's long since decided that booze isn't something she needs in her life— dominating force it once was—the old, unmarked bourbon bottle fills her with anticipation.

If anything, she deserves a drink. A celebration of their survival, at the very least, is in order.

"I'm salivating," she says bluntly.

"Why don't I skin a weasel and you make us some whiskeys on the rocks?"

Momentarily distracted, Mel says, "We don't have any ice."

Richard, already reaching for the hunting knife, pauses and

stares at her playfully. "I think you can figure this one out."

"Ah," she says, remembering that their tiny cabin is surrounded by snow.

While a weasel cooks on the stove, they clink jars of bourbon. Her once-stalwart tolerance has been obliterated by time. After a single drink, a familiar warm glow returns to her. The bourbon is rich and smoky, probably expensive, definitely strong. They decide to drink slowly, just two shots apiece, maybe three, then pop the cork back in the bottle, save some for later. It's not as if they can just hop down to the liquor store and grab another bottle.

"I imagine he was saving it for a special occasion," says Mel.

"A big hunt," says Richard, smacking his lips in appreciation.

"Maybe. Or his birthday. Something like that. Can you imagine that? Spending your birthday here, all alone, just you and the dogs, year after year?"

At this, Richard splutters into his whiskey.

"What day is it?"

"I have no idea."

Richard puts down his bourbon. The jar clatters on the worn wood tabletop. Scowling at the pain, he gets to his feet.

"What are you doing?" Mel asks.

Richard doesn't answer, but shuffles to the corner of the cabin and consults the bundles of sticks leaning against the window.

"How many days are there in February?"

"Twenty-eight."

"This wasn't a leap year?"

"No, I don't think so."

"Then I believe it's March twentieth."

"So?" she says, sipping her bourbon. "You have work tomorrow or something?"

The warmth is like an old friend. Maybe alcohol does deserve a small place in her life after all.

"It's my birthday tomorrow."

She laughs and slaps the table. "Well, you found this bottle for a reason! Tonight we celebrate!"

"What about just having two drinks and calling it quits?" A grin forms on Richard's face, his unruly beard splitting in two.

"We didn't have any bourbon before tonight, and we were doing just fine. I reckon that if we don't have any bourbon tomorrow, it won't be the end of the world."

How much her vocabulary has changed, spun and shaped by the lathe of time and circumstance. Never would she have dared use the words "I reckon" in New York.

She doesn't mind it. In fact, she likes it.

"I'll go get us some ice," she says, pressing her hand into his shoulder. "I reckon."

Richard sits down at the table and spins the cork between his fingers.

"Tomorrow, I'll be forty-nine," he says to himself.

Two drinks turn into four. The fire crackles merrily in the stove. Their bellies are full of weasel meat and bourbon, and they take turns singing songs.

Richard sings a few Tom Petty tunes. Bruce Springsteen. His boozy baritone is imperfect but pleasant.

She sings late-eighties pop hits. Bon Jovi, Prince, Blondie. Her voice reminds Richard of the sound a weasel makes when its leg is caught in a steel trap. He says as much. She's not offended by the comparison but instead chokes on her drink.

The night grows long. Laughter fills the cabin, and the place feels like home. There are only two of them in attendance, but it's the best birthday party she's ever been to.

She goes out to take a piss. The moon is high. Squatting beneath the starry skies next to the pee tree, her urine cutting a mineshaft into the snow, her mind drunk and light and airy, she feels confidence growing in her chest. Maybe it's the moon. Maybe it's the pride of being a provider, a hunter-gatherer, of catching their dinner. Maybe it's the approximately six shots of bourbon.

When she returns inside, there's a snowball in her hands, with a pine twig sticking up from it like an unlit green fuse poking out of a white bomb. She holds it carefully, as though it might explode.

Richard sits on the musk ox hide by the fire, whiskey in hand.

"What do you think you're doing?" he asks.

"It's probably around midnight," she says.

"And?"

"That means it's your birthday."

At that, she lights the twig candle in the fire and begins to sing. Not jokingly, like when she did her horrible impressions of Bon Jovi and company. But sweetly, sincerely, softly, almost a whisper.

"Happy birthday, dear Richard," she sings, walking closer to him, proffering her snowy faux cake. "Happy birthday to you."

It's her best impression of Marilyn Monroe.

Richard doesn't laugh. He leans forward, taking a second to think of a wish.

Their wishes probably aren't the same at that moment. Richard probably wants to go home. She's not sure if she wants that anymore.

He blows out the candle and looks up, grinning.

"Thanks, Me—"

But at that point, she's already there, shushing him quiet, her hands cupping his beard, her lips finding his.

She didn't know what to expect. Maybe that she'd wake up to him asking for a second helping. It had, after all, been a long time coming. Months of tension, all bottled up, finally uncorked with the help of a bourbon bottle.

But when the chirping birds, with no regard for her hangover, wake her up and she reaches for him, all she gets is a handful of musk ox fur. She opens her eyes. Richard is gone.

She tries to fall back asleep but can't.

She curses the birds and gets out of bed. Naked, she tends to the fire. It's nice to walk around in the nude again.

A grin accompanies the hangover that throbs at her temples. She can't believe it finally happened. But for some reason she's nervous, too—nervous that Richard might be out for a walk, cursing himself for being weak. Nervous that he'll blame the booze and it won't happen again. Nervous that it doesn't mean to him what it means to her. Nervous that she's right for being nervous.

The fire crackles. She picks up the bottle and shakes it. About a quarter remains.

She makes herself breakfast, sipping tea as the hangover slowly relinquishes its hold on her mind. When Richard still hasn't returned an hour later, she throws on her coat, wraps a beaver pelt around her neck like a scarf, and tromps out to the lake.

It's as if the sun got laid for the first time in a while, too. Bright as fire, it illuminates the snow, slashing diagonal shafts of light through the pine trees.

She takes the tent pole to probe for the snowmachine, if only to have something to do. The rhythm of it—placing the spike into the snow, pushing it hand-over-hand through the layers of the snowpack, feeling the tip smack into the ice, retrieving the pole, doing it all over again—helps her think.

She replays the night's events in her head.

Her fingers gripping the musk ox hide.

She pushes the spike into the snow, down to the ice, and retrieves it.

The cot creaking, Richard's panting.

Again she pushes the spike into the snow, down to the ice, and retrieves it.

A long-awaited duet played by firelight. So much sweat that afterward they stood out in the cold night, wearing nothing but each other, looking up at the stars as they cooled off, passing the bottle back and forth.

She pushes the spike into the snow, down to the ice, and retrieves it.

She's never been much of a cuddler, but they fell asleep entwined on the small cot. The sex was good—great, even. She expected that. What she can't believe is that they shared the cot. That, drunk or not, she slept through such close contact.

Again she pushes the spike into the snow.

The last thing she expects to hear is the *thunk* of metal on plastic. Like a pirate's shovel striking a buried trunk, though, the tip of her tent pole stops several feet above the ice.

She freezes, shocked from her reverie, as if she'd been asleep and was suddenly doused with a bucket of ice water.

This has to be it. She's found it. The snowmachine.

She double-checks to make sure, yanking up the pole, taking a deep breath, then probing again.

The second strike doesn't *thunk* this time—but it stops short. She's hit the cushioned seat.

It's less than two feet below the surface.

Oblivious to the cold on her ungloved hands, she scrapes through the slush, exposing a sliver of red plastic, a corsair catching the shimmer of a treasure long thought lost.

Mel looks around and takes her bearings. Richard must have probed this exact spot half a dozen times or more. Maybe the snow just needed to melt a little bit? Maybe he'd struck it when the ice level was higher and didn't realize it?

However he'd missed it, she's found it now. The question is, what to do?

It would be easy to dig out. She could do it herself. She could surprise Richard.

They could be home tomorrow.

Had she struck the snowmachine a month ago, even a week ago, the answer to that question would have been simple: Dig the thing out and get the hell out of there.

She leaves the tent pole sticking straight up from the snowmachine. Then, from a tree on the side of the lake, she breaks off a small branch and replaces the pole with the branch, so it looks as if a small tree is blossoming from white earth.

She folds up the tent pole and makes her way back to the cabin.

Richard returns a couple hours later.

"Good morning, birthday boy," she says. "Or should I say good afternoon. Where have you been?"

Richard hangs up his coat.

"Mel," he says, and turns toward her, wringing his hands. "About last night."

"Don't say it," she says, reading his body language.

He takes a step closer. "It can't happen again."

"Don't you want it to?"

"Of course I do. You're incredible. You're young, gorgeous. But my wife—"

"Your wife isn't here." Mel's voice is tinged with anger. "Your wife probably thinks you're dead. She's probably out there dating someone already."

Richard's voice turns cold. "Careful, Mel."

"Or what?"

Richard sighs and begins to remove his boots.

"It was the booze, Mel. I shouldn't have drunk so much."

"Oh, bullshit," she says, suddenly feeling disdain cloud her fondness for him. "It wasn't the booze. The booze is an excuse, that's all, something for you to use in an apology if you have to. But tell me the truth—you wanted this just as much as I did, right?"

A pained expression flashes across Richard's face. Then a look of stout resolution.

"It was the booze, Mel."

She grabs the bottle and hurls it at him. He catches it, surprise etched on his face.

"Well, there's a few shots left," she says, putting on her own boots. "In case you need another excuse."

He was just like the rest of them.

Without knowing exactly what she's doing, as if someone else is steering her body, her eyes blurred with tears, she walks toward the lake again.

There's a shovel in her hand.

It's time to get out of here.

To get off this godforsaken desert island.

She's angry. She feels taken advantage of. But it's different from all of the times she's been taken advantage of before. Different because she cares for him? Or different because the new Mel, the reborn Mel, doesn't take any shit?

She sees the branch that she'd placed earlier that morning. It may as well be a lighthouse, steering her ship to harbor.

But he chases after her.

"Mel!" She hears him yell. But she doesn't stop. She doesn't want to hear it.

The sun is high now. She's up to her knees in the snow, sweating profusely with the effort of wallowing through the slush. A drip of sweat trickles down her forehead, joining a tear on her cheek, the confluence of two rivers.

But still she doesn't stop.

"Mel! Wait!"

He catches up to her. His height seems amplified since he's on snowshoes, standing on top of the snow while she sinks into it.

He eclipses the sun for a moment, a wooly silhouette. She tries to step around him, but she can't move fast enough in the slush.

"Would you just wait a second!" he yells, gripping his back. "I can barely move."

"You're fifty now," she spits. "An old man."

"Forty-nine. But I concede your point."

"Would you please get out of my way? I have places to go."

"Where are you going? To dig me a grave?"

"If you must know—"

"Look, Mel." Richard gets down on one knee so he's at eye level with her. The sun glares into her eyes, and she squints.

It would be easy to take the shovel and crack him across the face with it.

"I'm no good at this," he says quietly. "You can ask my wife. I was no good at this twenty years ago, and I certainly haven't gotten any better with a lack of practice."

He sighs deeply and looks at the trees, the mountains, anywhere but at her.

"Do you remember when you dug me out of the avalanche?" he asks.

She doesn't answer. He's stalling. She isn't going to give him the luxury.

"I don't know how to do this. I've never—I've never cheated on my wife before."

She starts to speak, to say that it's not cheating, that the circumstances have changed, that his wife probably thinks he's dead, that soldiers in war, thinking they might die any day and never return to see their wives and families, often take new lovers the night before a battle.

But he keeps going. A flow of words. As if, should he stop, he'd never be brave enough to speak them again.

"I love my wife. You know that. I love my children. I'm not sure how to put this. But I care for you, too. Deeply. You've become more than a friend to me. And I lied to you. Last night wasn't the alcohol talking. You were right. The bourbon was an excuse, if anything. I'm a man trapped with a beautiful woman in a cabin in the middle of the woods. You think I haven't thought of that? You think I haven't seen you? That I haven't wanted you?"

At this, he laughs.

"No. A blind man would notice you. You make me feel young. I've wanted you since we met."

"When I was passed out and naked in a sleeping bag? Creep."

"No, no, not since we met. But shortly after you smashed that ptarmigan against a tree."

He pauses, searching for words. The shovel is heavy in her hand. Tell him about the snowmachine. Tell him now. But she can't find the words.

"And if we do get out of here, I'll have to explain my behavior to my wife. I won't think of it as infidelity. At least for now, I can't.

I guess I have to think of this as a parallel world. A world where all that exists is you and I and this cabin."

He leans forward now, taking her free hand in his.

"I went for a walk this morning. A long walk, despite my freshly tweaked back—thanks for that, by the way. I told myself what I had to do, resolved myself to it. But in the back of my mind, I knew that what I had to do, or what I thought I had to do, wasn't what I wanted. Does that make sense?"

He doesn't stop long enough for her to answer.

"I guess what I'm trying to say is that when you threw that bottle at me and stormed out, I realized I couldn't handle this without you. And after last night, which meant more to me than I think you know, it would be impossible to return to a previous version of ourselves."

He takes another deep breath.

"Holy shit, I'm not very articulate at this."

Finally, she responds flatly, "You're doing great."

"Thanks," he laughs. "What I'm trying to say is that I want this. I want you. I'm not sure what that means, I'm not sure how I'll remedy that if we ever get out of here. But I'm sure that I want you."

"You're sure it isn't just the whiskey?"

He laughs again. "I'm sure. I'm sorry I said that." He pauses. "Can I kiss you now?"

She thinks it over, considering briefly denying his request, then drops the shovel as if it were cursed. And for the second time, she's shushing him, her hands cupping his face, her lips finding his.

When they come up for air, she says, "I feel sorry for you."

"Why's that?"

"Your poor back," she says. "It'll never be the same."

They walk back toward the cabin, leaving the shovel forgotten, half-buried in the slushy snow, just steps away from the buried snowmobile.

Their ticket home.

Chapter 23

Rusty left Alaska running like something was chasing him. He swore he'd never return. But here he is, at the edge of the river that runs through his nightmares, second-guessing his decision to leave paradise, standing face-to-face with his brother.

Rusty's breath crystalizes in hot, ephemeral clouds. The whir of helicopter blades fades into the distance, and they trigger a memory - Bishop's bush plane, careening off the cliff. He shivers, despite the wool beanie and puffy jacket he just bought in Anchorage. He misses his wife, his kids, his little slice of heaven down south where the weather is warm. Where you don't need to fly in by bush plane or helicopter, where you can grab a beer while barefoot, where you don't need to live with steel-edged grit, where life isn't kill or be killed. Where you can just be, and that's enough.

The sun dips over the range, tinging peaks pink and purple with alpenglow. Alaska has some things going for it, but not enough for him to want to stay a second longer.

Rusty looks his brother in the eye.

Tomorrow, he'll make right the evil that keeps him up at night. The one misdeed he'd kept from his wife.

"Rusty," says James, his mouth agape.

"Hello, James," says Rusty. "It's good to see you."

"What the fuck are you doing here?" asks James, not unkindly.

Rusty laughs and claps a hand on his brother's shoulder, careful not to touch the rifle. He has no desire to touch a gun ever again.

"Is that how you greet me after fifteen years?"

"You're—" says James, trying to overcome the shock. "So tan."

Rusty laughs even harder. "And you look like you haven't shaved since I left."

James, as if remembering his manners, says, "C'mon in. I've got some moose loin I've been saving for a special occasion."

Rusty groans. "You dog. If there's one thing I miss about this place, it's the game. We've got nothing like fresh moose loin down in Nicaragua."

"Nicaragua!"

Rusty shoulders his duffel bag. "There's much to tell. But fear not, I brought whiskey."

As the whiskey pours, so do the stories.

Rusty tells of his exodus from Alaska. Of his days in Mexico, of partying his way to rock bottom, of falling in love with surfing. Of wild whores in the cities and wild waves on the coast. Of staying with coffee farmers in Guatemala, falling in love with Nicaragua, falling in love with his wife, starting a family, building a bar, making a life.

James, in turn, tells of the dogs, how he learned to train them, how he became their master. Of hunting moose, of shooting a grizzly that was so close he could feel its rancid breath, of books he's read, of repairs to the cabin he's done, of visits to town. And always, back to the dogs—who they are, how they behave, their personalities, their positions in the pack.

Some dogs sit quietly by the fire, others loll in their kennels. The brothers drink and eat and talk late into the night. And for a minute Rusty thinks his brother has changed, that he might convince him to leave this dump, to meet his niece and nephew and sister-in-law.

He's wrong.

Rusty takes a sip of his whiskey, swirls it around in his mouth, swallows, and sighs, gathering the courage to speak.

As if sensing that his brother is about to tell him something significant, James leans back in his chair. Rusty feels his brother's eyes narrow on him. Without saying a word, the night goes from lovely to uncomfortable. Then James speaks with such a coolness that, despite the roaring fire, the temperature drops well below freezing.

"Why are you here?" asks James, his voice raspy, quiet but cutting, like steel dragging across a whetstone. He hasn't talked this much in years.

Rusty raises his eyes, meeting his brother's cold, questioning gaze.

"Speak," says James. "I haven't seen you in fifteen years, but I can tell when you're holding back."

"Well," says Rusty. There was no use beating around the bush. "I suppose I came for three reasons."

"Number one?"

"To make sure you're alive."

"Check. Number two?"

"I want you to come to Nicaragua. To meet my family. We've got a little guest cabana in the back. It's simple but nice. Nicer than this," he gestures around the dark cabin, hoping that his brother doesn't take offense. "And warmer, too. You wouldn't believe it. No more bearskin rugs or beaver pelt coats. Just board shorts and sunscreen. I'll even teach you to surf."

James doesn't say anything. So Rusty keeps on.

"You've been here a long time. But you don't need to worry about the cops or anything. I've looked into it. The case has no suspects. I went to the embassy and got a new passport and never got flagged. We're in the clear."

"I'll never leave Alaska," says James quietly. "And it's not because of the cops."

This time, it's Rusty's turn to stay silent.

"This place has been good to me," said James. "In ways you cannot imagine. It sounds like in Nicaragua, you've found peace and purpose. Yes?" Rusty nods. Looking into the fire, James continues. "I have these dogs, this pack, this cabin. And these endless mountains, in which I can exist for days without saying a word, months without seeing a soul. It's religion, meditation. It's… peace and quiet."

He gets frustrated, unable to articulate exactly what he means, and smashes his metal cup down onto the wooden arm of his chair, denting the thick tin as if it were a beer can.

He fingers the dent with a calloused thumb.

"It's an old-fashioned life. I don't use the internet. I have no idea what's going on in the world. I'm disconnected. I live under a rock, some might say, but I don't reckon I'd rather be anywhere else."

Finally, Rusty speaks. "So, you're content to stay here and watch the world spin?"

James chuckles. "You don't get it. I don't watch the world spin. I'm only aware of the world's spinning due to the seasons, the rise and fall of the sun, the falling of snow, the melting of snow, the blooming of flowers. The birds that come and wake me up, the bear tracks that suddenly appear in the mud. I'm not an observer anymore," he says, pleased with the direction of his monologue. "I'm a participant."

Rusty finds himself nodding. It actually makes sense. Strangely, his brother's Alaskan existence parallels his own connection between self and surf. Maybe the Connelly brothers weren't meant for cities. They'd been brought up in one of the world's biggest, but Rusty wonders how they would have turned out if they'd had a different upbringing, if instead of being raised in the slums, they'd grown up in the fresh air.

"And the third reason?"

This is the trickiest of them all.

"I want to go to Jean Pierre's cabin."

James' back stiffens. Before he can ask why, Rusty looks into the grate of the fireplace, at the dancing tongues of hypnotic orange.

"I want to ask for forgiveness."

Killing Bishop, Rusty always thought, was an idiotic move.

"How the fuck are we going to get out of here?" he asked James as he stirred yet another depressing pot of oatmeal for breakfast. The sugar was nearly gone after James had spilled a few cups, drunk and high, trying to fix himself a batch of pancakes for dessert one evening, and they'd been rationing accordingly.

The sun was shining—a nice change from the depths of winter, when they woke in darkness, went to sleep in darkness, spent most of their waking hours in darkness. They'd read through the books. Rusty had whittled enough spoons to outfit a soup kitchen. He was sick of the cabin, sick of his brother, and there was no way out thanks to James. The sun, pleasant as it was, happened to be the source of his woes.

He jabbed the wooden spoon he was holding at the window above the sink. "Would you look at that? The icicles are melting. You remember what Bishop said? When the snow starts to melt, you can't land a ski plane here. Not that anyone's coming."

James oiled his rifle by the fire. He was becoming a better shot and often went hunting for multiple days at a time. It seemed to give him a pride that Rusty didn't get at all.

"You can land one of the planes with the big rubber tires."

"Oh, yeah," said Rusty, laughing spitefully. "And how are you going to book us a flight?"

James sighted down the barrel of the rifle and spoke with a vexing authority.

"We don't need a plane. We'll go to the Frenchman's house. The one with the dogsled team. We'll ask him for a lift. Then we'll resupply, get all the things we need for summer, and come back."

Rusty was silent, fuming over the oatmeal. It was starting to burn and stick to the bottom of the pot. He chiseled at the glop, cursing this godforsaken place, knowing that if they ever did get back to civilization, he would never come back.

The hike to Jean Pierre's cabin took two days. At night, Rusty was supposed to keep watch for wolves, but he fell asleep with the rifle on his lap and woke up to James' boot driving into his ribs.

They found a set of sled tracks and paw prints and followed

them south, remembering the flash of roof they'd seen from Bishop's plane, the scratch of Bishop's voice through the headset.

"He's a long walk southwest from my cabin if you follow the river—twenty-five miles or so, down on a little pond there, right where it meets the Hope—if you need to borrow a cup of sugar."

They heard the dogs barking before they saw the cabin.

Rusty had never heard anything like it; it was a savage, orchestral sound, each dog with its own tone and pitch, melting over one another like the sounds of a city. It made him skittish. He slowed down, but James pressed on, calling over his shoulder, "Don't be such a pussy."

"What if those dogs attack us?"

"I've got a gun."

"What if he's got a gun?"

"It's Alaska," said James before he disappeared into the trees. "Everyone's got a gun."

Sure enough, Jean Pierre sat smoking a pipe on the porch, a shotgun across his knees, six or seven dogs at his feet.

When he saw the brothers approach, slowly stamping through the woods and into the clearing, he stood up, raising an arm in greeting. James and Rusty mimicked the gesture, and the Frenchman slowly walked down the steps to greet them.

He wore a pair of leather pants, obviously homemade, that reminded Rusty of Bishop's jacket. A heavy woolen sweater completed the ensemble, with leather suspenders that kept the leather pants from falling down. JP was younger than Bishop, but old nonetheless. Gray hairs threatened to overtake the black that remained in his long locks, which he'd tied back into a rough braid. His beard and mustache were the same, more salt than pepper, and they likely hadn't been trimmed in nearly a decade. The mustache, at least, was neatly combed off his upper lip. Unruly eyebrows, scraggly as blackberry brambles, cast shadows over eyes that, as they got closer, Rusty realized were clear blue, like the ocean. All things considered, the man looked like a cross between a classic

Alaskan pioneer and a French corsair. As the brothers approached, the Frenchman spoke in his mother tongue.

"*Mon nom est Jean Pierre, appelle-moi JP. Qui es-tu et que fais-tu ici?*"

The brothers were silent, unsure of how to proceed. Rusty took the opportunity to cast his brother's plan into the dirt.

"Didn't think about this, huh?" he whispered, "That he only speaks French."

"Would you shut your goddamn mouth?"

"Gentlemen," said Jean Pierre. "I speak English as well."

"Ah," said James, surprised. In English, the Frenchman's flamboyant, aristocratic air was even more evident.

"Ah, indeed," said Jean Pierre, smiling broadly. "I have lived in America for much of the past decade, and in England before that. I have learned to speak the language to the best of my abilities."

It was odd to hear such speech so far from civilization, especially, Rusty realized, after five months without so much as speaking to a stranger. The shock, it seemed, made "Ah..." all the brothers could muster.

Noticing their confusion, Jean Pierre continued.

"What I said in my first language, dear boys, is that my name is Jean Pierre. Call me JP. Who are you and what are you doing here? The fact is, it isn't exactly common to have visitors here, at least not without the buzz of bush planes first, which I did not happen to hear as you approached. I must admit, I do prefer my dogs to those dreadful machines."

He looked fondly at his dogs, who, realizing the strangers were not a threat, had ceased barking and lay back on the porch.

"We're your new neighbors," said James, extending a hand. "I'm—Stephen, this is my brother—"

Before James could finish, Rusty chimed in. "Rusty Connelly, from Queens, New York." He gave a sideways look to James, who clearly wasn't pleased that he'd used his real name. "Nice to meet you."

The Frenchman beamed and shook both their hands. Despite his life of seclusion in the woods, the Frenchman tended to his hands with a lavender ointment every night before bed, and though well calloused, they were fragrant and supple. "New neighbors, my, my, how exciting. Whereabouts are you located?"

"Twenty-five miles up the river," said Rusty. "We're renting Bishop's place for the winter."

"Ah, Bishop, speaking of dreadful machines! That scalawag of a bush pilot! Any friend of Bishop's is a friend of mine. Quite a hike you boys have been on. Come in, come in, let's have a drink. Tea? Whiskey?"

"Whiskey would be great," said James. "And I'm not sure if you have hot food to spare, but we just walked a long ways."

Jean Pierre laughed and ushered them up the stairs and into the cabin.

"What kind of host would I be if I didn't feed my tired guests? Here, take off your boots, sit down, make yourselves at home. Pardon the mess, we weren't exactly expecting company."

He winked and poured three whiskeys.

The brothers removed their boots, accepted the drinks, and took their bearings. The cabin was tidy and well maintained, despite the dogs.

Jean Pierre raised his glass and said, "To Bishop, my favorite and only neighbor, and his new tenants."

James grinned and said, "To Bishop," before downing his drink.

Rusty said nothing but tipped it back all the same.

James took the words out of his mouth.

"That's some fine whiskey, sir!"

JP nodded, winked, and poured another round.

"A friend of ours distills this outside of Glacier Point. Bishop brings it to me by the crate." He gestured to an open cabinet high above the kitchen countertop, which was completely full of label-less whiskey bottles, all with corks sealed in black wax. "He makes moonshine, too, but it's too stiff for my liking."

"We've tried it," said Rusty, smiling sadly at the memories.

"Bishop always prefers it. How is that old man, after all?" said Jean Pierre.

Rusty opened his mouth, but James stepped sharply on his toe under the table.

"Well, Jean Pierre, to be honest, that's why we're here," said James. "Bishop was supposed to come back and get us about a week ago for a resupply and a visit to civilization. We're all out of a few things, whiskey included."

"A predicament no pioneer should ever face," said Jean Pierre. "You're welcome to take a couple bottles from my supply, but I assume you didn't hike twenty-five miles for a liquor run."

"No, sir," said James. "We were worried about Bishop. Punctuality isn't his strong suit, but it's unlike him to be a week late. We were hoping we could get a lift with you back to civilization before the snow melts."

At this, Jean Pierre glanced out the window.

"Yes, the snowline is starting to recede," he said. "I've likely got only a few more weeks where that trip is in the cards for me. I've actually been planning my own resupply trip for next week."

He nodded at a stack of crates, boxes, and burlap sacks stacked in the corner of the cabin.

"I was planning on taking six dogs," he mused. "But if I take ten, and leave a box or two behind, I should be able to bring you both to town."

"That would be amazing," gushed James.

"Thank you," said Rusty. "Sincerely."

"Don't mention it. Now, why don't we have a couple of drinks? I just took down a Dall sheep, got the start of a stew brewing. You boys can sleep here tonight, and tomorrow I'll bring you back to Bishop's. In, let's say, four days, I'll come to get you, and we'll make the trip back to civilization."

"That sounds perfect," said James, trying to keep the glee out of his voice. "Thank you again."

"Now that the pleasantries are behind us, let's drink! It's not often I get to practice my English. These damn dogs only speak French!"

Hungover and full after a breakfast of sheep stew and hash browns, the brothers got a ride back to Bishop's cabin with Jean Pierre.

James observed carefully as JP harnessed the dogs, and asked several questions about pulling capacity, distance, how much the dogs needed to be fed.

Jean Pierre gladly answered all of his questions.

"You certainly are curious," he noted, amused.

"As my brother said, we're from New York. We've never met a dogsledder before."

The four days passed slowly, but Jean Pierre came on time. Rusty packed everything he might need, though he left most of his belongings. He wanted James to think he'd be returning to the cabin. As Rusty was loading up the sled, tying his bag securely to JP's neatly organized bundle of boxes and thanking God that they had a way out, he heard the sound of a gunshot and shattering glass.

Rusty dropped the half-lashed bag into the snow and ran to the cabin. The dogs tied to the sled groaned and whined and barked, clear that something wasn't right. As soon as he heard the shot, he expected to find James looking down the barrel at the dead Frenchman. But instead, Rusty charged into the cabin only to find the two men grappling on the floor. There was a bullet hole through the window. JP cursed in French while James wrestled him with a frenzied look on his face.

"Rusty!" he grunted.

Rusty froze. He didn't know how to react. Dogs were barking furiously. The rifle was at his feet.

"Pick up the gun, you dumb motherfucker!"

Rusty picked it up and with quivering hands pointed it at the tangle of limbs below him. For a second, he aimed at his own wild-eyed brother, then shifted it slowly to aim at JP. The Frenchman looked up at the barrel, stopped wrestling, and lay back on the floor. Breathing heavily, he scooted back against the kitchen cabinet, wiped at his cut forehead, then checked his fingers for blood.

"Why are you doing this?" he asked.

"This wasn't my idea," said Rusty.

"No, it was mine," said James, standing up. "I thought I might have to kill you when my idiot brother here used his real name. The fact that you have a way out, with these dogs of yours, well, that was just more reason to do it."

Rusty's hands were shaking.

JP looked up into his eyes. "My son, you don't need to—"

James scoffed, "Oh, save it, you French fuck. We've got to do you, same as we had to do Bish—"

"We didn't have to do Bishop!" yelled Rusty. He turned and once again pointed the gun at his brother.

"You killed Bishop? *Merde.*"

The Frenchman crossed himself. Blood dribbled into his eyes. Rusty ignored him, indignant with anger.

"And *we* didn't do Bishop. *You* did Bishop."

It was the last thing he said to James for fifteen years.

James' eyes narrowed. "You shouldn't have said your name, Rusty. I know you did it to make me mad. But you sealed his fate. And yours."

He looked past the barrel, into Rusty's eyes.

Rusty might've been taller, but he was no match for James in a manic state. Like a snake charmer, James reached out a hand, grabbed the barrel of the rifle, and swung it back toward JP.

"This is your responsibility now," said James, speaking quietly into his brother's ear.

Rusty could barely see. Tears filled his eyes. The dusty, dark cabin felt like a prison. There was movement from the ground as the Frenchman tried to stand up and run. The action spurred a reaction, and Rusty's finger squeezed the trigger. He barely aimed, but that close, he couldn't miss. Blood spattered across his face, and he dropped the gun.

"I want to ask forgiveness," says Rusty. He looks up at his brother, the man who'd made him a murderer.

I want to ask forgiveness, he thinks to himself. Because time, though it helps, doesn't heal all.

Chapter 24

Richard lies on his back, the splintery wood rough on his bare skin. He grabs his knees and tucks into a tight ball, like a gymnast or a diver. Grunting, he rocks back and forth. Feeling more like a beetle unable to flip onto its stomach than any sort of aerial acrobat, he rolls against the creaky floorboards. After a while, the repetitive movement begins to untie tangled knots of muscle along his spine.

It's painful, but it's progress.

From his contorted position, he studies the punctures and perforations that decorate his threadbare boxer briefs to distract himself from the tightness. Like the bundle of notched sticks in the corner of the cabin, his mangy skivvies tell time. It's been more than four months since the crash. Luckily, given his current arrangement with Mel, the larger exhibitory holes don't expose anything she hasn't already intimately encountered.

The pain in his back is duller these days—no longer does he feel screws twisting between his vertebrae with every step. Still, he has to take it easy. A simple action like opening a cabinet or skinning a rabbit—let alone tending to Mel's youthful libido—can cause him to buckle with spasms.

His snow pants hang to dry above the fire, as do his long underwear, which are worse off than his boxers. Pretty soon, it will get so warm that he'll have to resort to wearing his long underwear when he's out hunting and trapping. If they still aren't rescued by summer, he'll cut off the legs and turn them into Daisy Dukes. What a sight that will be.

Outside, like the beasts and the birds, the mountains are ruffling their feathers, poking their heads out, tasting spring on the air. Southerly aspects are in the midst of their shedding cycle. With the sun rising higher each day, water permeates the snowpack, weakening bonded layers, and wet avalanches sweep down steep bowls and gullies, exposing the dark rock and dirt below. Southerly faces at lower altitudes are likely already patchy and impassable. Even with a working snowmachine, exiting the valley would probably be feasible only by hugging the shaded northerly areas—and how long that shaded snow will stay, he doesn't know. By Richard's estimation, without a fresh storm they'll be trapped within weeks, maybe less.

But perhaps due to the plethora of food at their disposal, or his newfound footing with Mel, or his indignation that a rescue team has yet to bring them home, or the fact that in the eyes of the world he's likely nothing but a frozen corpse, escape no longer seems a primary concern. When his thoughts wander toward the real-world repercussions of the spring shedding cycle, Richard feels the philosophical equivalent of a shrug.

Is this a strong man coming to accept the hand he's been dealt? Or a weak man lost between the legs of a younger woman? Richard doesn't know. Bothered that he isn't more bothered by the coming of spring, he grunts and rolls more vigorously, when there's a knock on the door.

Richard laughs. Never tiring of Mel's sense of humor, he plays along.

Still stretching, he shouts, "C'mon in."

The door creaks open. Two men stand in the doorway. Richard can't make out their faces—they're backlit silhouettes against the sunlight—but one is tall, the other shorter, both broad-shouldered.

"Hello," says the taller one, somewhat awkwardly.

Dumbfounded, Richard leaps to his feet, ignoring the shooting pain in his back. Suddenly embarrassed by his paltry attire and unsure of what to say, he simply stands there, his hands shielding what his fishnet boxers don't.

"We're sorry to bother you," says the taller man quickly. "Why don't you let us know once you've dressed?"

The stranger shuts the door. Richard rushes to put on his still-damp snow pants.

Who are these people? What are they doing here? How did they arrive without a helicopter?

The last question is answered after Richard throws on his shirt, shoves his bare feet into his boots, and steps outside. The sun is high and bright, and after Richard's eyes adjust to the light he makes out a dogsled parked at the edge of the forest. Not for a second does he guess the truth: that these Chinooks and huskies are descendants of Jean Pierre's own team, the dogs Mel has read so much about. His only thought is that their prayers—the prayers he was just contemplating, the prayers that have been lacking in recent weeks—have been belatedly answered.

The taller man stands on the porch, looking out over the mountains, his fingers drumming the railing. A small duffel bag is slung over his shoulder. He's wearing a seemingly brand-new puffy jacket, unzipped, and when he turns to Richard it's clear he's not broad-shouldered at all. Rather, he's wiry and lean, like a runner. Tattoos creep up his neck like ivy tendrils on a trellis, and his face is tanned, a shock of hair bleached blonde by the sun. Richard can't help but think that he's out of place, more suited to the beach volleyball courts of California than the wilderness of Alaska. On the other hand, his companion, yet to say a word, looks like a born-and-raised frontiersman. Built like a badger, he leans silently against the railing, a hand-stitched fur cap matching his coat. His hands, presumably well-versed in manual labor, stroke at an otherwise unkempt beard. A hint of a grin plays on his lips.

"Howdy," says Richard, unsure of what to say. He offers his hand to the taller stranger first. "I didn't expect any visitors—my, uh, girlfriend is out checking the trapline."

Girlfriend. How strange. He hasn't uttered that word, at least not about his own relationships, in years.

"No problem," says the stranger, shaking Richard's hand. Ropy veins twist up his thin yet powerful forearms. A quick smile forms in the corners of his mouth. "We didn't mean to sneak up on you. I can imagine there's not too much traffic around these parts."

"Less than you might think," says Richard.

"I'm Rusty."

"Richard."

"This here is my brother," says Rusty.

Richard turns to the shorter man, who grips his proffered hand tightly and smiles broadly, exposing yellowed teeth.

"James," the man says, his green eyes twinkling. "Delighted. Absolutely delighted."

"My pleasure," says Richard.

"You must be wondering why we're here," says Rusty.

"You're not wrong," says Richard. "Are you two all right? Are you lost? Do you need food?"

"No, no, nothing like that," says Rusty. "We've got plenty of food on the sled. We only came to see the cabin."

"It's not my cabin—long story—but it sounds like you might know that. Can I get you some tea? I'm afraid all we drink is snow melt or pine needle tea."

At this, Rusty scoffs. "Pine needle tea! And I thought we were desperate back in the day. We've got coffee." He pats his duffle bag. "Mind if we brew some up? Dogsled travel just isn't my cup of tea. Or coffee, as it were. And I'm jet-lagged like a motherfucker."

Richard grins. "There's a hot kettle on the stove already, and I haven't had a cup of coffee in approximately four months and five days. I wouldn't mind at all," he says. "Please, come in, make yourselves at home."

The brothers follow him inside. The cabin is dim, and it takes a moment for their eyes to adjust. Richard busies himself in the kitchen, hunting for a few clean baked bean cans.

James whistles. "It's been a while since we've been here, eh Rust?"

Rusty shoots his brother a furtive look but otherwise ignores the jibe. "Thank you for the hospitality. We didn't mean to barge in. Didn't think anyone would be here, to be honest."

"It's no problem. Thank you for bringing coffee. Although I've just realized," says Richard, cans in hand, "I don't have a coffee filter."

"Nor do I," says Rusty, "but this should do."

He withdraws a bandana from the duffle, then pulls it taut over a tin can and shakes a generous mountain of coffee on top.

Richard collects the kettle and pours hot water over the coffee. The aroma makes him salivate and nearly brings tears to his eyes.

"You have no idea," he says as Rusty scoops out another helping of coffee onto the bandana and readies a second mug, "how good that smells to me right now."

Rusty chuckles. "It's from the town I live in, Santa Catalina, in Nicaragua."

"You were too tan for Alaska."

"I lived here once," says Rusty, almost ruefully. "A long, long time ago."

"We used to be roommates," says James, as he accepts a tin can with a curt nod. "Thicker than thieves."

"What brings you back to Alaska?" asks Richard, grimacing as he lowers himself onto the cot. "Forgive me, I need to sit myself, my back is killing me. Please, take a seat."

At Richard's behest, Rusty takes the chair. James opts to stand, and eyes Richard curiously over the steam spiraling up from his coffee.

"I came to visit my brother," says Rusty.

"I live just south of here, about twenty-five miles down the Hope," says James. "The journey takes half a day with the sled dogs. A day, maybe two if you're walking, depending on the snow."

"Did you know Jean Pierre?" asks Richard.

"We didn't know him well, but he was our neighbor," says Rusty, blowing on his coffee to cool it. He takes a sip, winces, and places the can back down on the table. "But that's the reason why we came to the cabin, to pay our respects to Jean Pierre."

"So, he's dead then?"

Rusty nods, exhaling deeply. "He is."

Richard leans forward, intrigued. "How do you know? We found his journal, and it just cuts off one day as if, poof, he disappeared."

"I know," says Rusty, shifting in his chair. Then, with a forced smile: "Look around," he gestures to the tiny cabin, the crackling stove, the mountains beyond. "Who would leave this place willingly?"

"You might," says James, chuckling. "But not Jean Pierre. He was a real mountain man."

Again, Richard misses the look Rusty shoots his brother—his focus is locked on the piping hot brew. "This is much better than pine needle tea," he says.

Rusty laughs, "I can imagine. May I ask how you ended up here?"

Richard takes another sip of coffee. But before he can tell his tale, James speaks.

"You're from Glacier Point, aren't you? A friend of Al Bogle's?"

At this, Richard perks up.

"Al is a dear friend."

"And your girlfriend's name is Mel?"

Richard is momentarily stunned—all he can do is nod.

Rusty turns to his brother, "How the fuck did you know that?"

James grins. "Bogle came a few months back, in a government chopper. He's Search and Rescue. Whole state of Alaska's been looking for these two, sounds like."

Richard shakes his head. "Let me guess: they thought we were farther south?"

"Sure did," says James. "Matter of fact, they thought you weren't together. They told me where they thought you were, and I scoured that land for you, must've checked 20 miles in every direction, more or less. Didn't find so much as a snowmachine. Figured you got swallowed up by this winter we've had."

"It's been a deep winter, deepest I've seen, and that's mighty kind of you," says Richard appreciatively, touched that a complete stranger would go out of his way to look for him. "Both Mel and I were miles and miles off our respective courses. I was afraid they'd never find us—and I guess they never did. Let's see, how'd we get here—it's a long story."

He takes another sip, then starts from the beginning: separating from Jim, watching Mel crash into the ice, diving in after her, living in the quinzee for nearly a week, losing the snowmachine in the snowstorm, finding the cabin by the grace of God. The coffee is nearly cold when he finishes.

At the end of his tale, Rusty shakes his head.

"Hot damn, I'm glad we found you. Looks like you got your ticket home," says Rusty.

"Those dogs of yours? They can make it back to the road?"

Rusty looks at his brother. "James?"

"Indeed," James laughs. "They can certainly bring you and your girlfriend home, ideally one at a time. I've got a few more snoozing back at the cabin, but the two of you together would probably exhaust the dogs. It's a long way back without an engine. But what we'll do first is call Bogle."

James checks his coat pockets and shakes his head. "I must've left my sat phone at the cabin, silly me. But we can ring the National Guard tonight, let 'em know you're all right. Tell your family you're alive. They'll send a helicopter immediately. And if for some reason I can't get ahold of Bogle, I'll take you out myself."

It's over. They've got a way out. Finally. The exit sign only appeared after Richard stopped looking for it. He exhales, stands, walks toward James, and hugs the stranger tightly.

"Thank you," he says, tears beginning to fall down his cheeks. "You're the answer to our prayers."

James stiffens, then lets Richard embrace him, patting the

bigger man clumsily on the back.

"More like a devil if you ask my brother," he jokes, winking over Richard's shoulder at Rusty.

Richard returns to the cot, and his thoughts turn to his wife, his kids, the funeral they may or may not have had. He thinks of Jim, the betrayal that blew this whole thing out of proportion. And he thinks of Mel.

He has a life to rebuild, a family to provide for, amends to make, trust to earn—she has what? A career she clearly hates, a complex relationship with her family that she's only alluded to. She's complained often about dating, and never described anything remotely resembling romantic love. Several times over the past few weeks, ever since they began to share the cot at night, she's said things that make him think she wouldn't mind missing this ride.

Doing the dishes after a meal of moose steaks. "This is the most serious relationship I've been in since college." That one caught him off guard.

Leaning into him, still panting, covered in sweat. "I could stay here forever."

Not just typical pillow talk, caught up in the moment, the line between reality and fantasy blurred by endorphins, but a real, conscious declaration that what's in front of her is much more appealing than what she left behind.

How to break this news to… his girlfriend? That's what he called her just minutes ago. His mistress? His roommate? And how can he explain this to his wife? That holed up in the wild he found solace in a younger woman? Suddenly, all of his justifications seem flimsy; the scaffolding he's built up to buttress his infidelity feels wobbly, insubstantial, as if it all might come crashing down at any second.

But justifications to his wife, he realizes, are still days away, and Richard returns his attention to the present. "You should stay for dinner. We've got some moose. Mel will be back any minute, and I'm sure she'd love to meet you both.

Rusty seems interested, but James cuts in. "We've got to get back—I haven't fed the dogs."

"We've got plenty of meat," says Richard. "More than enough for the dogs. We've been stocking up, but it doesn't seem as if we'll need it much longer."

James shakes his head. "It's mighty kind of you, but the rest of the pack is at home. They won't forgive me if I leave 'em locked up overnight without dinner, and the place will stink like a sewer by the time we come back."

"Fair enough," says Richard.

"We'll call Bogle as soon as we're back, see if they can send a chopper tonight. If not, I'll bring you home with the dogs. Either way, you and Mel pack up. Assuming the weather's clear, I wouldn't be surprised if we got you home tonight, tomorrow for sure."

"That is incredibly kind of you," says Richard. "Hopefully Bogle answers. I don't want to make trouble for you and the dogs."

"It's no trouble. Worst comes to worst, we'll get you home." James grins. "I need to head to town anyway to stock up on supplies. Besides, this sounds like a great chance to get a picture of myself on the front page of the newspaper."

Richard laughs. "That happened to me once. Long, long time ago. It's a funny feeling."

"I bet," says James, no longer grinning. Richard doesn't notice. He's busy writing his wife's cell phone number down on a page torn out of *Robinson Crusoe*.

"This is a strange request, but please, when you call my wife, tell her I'm alive, and that I miss her and the kids immensely. But don't mention Mel. You can tell her we're both alive, but anything beyond that—I need to face that head-on, in person."

Rusty takes the paper and winks. "I understand completely. What happens in the bush, stays in the bush." As an afterthought, he hands Richard the bag of coffee and the bandana. "Take this— no, don't worry, we have more back at the cabin. Something tells me you and Mel won't sleep much tonight—enjoy a cup on me in the morning."

The sun is still high when Mel returns from checking the trapline, a beaver lashed to her knapsack. Richard catches her staring incredulously at the sled tracks, the paw prints, the small mountains of dog shit—glaring clues to the brothers' visit, but ones she might've missed four months ago, before her hunting senses were honed by the Alaskan wild.

"Our neighbors, from just down river."

"We have neighbors?" she asks, sardonically.

Richard smiles. "That depends. If you call twenty-five miles away neighbors."

"No shit," she says, shaking her head. "No wonder we haven't seen them before."

"They were two brothers, James and Rusty. Nice guys. James lives here full-time, Rusty's visiting from Central America. They were friends of Jean Pierre's. They're going to call Search and Rescue if they can, and if they can't get in touch, they'll bring us home on a dogsled. And best of all, they left us some coffee."

She takes it well. Better than he thought she might. They'd been saving a splash of bourbon for a special occasion, and decide to finish it off. "I think this qualifies," she says. They watch the sunset over the peaks, passing the bottle back and forth.

"I can't wait to see my mom, my dad, let them know I'm all right," she says.

"My kids," says Richard, emotion threatening to overtake him. "I can't wait to hug them." He changes the subject, if only not to lose himself to tears. "Your first meal back, what'll it be? Something vegetarian?"

Mel laughs. "I do miss vegetables. A Caesar salad—the biggest Caesar salad in Anchorage. Or Indian food: massaman curry or garlic naan. Or Thai: pad thai. And definitely a chocolate milkshake. You?"

"My wife's famous baby back ribs, with homemade barbecue sauce," he says. "And coleslaw. And scalloped potatoes. And a tall, ice-cold beer."

She stiffens at the mention of his wife. Richard notices, but he doesn't apologize. Anne is the love of his life, his soul mate, the mother of his children. He always intended to return to her. If she'll take him back, that is.

"Will you go back to New York?" he asks, changing the subject once more.

Mel ponders the question, staring out at the horizon, imagining a skyline of skyscrapers instead of summits.

"For a spell, at least," she says, unwilling to speak the truth—that she doesn't want to leave Alaska. That she found the snowmachine, and left it buried. That this cabin has felt more like home than anywhere else she's known.

Chapter 25

The dogs pant and pull, yip and strain, the wind at their backs. The sled track is Rusty's road to redemption. He hasn't been this happy in years, despite the joyous life he lives in Nicaragua. His heart is full, his soul on fire. He returned to JP's cabin to atone for his sins, and his pilgrimage will save two lives. Is that not a sign? The sun is setting over the mountain range, a vivid ómbré of purples and oranges and reds that reminds him of evening surf sessions in Santa Catalina, and that feels like a sign, too. When he returns to Central America, the specters of his past may have finally faded. His unforgivable sin will never be absolved, but peace, the elusive state of being he's been stalking like a hunter for well over a decade, seems within his grasp.

They arrive home at dusk. After the dogs are fed and a fire roars in the woodstove, Rusty checks his watch. "James, where's the sat phone? It's late, but we ought to call Richard's family. They'll want to know."

James pats his coat pocket. "It's here, in my jacket."

Rusty is confused. "You've had it the whole time?"

"Yes," says James, grinning mischievously.

"Why didn't you let him use it then?"

"Because I don't want search and rescue to come back."

"Why the hell not?" Infuriated, Rusty sputters: "Don't you

get it? I went back there to ask for forgiveness. God, the universe, whatever—something bigger than us, something is allowing us to make things right."

James paces toward the fire, then back again, cracking his knuckles.

"Did Richard look familiar to you?"

"Like every moose-fucking Alaskan I've ever met in this godforsaken state."

"That man, believe it or not," says James, "is responsible for this limp."

He sits back in his chair and kicks out his leg, stretching his knee and massaging the tendons.

"What the fuck do you mean?"

"His name is Richard Maynard."

James rises and rummages in a drawer in the kitchen, removing a crinkled piece of paper that he hands to Rusty. It's the photo Bogle gave him. A well-worn crease cuts like a scar diagonally across Richard's portrait, separating head from shoulders like an origami guillotine.

"You want me to believe he's the cop who shot your leg?" laughs Rusty, incredulous. He can't hide his impatience, his derision—his brother has finally plunged headlong into madness.

James ignores the condescension. "No, he wasn't a cop. He was there on vacation. His honeymoon, actually."

Deeper from the drawer James pulls another piece of paper, a yellowing newspaper clipping.

Rusty has seen it before. Years ago. He'd grabbed it surreptitiously from a newsstand on their way off Long Island.

The headline jumps out at him. "Honeymooner's Haymaker Nearly Thwarts Escape of Jewel Thieves."

He scans the article: "The robbers made off with an estimated two hundred and sixty-five thousand dollars in cash and jewelry, including a single diamond ring worth ninety-five thousand dollars. At this time, officials have noted that they have no suspects, but they do have DNA evidence from blood spilled at the scene, thanks to a punch thrown by Richard Maynard, an Alaskan tourist visiting New York on his honeymoon.

"After Maynard's brave and selfless actions, NYPD Officer Harold Romanoff, forty-seven, was able to open fire and hit one of the perpetrators, likely in the leg or knee. Hospitals in the region have been warned and are requested to notify NYPD of any gunshot wounds.

"Romanoff took fire himself and the father of two remains in critical care."

The article goes on, interviewing Maynard about the events. Rusty holds the two pieces of paper next to each other. In the photograph, a slightly less scruffy Richard smiles back at him. In the newspaper clipping, he's much younger, a hero, with police lights casting him in a dramatic glow.

"No way," says Rusty.

James nods, smiling wolfishly.

"The chances are infinitesimally small," says James. "You had a better shot beating out the rest of our brothers and sisters as a sperm. But it's as you say. God, the universe, something greater than us, has brought us together."

Rusty looks up from the photographs and stiffens.

"Even more reason to turn the other cheek. We should save them," Rusty says.

At this, James guffaws loudly.

"Save them? For getting me shot? For putting my DNA in the NYPD database? For forcing me to leave New York with my tail between my legs and live in the wilderness?"

"No one is forcing you to live here! You don't get it, do you? They don't have your fingerprints, and no one is checking for your DNA. Come to Nicaragua with me! Start over."

"I'm never leaving here," says James, darkly. "And neither is Richard."

"What are you going to do? Kill him?"

"I'm going to do—"

"What has to be done?"

Rusty echoes the words his brother has spoken to him on too many occasions to count, sick to his stomach.

"No," says James, aware of the jab. "I'm going to do what I want to be done. I'm going to have a little talk with Richard. Make him realize how his actions impacted my life and how, in turn, they brought his own demise."

"And the girl?" asks Rusty, now livid, shuddering with rage. "You going to kill her, too?"

"No," says James calmly. "It can be lonely out here, just me and the dogs all winter. You miss some things—the touch of a woman, for one. I'm going to invite her here to live with me. Well, invite isn't exactly the right word. Oblige, maybe. She's rather pretty, isn't she?"

Rusty's jaw drops. "You've lost your fucking mind."

James collapses into dark laughter.

"Don't worry. I'm not going to do that. I'm not some sort of sicko. But yes, I'll kill her, too. I can't exactly let her go after I take care of Richard, can I? Consider her a casualty of war. Plus, the beautiful thing is, according to the media, they've been dead for months now."

Rusty, disquieted and aggravated but not done swinging, counters. "Don't you get it?" he says, pleading now. "This is your chance. Your chance for redemption. Your chance to make amends."

"Amends?" says James, his voice biting with scorn. "This is my chance for one thing and one thing only: revenge."

Rusty yells, an unintelligible battle cry, unable to sound out the words threatening to burst forth from his gut. With a lunge, he raises his right foot and smashes it into his brother's chest. James crashes backward, breaking the chair, and Rusty dives toward the doorway.

By the time James extricates himself from the broken chair, fury in his eyes, Rusty is panting, holding the rifle, pointing it for the second time at his own blood.

"You'd kill me before I kill them?"

"If it would stop more unnecessary harm," says Rusty, resolutely. He will not tolerate another murder. No, he will not stand for it. "I'd sooner die myself."

"This doesn't need to be your battle," says James. "You have another life, a wife, kids. But this is my world. We did what we had to do back in New York. And I've lived every goddamn day since with this limp, a reminder of what I used to have, what I lost." James begins to spit; were his cheeks not veiled by a beard, Rusty would see the blood rushing to them. "And now the motherfucker responsible is delivered to my doorstep and you wanna play some biblical game of forgiveness?"

"Is that so hard, to forgive?"

"I'd never forgive you if you kept this from me."

"I've never forgiven you for what you made me do."

It's a relief to say.

James tilts his head and eyes Rusty pensively.

"That's what this is about? Your inability to come to grips with your own actions?"

James takes a step closer. Rusty grips the gun tighter. He can feel the perspiration on his forehead.

"That's it. You're terrified by the truth. You, my brother, are a murderer. Same as me."

"Shut up."

"In fact, you did it with that very gun. You shot Jean Pierre, point-blank."

"Shut the fuck up!"

"Do you know why you did it?"

"I didn't mean to do it."

James' voice softens. "You did it because you were protecting yourself. You were protecting me. We're family. Only blood we have left. And you want to spill that? For what? Some bullshit."

"It's not bullshit."

"You did the right thing. Jean Pierre was our only way out."

"I didn't need to kill him. He was going to take us home!"

"It was the right thing to do."

"It was wrong!"

"Wrong is right sometimes. Like right now."

"He didn't need to die. And Richard." He nods toward the photos. "He doesn't need to die. And that girl. She doesn't need to die either."

James sighs. "They don't need to die. But they will. Because I want them to. And unless you kill me yourself, that's what's going to happen."

James takes another step closer. The barrel presses into his chest.

"This is your shot," he says. "Take it—or don't."

Swiftly, James reaches for the gun, getting his hands around the barrel. Rusty sees it coming but can't bring himself to pull the trigger. He yanks backward and manages to hold on to the gun. James leaps sideways and, with a practiced kick, unlatches one of the kennels and yells, "Chase!"

Rusty sees a flash of fur and fangs spring toward him before unloading the rifle on instinct. It goes off like a firecracker in a steel drum, rattling his eardrums. Acrid smoke fills the cabin. The animal goes limp in midair but still knocks Rusty over.

James curses and kicks open two more kennels as Rusty pushes off the dead Chinook, which weighs him down like a lead blanket. It's warm, heavy, and wet with blood. There's no time for remorse as the two sled dogs, furious to see one of their own slain, launch themselves at the intruder.

Rusty releases the rifle, covering his head with his hands as he feels them rip into his calf muscles with their long fangs, bite into his back, paw at his arms.

Undoubtedly, one of them will find the way to his throat.

Visions of Victoria. A jungle he will never return to. A family he will never see grow.

But he hears a sharp whistle, and the dogs, panting, galled at being deprived of their prey, retreat.

Through his fingers he sees his disgusted brother standing over him.

Blood drips down his arms, his forehead, into his mouth.

But before he can register the taste of his own blood, before he can say so much as a syllable, the brown butt of the rifle swings down in slow motion. It rams into his temple, and the curtain drops.

Rusty wakes up, cramped and sore. His head is throbbing.

It takes him a while to realize where he is. That it wasn't all a bad dream. There, in the middle of the cabin floor, is the Chinook, dead, sprawled out like a bearskin rug.

Through some sort of metal lattice, he eyes the dead dog and shudders. Sadness sweeps over him. No, he hadn't meant to kill the beast. But it had seemed his only choice.

Jesus, he sounds just like James.

"I did what had to be done."

The smell of dogs and death overwhelms his senses and he begins to feel nauseous. Vomit creeps up his throat, threatening to spill out.

He cannot move his hands or his feet. They aren't bound, but still, he's stuck. He realizes that he's not tied up but locked in a kennel, imprisoned in the very home of the dog that lies dead on the floor.

His head still throbbing, Rusty closes his eyes and attempts to find sleep.

The rattling cage wakes him.

Through a bleary eye he sees his brother's beard, his seething eyes, and the barrel of the rifle banging against the steel bars.

"Good morning, brother. Rise and shine. How did you sleep?"

Rusty wants nothing more than to stretch his cramped limbs.

"Are you going to let me out of here?"

"I will," says James. "Of course I will. I don't want you locked up in here any more than you do. But you had to be punished."

"That thing was going to kill me."

"Only if I'd let him. If I let you out, will you attack me again?"

"No."

"Will you allow me to return to Jean Pierre's cabin?"

"Yes."

"Bullshit, I'm afraid," James chuckles. "You're as bad a liar as you are a murderer. You've made your bed. Now you're locked in it."

To a soundtrack of Rusty's pleading and cursing, James prepares his things. Much as he would before a hunt, he oils his gun, sharpens his knife, packs provisions. Out in the yard, he ropes up a team of dogs. Rusty hears him whistling as he does it, like nothing's even remotely amiss. It's the whistling that does it, that causes him to lash out with the heel of his hand, bashing the metal door of the cage.

There's a small lock on the latch, not that he'd be able to pick it—he can barely stick his fingers through the metal grate. However, when he bangs the door, he notices that the latch itself is loose. He jostles and jiggles the door—sure enough, there's some play. Rusty bets it was screwed into the wooden wall years ago and hasn't been tightened for ages.

While James bustles around the cabin, preparing his gear, Rusty puts on a show. He yells, pleads, carrying on until his voice is hoarse.

However, when James is out of the cabin, fiddling with the dogs and the harnesses, Rusty is all business. Carefully, he shifts his weight, curling away from the door so that his boots are up against the metal grate.

When James enters, presumably finished with his preparations, it looks as if Rusty has curled up in defeat.

"Rusty," says James. "I know you're not asleep."

"Don't do it," says Rusty, his voice muffled in the kennel.

"I'll be back tomorrow," says James. "In the meantime, don't move."

He hears the cock of the rifle, the click of the lock, the creak of the hinge. Then the slosh of water, a bowl dropping onto the thin blanket.

"Enough to make it through the night, at least. If you've got to piss, do it in the water bowl, or shove your cock out the slats and piss on the floor for all I care. If you've got to shit, do it in the corner. That's what the dogs do. But I recommend you hold it for your own sake."

Rusty could kick, hard, and knock James off balance. He thinks about it, but he knows that his brother won't hesitate to pull the trigger.

James laughs knowingly.

"Thought you might try something there. Should've known better."

Again, the door creaks, the latch snaps, the lock catches. Rusty hears James give it a couple tugs, and then, satisfied, his footsteps receding as he heads toward the door.

Before he leaves, though, James pauses in the living room.

"He was a good dog, a loyal dog. The head of the pack. I loved him dearly. Do you know why I'm going to leave him here tonight?"

Again, Rusty doesn't answer.

"Because, funnily enough, you've killed that dog before."

The cryptic words are punctuated by a slamming door, and James is gone.

Rusty hears the spurring shouts of his brother, the yapping of the dogs as they excitedly leave the homestead. The dogs left behind howl as their master pulls away.

Rusty, however, does not howl. He sits up as much as he can in the cramped quarters of the kennel and kicks at the grate.

The latch rattles but doesn't submit to the double kick from his boots. Pain rushes through his right ankle and up to his knee.

"Fuck!" he screams at the pain.

Over and over again, he kicks. But the screws don't yield. On the verge of giving up, he slumps even lower, so that his head is touching the back wall of the kennel. From this angle, Rusty realizes, his knees are bent, and his toes are pressed against the door. He won't have as much space to wind up, but he'll have more follow-through.

Buttressing his arms and pressing his palms into the back wall like he's doing a headstand, he coils up like a spring, and with a guttural yell, kicks out his legs.

In a flurry of splinters, the latch wrenches off the wall. One more kick and it's hanging askew from a single, discombobulated screw. A final kick and it travels halfway across the room, landing squarely on the back of the dead dog.

Wincing, he emerges from the wood and metal prison and unkinks his beleaguered body, wishing that Victoria were there to work her elbows into his muscles.

No time for realigning his battered spine, not now. James is fifteen minutes ahead. By the time Rusty gets a sled set up—assuming there is a second sled—he might very well be too late.

He's banking on the fact that James, though a sorrowful hermit, is also desperate for human contact, and he won't bust into Jean Pierre's cabin guns blazing. He'll take his time explaining himself, like a cartoon villain with a taste for drama. He'd never kill Richard without a triumphant monologue, cliché as it may be.

Rusty hobbles to the shed as quickly as his throbbing ankle will allow, ignoring the blood leaking from the back of his calf and his forearms. There, he finds what he's looking for: a second sled. It's in poor condition, but it will do. The left ski seems as if it may break at any moment, and the handle is rotting. Rusty guesses that James abandoned this sled years ago, and perhaps keeps it only for parts. That would make sense, as the brake is missing entirely. Looking around the shed, Rusty finds a two-by-four, jams it into the snow, and says, "There. That'll be my brake."

Apprehensive, he rounds up the dogs. Two growl at him from behind the bars of their kennels. Three seem keen to join him as he shakes a dog harness like a tambourine.

By the time he's wrangled the dogs, filled up a water bottle, and stashed a handful of jerky in his pocket, half an hour has passed, maybe more. Plus, with only three dogs, he'll be moving slower than his brother. But he won't stop. He'll ride straight there, as fast as the dogs will carry him.

Before he leaves, he stoops down by the dead dog. He bows his head, scratches its ears.

"I'm sorry. I didn't want this."

Then, tossing the bent and broken door to the side, he gathers up the dog in his arms. It's stiff and lifeless, and he strains under the weight despite it being drained of blood, which has spread out over the hearth like a red rug.

He heaves the dead dog into the empty kennel and tenses up as he reads the hand-carved wooden placard above it: "Jean Pierre."

His brother's last words echo.

"You've killed that dog before."

The nausea that had threatened to overcome him in the tight confinement of the kennel finally does. Without time to move elsewhere, he vomits, splattering sick all over the floorboards. It intermingles with the pool of dog's blood in a rank mixture.

Wiping his hand on the back of his mouth, Rusty turns and walks out the door. He doesn't have time to clean up the mess. Plus, it isn't as if he ever plans to come back to this hellhole.

Chapter 26

All night and all morning, they listen for a helicopter that never comes. Richard stokes the fire for what he hopes will be the last time. Mel sits at the window, sipping her second coffee, alert as a watchdog. She hears the yipping before Richard does.

"They're here," she says. "Dogsled."

Richard squeezes her shoulder and glances out the window. "That's James," he says, a mix of emotions rushing through him. He's relieved, nervous, excited, and, oddly enough, a little sad. "This is it."

Together, they step out onto the porch to greet their liberator.

As James ties up the dogs, he recalls his first winter with the pack. Whenever he ventured near the Frenchman's cabin, the dogs grew skittish, howling to the heavens as if mourning their deceased master. James hated to see his bond with the pack jeopardized by a dead man, so he avoided this section of the Hope Valley for years. The passing of time weighs heavily on him now. His dogs are oblivious, each born after Jean Pierre's death. To them, it's a ramshackle cabin like any other. He's the only master they've ever known. And today, as if emphasizing that fact, Jean Pierre died for a second time, once again dispatched to the mountains in the sky by Rusty's reluctant rifle.

"You made it!" calls Richard. "We've been listening for a helicopter."

James looks up from his task to find Richard and Mel waving

at him from the porch.

"My sat phone didn't work, unfortunately," says James, climbing up the stairs. "I haven't used it in years, and I guess I fell behind on the payments. Don't have a credit card or even an ID these days. Not to worry, I'll get you both out of here."

"Rusty couldn't make it?" asked Richard.

"He's a bit tied up at the moment," says James. "And we can't all fit on the sled anyway, the other dogs needed to rest."

He shakes Richard's hand then turns to Mel, grinning. "You must be the girlfriend."

Mel arches an eyebrow and looks sideways at Richard. "Nope, I'm Mel."

"Bad intel, my apologies," James chuckles. "Y'all packed up?"

Richard, blushing, forces a laugh. "Not much to pack. We were ready minutes after you left yesterday afternoon."

"Good man. You still have some moose lying around? I could use a hot meal before we head out. Maybe some coffee, too. And the dogs could use a bite as well. Besides, the snow is pretty melted out at this point, the only way to make decent time on the sled is to ride at night, when the lower temperatures consolidate the crust. I have a powerful set of lights, and if it's all the same to you, we'll wait until dark."

While Mel cooks up a few moose steaks and Richard fixes coffee, James makes himself at home. He removes the rifle that's slung across his back and hangs his homemade fur coat from an iron hook. He takes a load off in the chair.

Richard hands James a cup of coffee.

"Thank you," says James.

"It's the least we can do," says Richard. "Will jerky work for the dogs?"

"Jerky's fine," says James. "But don't skimp. Those dogs eat more than you and I combined. I get hungry just driving that bitch of a sled, can't imagine pulling it," he says, accepting a plate from Mel with a grateful nod. "Thank you, darling."

Richard piles jerky in a bucket and, after affirmation from James that it's sufficient, dumps the smoked meat in the snow by the sled. The dogs descend upon it greedily, and Richard returns to grab a plate and cup of his own. He sits on the cot across from James, steaming cups of coffee perched on an overturned milk crate between them, and saws at his steak with his penknife.

The men grunt appreciatively at the tender, medium-rare meat—Mel's cooking has only improved—and she scrapes at the cast-iron pan in the sink. She thought about leaving the dish—this is their last meal in the cabin, after all. But there's a small part of her that wants to return someday. Maybe she can buy the land, get a snowmachine of her own, fix up the cabin. Buying the land might not even be necessary. Jean Pierre's been dead for years, and no one has come knocking. Out here, all she might need to do is stake her claim.

"Handsome rifle you have there," says Richard in between bites.

"Ain't she a beauty? Never leave home without her. Winchester Model 70 Alaskan. Grizzlies are starting to wake up now, can't be too careful."

"I saw a couple tracks downriver last week."

"In my experience," James pauses, washing a bite of steak down with a gulp of coffee. "Nothing puckers the asshole like a stare-down with a full-grown grizz."

"I've only gotten up close and personal with one once, and once was enough," says Richard. "A long time ago. I was salmon fishing. Nearly shit myself. Luckily, I had my forty-four on me, and she shuffled off into the bush before I needed to use it."

"Lucky indeed," says James. "I've faced plenty, and taken down a couple with that very gun."

"May I?" asks Richard, pointing to the rifle. It will take two full days to sled home, and he's eager to connect with their strange savior. A mutual appreciation of firearms seems like a good place to start.

James beams. "Sure can." He leans over and grabs the rifle, then quickly pulls back the bolt, removes the cartridge, and hands the gun butt-first to Richard. "This is Lorraine," he says.

"Lorraine," repeats Richard. "The pleasure's all mine."

He runs his hands down the gun—it's a beautiful rifle, well maintained, an old-fashioned model with an updated scope. He eyes down the sight.

"I had a Winchester 270 once, it was my grandfather's. Loved that gun. They just don't make 'em like they used to," he says.

"I agree with you there," says James, nodding sagely. "She's gotten me through fifteen winters out here. I upgraded once, then switched back to Lorraine. Felt like I was cheating on my wife—no offense." He looks quickly from Richard to Mel, who pretends she's not listening in the kitchen, then continues. "Something special about guns with history, guns with character, guns you know have seen some things. Lorraine's seen some shit, no doubt about it."

"I believe it," says Richard.

He hands back the gun, and returns to sawing the last of his steak. James accepts the rifle gently, like a mother would her newborn. He pops the cartridge back in the rifle, then pats the gun fondly.

"Matter of fact," says James. "Lorraine put a hole in Jean Pierre."

The skinny street dogs of Nicaragua look like cat food compared to James' sled team. In the radiant morning light, Rusty follows the river toward Jean Pierre's cabin, watching the three lithe, furred backs bend and strain. Their tongues loll, but Rusty won't let up.

Every minute that goes by is a potential double homicide.

He can barely stand, but he won't stand for it.

The sun's rays refract upon the mountains to the east, catching the corners of peaks, splaying through valleys, and he rides through light and shadow.

His water is long gone, and he's thirsty. He gnaws on a piece of caribou jerky, knowing that it will leave him thirstier still, but he needs the calories.

Using his belt for a whip, he cracks it into the air. The exhausted dogs push harder.

He has no gun, no weapons save for a hatchet he grabbed off the porch on his way out. He rides hard, belt in one hand, hatchet and reins in the other. The two-by-four fell off long ago. He has no brakes. That's just fine. He doesn't intend to stop.

No gun, no water, no brakes. But worst of all, he has no plan.

Only to stop his brother from cold-blooded murder.

That, he will stop at all costs.

But can he murder his own brother? If it comes down to a fight—and not a fight like the old days, but one with weapons, with lives on the line—will he hesitate? Will he be afraid to take the final step? Or will he execute his own flesh to save two innocent strangers?

Maybe this is why he returned to Alaska. To serve a higher purpose. To exorcise evil from these mountains, to bring Richard and Mel home.

He grips the hatchet tighter and swings the belt down. The dogs pound onward, exhausted and frantic, never having run so hard in their lives.

Surprise flashes across Richard's face, but he masks it quickly. "Excuse me?" he says.

James smiles broadly, then tilts back in the chair, the rifle in his lap.

"You heard me right," he says. "My brother and I were stuck out here—not unlike yourselves—in my cabin, which, at the time, we were renting from a friend of the Frenchman's. How that cabin ended up in my possession is another story entirely. Anyways, JP offered to take us back to civilization. But I realized I didn't want to go back to civilization. I wanted to stay here, in paradise, and the only way I could do that was with sled dogs. So we—or rather, my brother—shot the Frenchman, and I took the dogs for my own. The dogs you see outside? Those are the descendants of JP's old pack."

"Why are you telling us this?" asks Richard,

gripping his knife tightly.

"I'm telling you this, Richard Maynard, because believe it or not, you and I met once before. Fifteen years ago. It was a brief but momentous encounter, outside of a jewelry store in New York."

James grimaces and begins to roll up his pantleg, revealing a scarred knee.

"The encounter left me with a bullet in my leg, and you got your picture in the paper. I believe the headline read: 'Honeymooner Haymaker Nearly Thwarts Escape of Jewel Thieves.'"

Richard's jaw drops. His brain is buzzing, flooded with disbelief. New York? Hearing the headline triggers memories of his wife, his poor wife, who brought that Times edition back to Alaska, cut the article out with a pair of scissors, framed it, and hung it in their kitchen above the coffeemaker. He remembers how Anne finished the story countless times when she told it at dinner parties: "I think he set up that heist so we'd never have to go to New York again."

It was true. They hadn't been back to the city since. If he makes it out of here alive, that's the first place they'll go, back to New York, on a second honeymoon. But a reunion with his wife seems increasingly unlikely, as James clearly isn't here for a rescue.

"This is the second time," says James, lifting the rifle, "that I've aimed a gun at you. The difference is that this time, I know how to use it. And this time, I intend to."

For a moment, Mel is paralyzed with confusion. On one of their many walks along the trapline, she asked Richard if he'd ever been to New York. He told her about a few business trips, a shitty diner he liked, visiting museums, attending Jets games. But he never said anything about his honeymoon or a jewelry heist, and certainly nothing about a run-in with a gunman.

There's no time to wonder why Richard hadn't shared that story with her, although the answer is obvious—the conversation occurred after they'd transitioned from friends to lovers. There's no time to calculate the probability of James and Richard crossing paths fifteen years ago in New York and again here and now in Bumfuck Nowhere, Alaska. These thoughts are wastes of precious seconds. James has a loaded gun, aimed point-blank at a man she's come to love.

Her mind races. She needs a weapon. There's a kitchen knife in the sink, underneath the cast iron she's been chiseling away at, but it's duller than the men she used to date in the city. And what's she going to do? Throw it into James' jugular like a shuriken? She's not a fucking ninja.

She needs JP's shotgun. It's across the room, tucked in the closet where they first found it. She put it away last night. Mel tries to steady her breathing and formulates a plan, ignoring the question that threatens to overwhelm her: Assuming she can somehow distract James and get the shotgun, is she capable of using it?

James holds the rifle steady. Richard clutches his penknife, still shocked. James' smile is gone now, replaced by a grim but purposeful expression.

"Hands up, slowly, and drop the knife," says James

Richard does as he's told, lifting his hands and then tossing the knife onto the crate. The knife clatters on the plastic, and the open blade catches one of the cups and tips it over, spilling coffee on the rough brown floorboards. James can't help but look down for a millisecond, and that's enough for Mel to make her move.

With a guttural yell and a splash of dishwater, Mel yanks the cast-iron pan from the sink. In one fluid movement, like a discus thrower, she spins and heaves it toward James with startling accuracy.

James sees the pan coming and dodges backwards. Richard moves in tandem with the pan, ducking below the barrel of the gun. James pulls the trigger, but it's too late. The bullet rips into the wall behind Richard, detonating an explosion of splinters. Richard's ears are ringing like church bells, but he's already in motion, driving his shoulder into James, a move reminiscent of his days on the gridiron.

Mel, meanwhile, sprints to the closet. She grabs the shotgun and, despite her fumbling fingers, breaks it down and loads it with two shells. She cocks it and turns around, hoping to find Richard in possession of the rifle.

Instead, the rifle is on the ground, and both men are standing. James has the knife at Richard's throat and uses Richard's body as a shield.

"Easy now," James says, grinning wildly at her over Richard's shoulder, blood dripping from the corner of his mouth.

Richard grimaces, holding his right arm with his left.

"Are you all right?" asks Mel, her voice quaking from the adrenaline.

"I'm fine," says Richard. "I think I dislocated my shoulder when I tackled him."

James' breath is ragged, his heart pounds, but he speaks smoothly.

"May I suggest, Mel, that you put down the gun."

Mel stands there, vibrating with fear, the gun swaying back and forth in her hands like a tree branch in the wind.

She knows she'll never take that shot, never take that risk. A rifle is one thing, but a shotgun blast from this range? Richard will be peppered like a steak. Still, she can't put the gun down. It's her only bargaining chip.

She looks at Richard for help, for confirmation, for guidance. His own blade is pressed against his throat, to the point that she can see a faint trace of blood outlining the freshly sharpened steel.

Her arms will tire eventually, James knows. The girl is thin, the gun heavy. It's only a matter of time.

"I'm a simple man," he says slowly, like a congressman on the House floor, about to lay into a filibuster. "A simple man. I have my dogs, my cabin, my little life out here. But that doesn't mean I've forgotten the life I left behind, the life I could've had. I had to leave New York thanks to you, Richard. Alaska called to me, as it has to countless others. I came here, found this place. I killed the man who rented us our cabin, so you might say that I haven't paid rent in a while."

Richard takes this moment to try to run—all he needs to do is to jump out of the way so Mel can get a shot—but James is strong and expecting it. He grabs Richard's dislocated shoulder and muscles him back into place, then presses the knife even more tightly against his skin, so the red outline becomes a steady stream of blood.

"That was impolite," says James. "I'm in the middle of a story."

Richard grits his teeth at the pain.

Mel readjusts the gun.

"Are you tired, Mel?"

"Go fuck yourself."

"As you wish. Where was I? My brother killed Jean Pierre. He didn't want to, but he did it to protect me. I learned how to drive the dogs, and brought my brother, who refused to talk to me after Jean Pierre's death, to town. He left Alaska without saying a word. I hadn't seen him until a few days ago. But since then, I learned to love this land. I found more purpose out here than I ever had in the city. Some call the city a harsh reality. That makes me laugh. This, this is a harsh reality. Everything is harsh and real here. It's kill or be killed. Survival depends on you. There are no societal ideals here, no savings accounts or relationships or computers or falsified goals that humans have created to inject import into their piddly lives. Out here, my goals are the same as the wolf, the bear, the salmon. There is no pretense. Only survival. That is the harsh reality."

"Except the wolves and bears fuck each other," says Mel, more bravely than she feels. "And you're a crazy fucking hermit and, maybe I'm just projecting here, a chronic masturbator."

He ignores her, but the anger starts to show.

"But as devout as I've been to this temple of mountains, this sacred cathedral of rivers and sky, there's been a constant thought, a pea under my spiritual mattress, that's made it impossible for me to get comfortable. And that pea, Richard, is you.

"You see, I've never been a forgiving man. Vengeance suits me.

Since I was a kid on the playground, any bully who picked on me received his own medicine, but tenfold. And I've never had an act committed against me that so demanded vengeance as did yours," he says. "And I've been close to exacting that vengeance. I've driven by your house several times, a gun on my lap, only to see the gates, the kids, your wife. Too messy. I didn't need a five-person murder, the national press. But I thought about it. Wanted it. Needed it, in order to continue my life at peace."

The dogs outside begin to bark, as if they can hear their master's speech, and James smiles at the sound.

"The funny thing is, I gave up that dream. I told myself it was a waste of time. A great way to get myself shot—or worse, sent to jail. And so I let it go. For years, I let it go, and you rarely crossed my mind, save for on the coldest mornings, when my knee throbbed as if the devil himself were poking at the tendons with a pitchfork.

"But then, a Search and Rescue chopper came. Bogle showed me your picture, told me you were lost out here. And I knew that my time for vengeance had come. That, against all odds, my patience had been rewarded.

"And so, Richard, I'm going to take your life from you, not altogether unlike the way you took mine from me. Although, perhaps, as with the bullies of my youth, the punishment is greater than the crime. This, I suppose, is my nature."

The keen blade at Richard's throat is cold, but the blood that drips down his neck is warm. Gut-wrenching pain throbs through his arm, but Richard stays quiet, allowing the megalomaniac to spew his monologue. The longer James talks, the longer he stays alive.

He has to do something, but he isn't sure what.

If he moves again, James will tense up, the blade will rip into his neck.

Mel can't take the shot unless he jumps out of the way, and there's no way to do that without putting his life in danger.

James' beard scratches across Richard's neck. His breath is hot and foul. Richard looks up at the woman behind the barrel.

She's tough, and regardless of what happens next, she'll make it out alive. This comforts Richard. Should James draw the blade across his throat, he'll become a useless shield, and she can take her shot. James knows this, too—that's why he drones on and on.

"You'll be ok," he mouths to her. "You'll be ok without me."

Before she can respond, the door slams open.

There's a yell, and a gunshot.

Hatchet in hand, Rusty puts his ear to the door and hears the low murmur of voices. He's not too late.

With his good leg, he kicks the cabin door open and bursts into the room.

"Stop!" he yells.

The one-room cabin is frozen like a shoebox diorama. James has a knife to the throat of Richard, who seems to have a broken arm. There are signs of a scuffle in the living room—an upturned milk crate and knocked-over chair, a cast-iron pan and cups and a pool of coffee on the floor.

He sees Mel, shocked, behind a swinging shotgun, and the regret in her wide eyes as the trigger clicks back and the hammer strikes home and a bang loud enough to wake Jean Pierre from the dead fills the small cabin.

The momentum of the blast knocks Rusty back; he lets it take him away, one step, two steps, and he turns out the door, onto the porch. He looks down at red hands that clutch at his stomach. He looks out at the mountains, mountains that had caged him for not just a year, but his whole second life, and suddenly they seem not like bars to a prison, but like stairs, like that song, that beautiful song, like a stairway to heaven, and for once, finally, he does not feel trapped by them anymore.

Chapter 27

"No!" yells James, and the knife at Richard's neck goes slack. As Rusty spins and totters out the door, Richard growls and elbows James in the stomach, then lunges for the rifle.

Richard cradles the rifle against his chest with his single uninjured arm and pivots to face James. He clicks the trigger, but the rifle doesn't fire.

"Shit," says Richard, then grabs the barrel of the rifle and brandishes it like a baseball bat.

James speaks calmly, deftly tossing the knife from one hand to the other. "If you would allow me to remove myself and my injured brother from the premises, I would be much obliged."

"You're not exactly in a position to make bargains," says Richard. "She's still got another shell in that shotgun."

Without looking behind him, Richard steps to the side so that Mel, assuming she can still hold the gun straight, won't miss.

Every minute they do nothing, she's becoming a murderer.

She didn't mean to shoot him. She didn't mean to at all. But when he burst in, instinct took over.

She wants to take James up on his deal. Let him leave, never come back, take his brother and go.

As if reading her mind, James turns to her.

"You're not a killer," he says. Goosebumps form on her forearms.

"I might be already," she stammers, shaking under the weight of the shotgun, under the weight of what she's just done.

"Be strong, Mel," says Richard, stepping back slowly. "I need to pop this back in."

He puts the rifle down, grits his teeth, and raises his arm, bellowing in pain until the ball of the joint pops back into the socket. He rolls his shoulder, shaking his head, then reaches into the cupboard to retrieve a length of rope. "Fuck, that hurt. Keep the gun on him. I'll tie him up."

Richard edges closer, holding the rope like a cowboy approaching a particularly stubborn bull.

This isn't going the way James planned it, but if he's learned one thing from a life of survival, it's that plans often go awry at the worst times, and the ability to improvise is a most valuable weapon.

He recalls a summer day on the streets of Queens. They were playing stickball, and Rusty called his shots like Babe Ruth, pointing up over the parked cars and fences and saying, "This one's going to Brooklyn." James hurled fastballs and sliders that left Rusty slicing through the air. They stopped for Cokes at the corner store on the way home, taking a detour down to the pier to dip their feet in the East River.

"You could be a pitcher someday," said Rusty, back when he still admired his older brother, before he feared him. "Maybe not for the Yankees, but the Mets at least."

"Yeah, right," snorted James, pleased, watching the boats float by on their way to the Upper Bay. Even at thirteen, he had a notion that he'd never don a jersey and take the mound, he'd be a pickpocket, a grifter, a burglar, a bookie, a gangster. Be a cop or a criminal—that was what the kids were taught in Queens, if not explicitly in school, then by the generations who came before them.

James always thought the criminals seemed to have more fun.

With a grunt and a step forward, James brings down his arm and releases the knife from his fingertips.

He can smell the summer stink of the East River, hear the flutter of Coltrane's saxophone on a scratchy taxicab radio, feel the thump of a properly hit baseball soaring over the parked cars, over the fences, all the way to Brooklyn.

Richard closes his eyes and ducks, expecting the knife to come biting into his chest, slashing into his shoulder, piercing his rib cage, leaving him lifeless. But the only thing he feels is a semi-truck crashing into him, his torso smacking the floor, his head whiplashing back into the musk ox hide.

The knife may have missed its mark, but the semi-truck—which he now realizes is bearded, spitting, and furious—begins to punch him relentlessly.

Dazed, Richard rolls over onto his side, curling up into the fetal position to take the brunt of James' blows. His shoulder is still in agony. But as he turns, he sees Mel, kneeling on the kitchen floor, a look of shock on her face, blood soaking her shirt, the knife jutting from her side.

It was the perfect double play.

James batters Richard to a pulp, manic with contradiction. He's pleased with how well his knife throw was executed, furious that he hasn't been able to tend to his wounded brother.

The quicker he kills this motherfucker, the quicker he can get to Rusty.

Richard is curled up on his side, taking blow after blow, submissive as a beaten dog—then suddenly the man is a snarling beast, rising from the floor like he's channeling a grizzly.

Richard throws James off with superhuman strength and stands, panting, demons dancing in his eyes.

The two men square off, the small cabin a gladiator pit.

She lies on the kitchen floor. There's a blade inside her; she can feel steel sharp against her ribs. She doesn't want to look at it, but she does anyway, her gaze morbidly and magnetically affixed to the union of steel and skin. She watches her blood coating the silver blade, a rising tide of a red on a metallic beach. She looks at the blade and waits to die.

Nothing but Mel is on Richard's mind. He had sharpened that knife last week until it was keen as a razor. Now it juts out of her side, and with every second that goes by, she's bleeding out.

He faces James, unaware of his heavy breathing, his spasming back, his recent concussion, his throbbing shoulder. Adrenaline floods his nervous system. In an instinctual, almost subhuman consciousness, he understands that if he fails to subdue this intruder, all will end.

The rifle is out of reach. The shotgun is in the kitchen, at Mel's side, equidistant from James and him. If they both dive for it, it will invite a struggle near Mel, and that he cannot afford.

At his feet is the length of rope. He bends low quickly and picks it up.

"You're going to lasso me up and bring me to the sheriff?" mocks James.

In a cold voice that Richard doesn't recognize as his own, he says, "You don't deserve the courtesy."

A handful of rope in each clenched fist, he lunges at James before the bearded bastard can react, knocking him over.

James stumbles backward. Richard lands on top of him and projects his right knee into James' bum leg, methodically twisting the joint past its breaking point until he hears a crack, evoking a howl from James. With his left knee, he pins down James' flailing right arm. James' left fist bashes repeatedly into Richard's face and stomach, but it might as well be a petulant fly.

Richard presses the cord against James' neck until the frayed fibers cut at his throat. James' face flushes red. Veins bulge and pulse like kinked hoses. Eyes wide, he gasps and sputters. His free hand slowly ceases hammering at Richard's body and face, and he reaches upward, his fingers clenching and unclenching, like a falling man searching for a handhold.

But there's nothing to hold, nothing to grab on to, save for Richard himself, and there is no mercy left in Richard, none at all.

Mel wakes to Richard stitching her up. This time, though, she doesn't squirm at the sight of a stranger, but instead feels instantly relieved to see his familiar face.

"We've got to stop meeting like this," she says. "I've got déjà vu."

"I'm glad you're awake."

"How long have I been asleep?"

"Not long," he says.

"How many stitches?"

"Only forty-three this time."

"I assume it didn't hit any major organs? Since, you know, I'm alive."

"I assume the same."

She pauses for a second, then asks the burning question.

"Is Rusty alive?"

Richard looks away.

"After I subdued James and got you into a stable position, I went out to look for him."

"What do you mean, 'look for him'?"

"Exactly that. I followed a trail of blood. It was like tracking a wounded animal. He was in the middle of the lake, spread out, on his back."

"Dead?"

"Yes."

What he can't bring himself to say is that he watched blood trickle from Rusty's lips, that he listened to Rusty's last words, that he held the man's hand and felt it go limp, that he watched the shine leave Rusty's eyes.

"I've never escaped my sins," Rusty said, a tear on his cheek, a sad smile on his face. "It was too good to be true. Tell my wife,

Victoria, at The Rusty Nail, a bar in Nicaragua, '*Lo siento, te quiero, siempre.*'"

"What does that mean? Just in case I don't remember the Spanish."

"I'm sorry, I love you, always."

"He's gone now," says Richard softly. "There was nothing I could do but bury him."

He doesn't mention how he had to take the dogsled across the valley, to the melted southerly aspects; how, when he got to the snowline, he hauled Rusty's body onto the muddy, saturated earth, and scraped a shallow grave—a marathon of a task with one good arm—which he marked with a rough cross of pine boughs. He doesn't mention how he wiped the shotgun clean, pressed James' fingers against the barrel, the trigger, the butt, and then walked out to the lake, where Rusty himself had died, and dropped the shotgun through the fishing hole.

She doesn't ask about a grave, about the gun. All she can think about is that she's killed a man. Tears flood her vision.

"I killed him."

Richard's bloodstained fingers brush them away.

"You did what you had to do."

"He was a good man. He tried to save us."

"Good men always die," says Richard. "If his brother hadn't had a knife to my neck, you wouldn't have shot him. And if you hadn't shot him, for that matter, James might have killed us both."

"And James?"

"He's tied up. I left him locked in the shed for now."

She nods, as if this is the most logical way to handle their current situation.

"We'll harness all the dogs together and follow the river home. I wrapped up all the blankets and food. As soon as you're ready, we'll leave this place forever."

She nods and, exhausted by her newfound knowledge, falls back asleep.

Two days later, once Mel's fit to travel, Richard situates her on the sled, bundled up in the musk ox hide. It takes a while to get everything loaded up with his injured arm, but he manages through the pain.

The sun is high, but the evening is getting cool. They'll travel at night to make the most of the freeze. It's a cloudless sky, and they'll be able to navigate just fine.

"There's one more thing I have to do."

He trudges back to the shed. With the rifle trained on the door, he kicks it open, not worrying about the broken lock. He won't be needing it again.

Sitting with his back against the far wall, James has cut the rope that bound his hands on one of the sharp tools in the shed. Richard expected as much.

"On your feet."

"I can't."

"Lift up your pant leg."

James grimaces and does as he's told. The swollen flesh around his knee is black and blue and purple and yellow, like a rotten grapefruit.

"I can't walk."

Richard nods.

"Then crawl."

The rifle is unwavering.

James crawls back to the cabin, gritting his teeth at the effort, at the pain in his knee.

It takes them ten minutes to make the short trip to the cabin. Richard doesn't bother to help the man. He's sure James has a trick up his sleeve, and he'll take no chances. There's no hurry—the only thing he's racing now is the snowline.

After James crawls up the stairs, Richard kicks him in the flat of his back, puts the muzzle to his skull, and reaches down to frisk him. In his boot, Richard finds an iron railroad spike, and in his belt, a jagged piece of glass. He removes both, drags James into the cabin, and puts the contraband on the kitchen table. With a fresh piece of rope, he ties James to the chair, then pushes the chair close to the table.

"Are you going to wine and dine me now?" asks James.

Richard's answer is indirect.

"Your brother is dead. I'm taking the dogs. I don't imagine you'll be walking anytime soon. I've taken all the food we need and burned the rest. I've thrown all the traps and the shotgun to the bottom of the lake."

He unloads the rifle and places the round on the table. Then Richard silently repositions the shard of glass and the railway spike next to the shell on the table, like some torturous table setting. James eyes them hungrily.

Finally, Richard puts the rifle in the center of the table, like a centerpiece.

When James grasps the point of Richard's reorganizing, the look in his eyes is of pure hatred. But the madman seems to enjoy the madness he's kindled in others.

"You couldn't do it yourself," says James, laughing maniacally.

Richard disagrees. "You are responsible for the death of three men that I know of: the pilot, the Frenchman, and your brother. I could kill you without dirtying my conscience. However, I don't think you're worthy of an executioner's sympathies. If you want mercy, you'll have to take it for yourself."

James continues to laugh, but it turns into a snarl as he jerks at his ropes.

"There's no need to do that," says Richard. "You'll be able to cut yourself free. I made certain of that. But it will take you long enough that you won't hurt me or mine ever again."

"Fuck you," spits James.

Richard walks out and shuts the door. He trudges back out to Mel and the sled, exhausted.

"Let's get out of here," Richard says. "We've got a long road ahead of us."

Truth is, he just doesn't want to hear the shot.

Epilogue

Clean-shaven, in a black suit, Richard sits stiffly in the front pew next to his children.

In the casket is his beautiful wife, carved to a fragment of her former self by cancer.

It's a closed casket. She didn't want to be remembered like that.

Tears drip onto his suit jacket. He shakes as the priest gives his sermon, the words of which he doesn't catch. Sarah squeezes his hand. From behind him, a hand claps on his shoulder. Richard doesn't need to look, he knows it's Jim's.

The joy of exiting the wilderness dissolved into anguish when he learned of his wife's illness. The papers called, the TV stations, too, and he ignored them all. He stepped down from an active role at his company, gave his vice president full control. The merger fell through, but he didn't care. He focused his attention entirely on his family.

Six months and seven days. That's all he had with her.

On walks around the pond near their house, he told her everything, everything except the affair, though he was sure that she knew. He was never any good at lying. A confession and apology seemed selfish in the face of her imminent death. If she did know, as he suspected she did, she didn't say a thing. She had precious little energy, and she didn't aim to waste it exploring her husband's backwoods infidelity. At least that's how he took it. It made him feel a little less cowardly.

At the end of the service, he and the children stand outside, shaking hands and thanking tearful churchgoers.

Whispers of condolences. Hugs and embraces.

"Thank God you're home," says one. "For the children."

"Gone too soon," says another.

Obvious statements but said all the same. Such are funerals.

The suits and dresses blend into a river of black, and he hardly recognizes friends and family as they cue up one by one to offer their well-intentioned but largely useless thoughts and prayers. At the end of the line, however, is a face he recognizes immediately. Even though she's now clean, wearing makeup and a modest black dress rather than tattered snow pants or a dank musk ox hide.

"What are you doing here?" he says, bewildered, almost angry.

In response, too torn up to speak, she hands him a letter.

He recognizes the handwriting instantly.

Dear Mel,

We've never met, but I feel that in some ways you know me, and I know you. Richard has told me all about your time together in the cabin, and he speaks fondly of you, though I suspect he's left out certain parts so as not to pain me further on my deathbed. Yes, I am dying, as you likely know already. I wonder how your exit from the cabin would have played out had I not been sick, but I don't have the time, nor the pain tolerance, to torture myself with speculations.

I do not fault you—or Richard, for that matter—if my assumptions are correct. It is impossible for me to fathom the extraordinary circumstances of your survival. So while I am not strong enough to meet you in my current state, I am strong enough to extend an invitation: Come to my funeral. Richard is weakened almost more than I by my illness, and he will need the strength of a strong woman—which you no doubt are—to overcome my passing. In what capacity, well, that's up to you. He has no idea I'm writing this letter and would protest if he did. But I write this not just for

Richard—I write this for my children, too.

    Of course, only come if you so desire. Alaska has irrevocably altered your life—it would not surprise me if you never want to return, or, on the contrary, if you're already itching to come back. It's a land of extremes, after all. You already know that, better than most.

    So consider this a hello and a goodbye, forgiveness and a blessing, all wrapped into one. Were I to survive, we might be enemies. Seeing as I'm dying, I'd rather be friends.

    Sincerely,

    Anne

Richard looks up from the letter, baffled once again by the strength of his beloved wife, to see Mel in tears.

"This is Mel, then?" asks Caleb, quietly interrupting.

"Yes," says Richard, unsure of how to proceed.

Caleb solemnly extends his hand. "Thank you for coming and paying your respects to my mom. And for taking care of my dad in the cabin."

Richard nods imperceptibly, she takes Caleb's hand, and then Sean's, and then Sarah's.

She hugs Richard, and whispers in his ear, "I'm so sorry, Richard. For everything."

She straightens up and says, rather matter-of-factly, "I left my job, sold everything. I've got an Airbnb on Spruce Street, renting by the week, but I'm looking at cabins and land. Somewhere remote. I've even been thinking about getting my pilot's license, too."

She hands him a scrap of paper with her new address and a phone number on it. "I even have 907 area code now. I guess I'm officially an Alaskan." She smiles, then grows somber. "Anyways, when you're ready," she says. "I'm here."

She walks away from the church with his eyes on her back. She gets into her rental car and drives to the Airbnb. She could use a stiff drink, but she's trying to cut back, and besides, she can't afford a hangover. Tomorrow morning she's looking at open houses with her realtor. And tomorrow night, she told a devastated Marty that he could take her out for dinner as an apology—maybe she'll have a drink then. For now, she settles for a seltzer water with a slice of lime.

It was difficult to explain to her parents why she wanted to return to Alaska. Voices were raised, tears were shed. But the simplest explanation was that the place that almost killed her gave her life. They'll come visit. Someday, they'll understand.

Mel had tried to go back to work, tried to fit back into the city. She might've been able to force herself through it if it weren't for the newfound fame. Every newspaper and talk show wanted a sound bite, an interview with the pretty, young stockbroker who survived the snowiest winter on record in the Alaskan backcountry and exited under mysterious circumstances. They all wanted the scoop. Her coworkers treated her like a celebrity. People recognized her on the street. The Pierce family, too, reached out, wanting to mend fences and welcome her and Diane back into the fold.

"We want to make sure you're taken care of," said her grandfather, after tracking down her phone number.

"My mom's been taking care of me since Toulouse," she responded, and hung up.

That was the straw that broke the camel's back. The city that saved her suddenly felt claustrophobic. Her anxiety returned. But she didn't want to take meds again, not if she didn't need them, and she hadn't needed them out in the bush. So she ran, like so many others, to Alaska.

She steps out onto the balcony and looks out at the mountains. Imposing sentinels of the wilderness, just recently capped with the first snows of the season. It feels like home, more so than any city skyline.

She raises her plastic cup to the horizon and drains it.

END